Last Laugh

Also by C.K. Crigger

Painter's Bay Series
Buried Bones

Under Seige

The Woman Who Series
The Woman Who Built a Bridge

The Woman Who Killed Marvin Hammel

The Woman Who Wore a Badge

The Woman Who Beat the Odds

The Woman Who Inherited Trouble

The Woman Who Went for Broke

Novels
Ault's Heir

Black Crossing

Hereafter

Letter Of The Law

Liar's Trial

Lost Girl Lake

Madame's Daughter

The Yeggman's Apprentice

Yester's Ride

And many more...

Last Laugh

PAINTER'S BAY
BOOK THREE

C.K. CRIGGER

WOLFPACK
PUBLISHING
— EST 2013 —

Last Laugh
Paperback Edition
Copyright © 2025 by C.K. Crigger

Wolfpack Publishing
1707 E. Diana Street
Tampa, FL 33609

www.wolfpackpublishing.com

Paperback ISBN 979-8-89567-815-2
Ebook ISBN 979-8-89567-814-5
LCCN 2025945095

Last Laugh

One

The dining room of the Painter's Bay Hotel buzzed with conversation, mixing with the clatter of cutlery on heavy pottery dinnerware. As on most Friday evenings at the dinner hour, the first seating was packed with customers enjoying Rio Salo's succulent *Boeuf* Wellington. As an alternate on the menu, she was offering pork chops Alexander, but for the most part, they were being ignored.

Flushed from the heat of the kitchen, Rio traded the chef's apron that enveloped her thin body in a cocoon of heavy cloth for a frilly half apron and went out to speak with the customers. Her grandpapa had always done so, his personality pleasing the clientele. Glad-handing, he'd called it. Making the people feel important. Which they were, of course. Part of what had made the Painter's Bay restaurant a desirable destination.

When the second seating for service came around, she'd change aprons again and work in the kitchen. Such was the routine she'd grown used to in the months since reopening the hotel after her father died and her half brother, Eino, came home after two years away. Fortunately, he'd promptly left again. She didn't know where he'd gone and was glad of it. She only hoped he never came back.

Pausing at the entrance to the dining room, she surveyed first the diners, then eyed the niche where the small hotel bar was located. There were three stools, all occupied at present, and a space for men—and the rare woman—to stand and order their favorite tipple. Mostly, the men would take their liquor outside to the porch to await their turn for a table, at least when the weather permitted. The ladies generally sat in the lobby.

For now, Turner, the bartender, held sway, taking care no one drank past capacity. He was good about that. Looking over, he saw her and winked. Something to put a smile on her face that had been lacking before.

Still, she couldn't help but be aware of a certain discussion going on at the table nearest the doorway. The one where Mr. Masterson, the local banker and, in Rio's opinion, a self-important toady, had a couple fellows dining with him, all with their backs turned to her. They were unaccompanied by any women, although most Friday evenings the banker and his wife showed up together. Which meant this must be a business dinner.

The thing is, even from the back, Rio recognized the men with him. She'd first seen them in the early summer when her inheritance hadn't yet been well known. These out-of-towners had been attempting to buy the hotel in a deal seemingly instigated by either Eino or the old sheriff—she'd never figured exactly who or why—while using the banker as a go-between. Anyway, the investors, a certain Melvin Carver and his son of the same name, had been disappointed to learn she wasn't interested in selling. Mr. Masterson had been quite embarrassed by the whole chaotic situation, even though he seemed to think she should've been flattered.

He had apparently forgotten the lesson because here he sat with the same men, at the same table, all talking with the same loud voices. Didn't it ever cross their minds to wonder if the other patrons may have been able to overhear something that wasn't their business?

With a twist of her mouth, Rio cocked her head and unashamedly listened.

"I urge you to look around," Mr. Masterson was saying, overriding something Carver the younger blathered on about. "Do you see a place that is about to go under and is desperate to sell? I don't."

They were definitely discussing *her* business.

At least the banker could see business was booming. The Carvers didn't bother to so much as glance around. The elder man shrugged without answering the question.

"According to what you're saying, the young woman is apparently still holding on to the hotel. I'm sure it won't be hard to convince her to take the money, however. Five hundred dollars will seem like a fortune to her. Women have little concept of value. Truthfully, I wouldn't expect anything better of an educated lady from the city, let alone some little backwoods chit like the Salo girl. Most likely, she'll be dead broke by the new year."

3

"Admittedly, she is a decent cook," Carver Jr. said. "If she even does the cooking herself, as you say she does."

Internally, Rio huffed. So now he was casting aspersions on the banker's report, as well as her financial knowledge and her cooking. Fools, father and son.

Masterson's displeasure became apparent. "I suppose you're going to say you've had better beef Wellington anywhere? I beg leave to doubt it."

In other circumstances, or with anyone else, Rio might've appreciated the praise. She didn't care what Eldon Masterson thought.

Carver Sr. waved a hand at his son, flashing a rather gaudy ruby ring as he did so. "That's enough, Melvin. It won't matter in the long run. Now, Masterson, as I remember, she got rather testy the last time we broached the question. Do you have any suggestions in order to expedite making a deal this time around?"

Visibly reining in his pique, the banker shrugged. "Flattery, I suppose. That generally works with women. They all like to be complimented, whether on their beauty, their talents, or their children. At least this young woman can legitimately claim one of those choices. Or two, rather."

Carver Jr. sat up. "Two?"

"Yes. As you can see, she's a fetching little thing, as well as an excellent chef."

Fetching little thing indeed! She burned with anger.

As if sensing Rio's ire, Masterson raised his head to gaze around the room, causing her to shrink back.

But then she wondered why she bothered. This was her home and her place of business. She had a perfect right to be wherever she wanted. But the fact remained, she preferred to keep what she'd heard to herself. As her father had often said, "Knowledge will always put you at an advantage. Know what they know and you win." Why she thought she might need an advantage, she didn't know. She just did.

The evening flowed on without a hitch. The Golz girls, Eliza and Marie, flew around the room as if they had wings. In the kitchen, their sister, Blanche, worked together with Rio in a well-matched team. Outside, their little brother, Tommy, watched over the horses and buggies. And for this evening, one of the older brothers in a family with nine siblings manned the boats to and fro across Painter's Bay between the town and the hotel.

By closing time, Rio was exhausted. Friday night, with its special menu, always took more effort. The morning would come all too soon when she'd prepare breakfasts for the hotel patrons. Only three rooms of the five upstairs rooms were occupied tonight, but there'd be drop-ins at the restaurant in the morning. There always were.

Consequently, when the restaurant closed, and the guests had all retired to their rooms, she hurried to lock the front door and called Boo, her fluffy little white dog, in from his evening scamper before turning in herself. With all the lamps but her own extinguished, her key was in the lock of her office door when she heard a commotion at the front. Voices murmured, something thumped onto the porch floor, and the voices got louder.

The bell at the hotel door clanged, for some reason sounding extra strident.

For seconds she hesitated, torn between ignoring the clamor and answering it. Finally, her sense of duty as a hotelkeeper overcame her reluctance and, Boo at her side, she went to tend to business.

Opening the door, Rio held her lamp at shoulder height, the better to see who stood there. Beyond the first two figures, a stoop-shouldered man waited. His hand, she saw, was held toward them, palm out as if in expectation. The two in front pretended not to see.

Rio recognized him. Mr. Pellow, who owned a livery stable near the edge of the lake, had recently built a dock and had a couple of boats to rent. Upon occasion, he rowed the boats. This was one of those occasions, and he stood now awaiting payment for his service. And he probably expected a tip, considering the late hour.

Alas, he seemed to be waiting in vain, either for payment or for a tip.

As for the women, they ignored him. Both appeared cranky.

An uneasy feeling swept over Rio. One thing she'd learned during these busy days of handling the business of hotel ownership was not to let anyone play you for a fool. Another thing she'd learned was that not too much scared her anymore. The result, she assumed, of so many people wanting to kill her—and not succeeding. So far, though, not by want of trying.

Nowadays she went armed with a little .32 Iver Johnson pistol stowed in her specially made skirt pockets.

The woman in the lead tried to push past her. "Pay the man," she snapped.

Far from letting herself be pushed, Rio remained blocking the doorway. Boo, loyal friend that he was, let out a gruff warning bark at the woman, eyeing the hem of her skirt. No doubt with the intention of finding the ankle hiding beneath it.

The woman's lip curled. "Disgusting. Get that creature away from me."

Rio didn't move. The other woman stepped forward. For some reason she was carrying an umbrella and poked it tentatively at Boo. He, of course, dodged.

Mr. Pellow cleared his throat. "That'll be twenty cents," he said.

The first woman glared, at him and at Rio. "Pay him," she repeated and yes, she was speaking to Rio.

"No," Rio said, then added at the woman's irate astonishment, "Mr. Pellow is an independent business-man, not a hotel employee. I'm sure you must have seen as much at the dock in Painter's Bay. His fees are clearly stated there."

Right at the moment, she hoped the woman turned around and went back to where she'd come from. The hotel didn't need patronage from someone as rude as she, and, tired as Rio was, she had no inclination to kowtow to the woman, potential guest or not.

"The nerve." The woman glared like one of those black mamba snakes Rio had read about. "Get the manager. I'll speak to him. And..." she added with an imperious tilt of her sharp nose. "I'll see you fired. Impudent fool. I won't stand for it."

Meanwhile, her companion's lips tightened as she aimed the umbrella at Boo again, as if to skewer him with a sword.

Mr. Pellow's eyes had gone wide. He began backing away, evidently willing to forgo his twenty cents and a hard-earned tip in order to avoid any further acquain-tance with the two women. Unfortunately for him, Rio was just as fast and had less far to go. She shut the door in the women's faces, possibly even catching the pointed toe of the woman's shoe in the process.

There'd been a lot of luggage sitting on the porch, she noticed as the door closed. Evidently, they'd come for an extended stay. Not her problem, she decided. No law she knew of said she was obligated to serve such disagreeable people. Mr. Pellow would have to look out for himself.

Arguing voices carried to Rio from outside. She moved to the nearest window, where she had a partial view of the porch. From there, she could see Mr. Pellow shaking his head in disgust and heading back to his boat. He was alone. He may have gotten his twenty cents, but his attitude indicated no tip had been forthcoming.

Where, Rio wondered with a sinking feeling in the pit of her stomach, were those women?

Seconds later, the bell began clanging again and didn't stop. The women called out, loud and often. Boo barked. Inside of a minute, boots clumped down the stairs from the upper story toward her.

"Is the hotel on fire?" the man staying in room three demanded.

"What in the world is going on?" A very irritated guest from room five called from the top of the stairway. "What are those women screeching about?"

"Yes," the wife of one of the men chipped in. "Are we in danger?"

Rio held up her lantern so they could see her. "No," she told the man on the stairs. "The hotel is not on fire." She called out to reach the others. "The livery stable man rowed a couple women over and left them here.

I've refused them hospitality. As you can tell, they are not the kind of people I want in the hotel. But you're not in any danger." She hoped.

"Can't you make them be quiet? I'm trying to sleep." The woman was whining like a child.

"Yeah," said the man next to her. "Make them stop. Immediately. I mean it. You don't, I know four fellas who intend to stay here during hunting season who might be interested in hearing about this." A threat. He turned and shuffled away.

Indignant, Rio snorted. "Do you have a suggestion as to how? I can't bind and gag them."

The booted man cleared his throat. "Could shoot them. I hear you're good at that."

"What?" Her dark eyes glared at him.

"Or it might be better for everyone if you were to let them in for now and get rid of them in the morning." The only serious suggestion came from the man in room two, Eino's old abode.

"Really," she started, just as something thumped against the hotel entry door. Something that sounded remarkably like a battering ram. She spun around.

"Excuse me, please. Everyone, go back to bed. I'll handle this." One way or another, she determined. And to think she'd thought the foes she'd faced earlier in the summer had been bad.

Without waiting to see if they took her at her word, and with Boo still at her side, she trod back to the lobby and flung open the door just as another blow thudded against it. Only her quickness let her avoid the end of the bench the two women, one on each side, were shoving back and forth. The paint, fresh only a short while ago, had now become an immediate chore to redo.

"Stop that." She glared into the nearest woman's slitted eyes. The woman was about thirty, wore a cheap-looking felt hat, and a plain dark dress under a cloth jacket. Beyond her, a slightly younger woman—or maybe only a better cared for woman—held up a hand and examined the fingers of her elegant kid gloves as if looking for damage. How she managed to smile and sneer at the same time, Rio didn't know. Eyes the color of green grapes were narrowed to slits.

"Since Mr. Pellow has gone," Rio continued, "I'll allow you one night's lodging. There will be an extra charge for damage to the door."

The younger woman sniffed. "I'll have your best room."

Rio gave her a cold look. "The hotel is almost full tonight. The only available room will be two dollars for you both, plus fifty cents to repaint the door you damaged. In advance. Take it or leave it." She had no compunction at fibbing. She had two empty rooms upstairs, plus one on the ground floor. Pure irritation made her offer only the smallest as an option.

"Nonsense. I'll pay when my business is done, and I leave." The younger woman took another try at pushing past her. Unsuccessfully, once again.

Rio worked hard and was stronger than she looked. She stood firm.

"Madam," she said, "I think you'd better count yourself lucky that I'm a kind and thoughtful person. You, to the contrary, have proven yourself otherwise. The only reason I'm allowing you in is to keep your noise from annoying my other guests. You have my concern for their welfare to thank. If you refuse to comply, there will be consequences." Not that she knew what they'd be. She hadn't thought that far ahead.

What she did know was that with no sheriff or even a city marshal around to uphold the law, all she could do was trust her demeanor and words were convincing enough to keep the women from crossing a line.

In this case, it seemed to work.

For the moment. She had her doubts about how long it would last.

———

TO SAY Vesta White was displeased with the room the impudent female—her and her scruffy little dog—showed her to didn't start to describe her feelings. And then to put Bindle, her maid, in the same room with her was the outside of enough.

Looking around at the one narrow bed, it indicated Bindle would either have to sleep in it with her or on the floor. Vesta knew which she'd prefer, although she could foresee problems if she insisted. Her hair, for instance, wouldn't be properly done for weeks. Or a stain might appear on her favorite gown. Things of a similar sort had happened in the past until Bindle finally got over her aggravation. Usually, it required a monetary bonus.

For two cents she'd fire the maid, but Daddy insisted she be kept on. Vesta didn't know why.

It hadn't occurred to either woman to ask for a cot to be moved in. Of course, doing so would've taken the rest of the tiny room's floor space and Vesta would need that, both for her luggage and for spreading out her notes and maps. Everything Evan Salo—although

Quinn Callahan, the investigator, had said Evan's name was actually Eino—had told her, everything he'd talked to her uncle Robert about, was documented and included. Neither man had known of her efforts, but she'd always been good at ferreting out secrets. And this was one she intended to act on.

A genuine smile crossed her face before the state of the pokey room caught her attention again.

"Help me out of this gown," she snapped at Bindle. The maid was sweating after carrying up the most immediately necessary of Vesta's luggage. "I'm tired and want to go to bed." Her glare at the other woman was every bit as fierce as the one she'd directed at the hotel personnel. "I suppose you'll have to sleep beside me. Stay far to the side and outside of the sheets. I don't want you touching me."

Not that there was much room left 'far to the side.' And not that Vesta particularly cared.

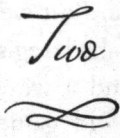

Two

Clouds gathered by morning. Thunder rumbled, and by the time Rio's puffy golden popovers were out of the oven, rain was coming down hard. It dashed against the kitchen window and flowed in streaks over the sill.

Apparently, the summer's drought was over, Rio thought as she dried Boo's feet and settled him on a rug by the cookstove. Good for ranchers and farmers, she supposed. Not so much for loggers or people in the hotel business.

"There," she said to Boo. "Is that better?" He didn't actually like rain and preferred to stay inside on rainy days. Especially if someone would throw his ball from the kitchen all the way to the lobby, a game of fetch he never tired of.

She'd made hash this morning using the leftover pork chops from last night's alternative entrée, gently mixing the meat with precisely cubed potatoes, onions, and plenty of herbs from her garden. The hash would be served with either milk gravy or her special ketchup, depending on the diner's taste.

Meanwhile, she pondered how to entertain the hotel guests. Most had come for the fishing, but this was a day when only the hardiest would venture out in the boats, and since most had registered to stay another night, she'd have to find a way to keep them happy. Maybe dig out some old games like Pit or Pigs in Clover. Better yet, a musical evening, and if enough people showed up, perhaps they could clear the lobby and dance.

"It's too bad you don't know a lot of fancy tricks." Rio gazed into her dog's soulful eyes. "I'd hire you to keep folks laughing." Afraid this might sound too critical, she hastened to say, "But I love you, anyway."

A chuckle came from the doorway. Male. Familiar. Welcome.

Rio looked up to find young Win Ferris peeking in. His hat dripped rain from the brim, and his coat was soaked through. Even so, he appeared none the worse for wear. And his arms were already open to catch Boo, who raced gleefully toward him.

"Win! Welcome! I didn't know you were coming." A smile, in short supply these last few months, lit her face. Her dark eyes, a surprising contrast to her pale hair, sparkled as she searched beyond the fourteen-year-old, looking for and hoping to see his older brother.

The space was empty.

"Are you alone?"

"Nah." Win, who'd dropped to his knees and was busy giving Boo a tummy rub while the dog wriggled in ecstasy, grinned at her. "We've got our own horses now,

Rio. Beck's putting them up in your barn. We figured that would be all right."

"Better than all right. I've missed you, Win."

He set Boo aside for a moment and studied her. "And Beck?"

Her naturally fair skin pinked. "Well, sure." She made it sound like an afterthought, but it wasn't. And watching Win, she was afraid he knew it. Had he seen the kiss Beckett had bestowed on her before he—and Win—left for Montana? She wondered. More than a month ago, now. Beckett'd had to finish rounding up the opium smuggling ring that had pressed on through Idaho into that state. As a federal customs agent, it was his job.

"Hang your coat by the stove," she said. "That's what the rack is for. You didn't ride horseback from Montana, did you?"

"Heck no." Dutifully, he deposited the very wet hat on a peg and hung the coat beneath it. "We caught a freight from St. Regis, riding in a stock car with the horses. So here we are." He grinned. "What's for breakfast? It sure smells good."

"Oh, you're hungry, are you?"

"Yeah, but I'll wait until Beck gets here."

Win, for all his slim build, had a healthy appetite.

Though Rio had more questions, the guests, with many complaints over the turn the weather had taken, had begun gathering in the dining room. First, the fellow who'd had the good sense to suggest letting those women stay the night so the guests could return to bed. Overheated tempers had soon cooled, except for Rio's own. Next, the couple who'd intended to fish and were loud in their disappointment but took a table in the dining room quietly enough. And last, the man who'd mentioned Rio's reputation with a gun.

Though he didn't know the half of it—and never would.

A few other wet and hungry men had gathered on the porch. Some were sportsmen, a few from the sawmill over across the point. And, surprising Rio because she wouldn't have thought Molly Clement ever got up this early, let alone be willing to ride in a boat in the rain, Dr. Clement and his wife.

"A childbirth," Molly whispered as Rio delivered steaming cups of coffee and a miniature pitcher of cream to their table. "A difficult one. James needed my help. I'm a pretty good nurse, you know, when I have to be."

Rio did know. She'd been the recipient of Molly's expertise herself when she'd gotten shot not so long ago. Molly and the doctor had provided wonderful care.

Win, after washing up and combing his hair, pitched in like the trooper she'd always found him to be and began helping serve up food.

So far, to Rio's relief, the woman and her maid from last night had yet to make an appearance. She'd be willing to bet on them creating a fuss when they did. Better to get breakfast service over with before they ruined it for everyone.

She finished with the last table and returned to the kitchen just as Beckett strode in. The porch door slammed shut behind him. Rio couldn't stop the involuntary move she made toward him. Knew he noticed too. His eyes, so dark they were nearly black, smiled at her, although his outward expression didn't change much. Softened a little, maybe.

He spoke to his brother. "Rio put you to work already?"

"Slave driver," Win mock grumbled.

A sort of peace came over Rio as they slipped into the easy ways with each other they'd developed during the summer. A peace that held as she dished up plates for the three of them and, after she took a quick turn around the dining room to replenish coffee, they sat to eat at the kitchen table.

But she'd barely taken her seat before the older woman from the night before barged into the kitchen as if she owned it herself. She glanced around, sharp eyes taking in the kitchen, contents, and menfolk. Eyes that settled on Beckett, widened a little, then narrowed.

"Huh," she said. "Is entertaining men friends tolerated in this establishment?"

Beckett looked at Rio, one eyebrow lifting in question. Win did too, his face much more expressive than his brother's.

Rio sucked in a breath before taking a leisurely bite of pork chop hash. She chewed, then swallowed. Could've used a bit more celery, she decided, and she preferred it with the brown gravy. Only then did she turn her head toward the woman.

"None of your business," she said. "The dining room is across from the stairs, as I'm sure you could see. Find a table. I'll be with you in a bit."

"Miss White requires her breakfast in fifteen minutes," the woman said. "Served on a tray in that shabby little room. She requires a pot of oolong tea, two poached eggs, and one slice of brioche bread. I'll have whatever you're eating, also on a tray."

"I don't do individual menu selections," Rio said,

although that wasn't necessarily true. It all depended. At certain times, for instance, when the Golz girls were here to help. Whoever this woman was, and she hadn't yet heard a name, to Rio's way of thinking she was no one special. But Rio'd been right on the money in figuring there'd be some kind of stink. This conversation seemed a wind-up to war.

"And I don't do room service," she continued. "You both will need to eat in the dining room. You may tell Miss White so."

Turning away, she took a rather large bite of popover and didn't taste a thing as she chomped as if grinding stones. Meanwhile, the name *White* percolated slowly through her mind with chilling effect. Her fork clattered onto her plate.

White? This couldn't be part of her half brother Eino's mother's family, could it? Barging in as if she was entitled to the place? What would any of them want here, anyway? She'd found the money and bearer bonds Eino had stolen from his uncle. All of which Quinn Callahan had returned to a Mr. White. She'd never heard the man's first name, and when he'd written a note to say Quinn had delivered, he'd signed as R.B. White. She had no idea what the R.B. stood for.

Beckett's hand felt warm, almost hot, as he reached out and covered hers. "Easy," he breathed.

For long moments, the woman stood in the doorway, her breath rasping in and out. Finally, she snapped, "You'll be sorry," before whirling, footsteps loud as she retreated.

Win stood up and went out to where he could see her ascending the stairs. "Who was that? She ain't what you'd call polite, is she?"

No longer hungry, Rio pushed away her plate. To her own surprise, a wry laugh bubbled forth. "And to think she's only the maid."

Win glowered. "You mean there's more of them?"

"Just the mistress and her maid." Her nose wrinkled at the sound of that. Like they were upper-class British maybe, which she could tell they were not. She met Beckett's eyes. "The maid, she called her employer Miss White. Eino's mother's maiden name was White. And the last name of the man to whom Mr. Callahan returned a fortune. The way she talked to me. Do you suppose..."

Beckett was quick. "Are you thinking she's one of those Whites?"

Win, sitting at the table again and being plenty quick himself, grunted. "What do you suppose she wants?"

Exactly what Rio had been wondering. "Whatever else, it doesn't seem to be making my acquaintance and being friends."

"No. I noticed that from the way the maid—you're sure she's the maid?—talked to you." Beckett didn't appear certain.

"That's my impression."

"From the way she gave the order, she expected to be obeyed without question. And no please, no thank you. Have you had words with her before?"

A little embarrassed by the admission, Rio nodded. "Oh yes, indeed. Miss White and her maid turned up after closing last night. First, they tried, and may have succeeded, in bilking Mr. Pellow out of his fare when he brought them and their luggage in his boat. Next, the maid tried to skewer Boo with an umbrella, and Miss

White threatened to have me fired. I decided not to put up with their blather and closed the door in their faces."

Win grinned.

"Yet here they are," Beckett said.

"Yes. You see, they stood outside and started yelling and ringing the bell and finally, used the bench to try battering down the door." She turned to Win. "And ruined the paint job from summer."

Win scowled as Rio continued. "The rest of my guests put up a fuss, so I finally had to let them in. Not that I've received a dime, so far, and am pretty sure they'll skip without paying if they can get away with it. But the funny thing is..." She broke off, not really wanting to say more.

Beckett insisted. "Is what?"

"Funny that she seemed sincere in thinking she could get me fired. If she is one of Eino's family, wouldn't Quinn Callahan have let it be known how things worked out around here?"

"You'd think so."

"Most people would be grateful and treat you nice," Win said. "After all, it's you who got their money back for them. Even that Italian guy turned halfway decent."

Rio's lips twisted. "That Italian guy scared me half to death." For more reasons than one. "Anyway, forget her. I want to hear your news."

She got up, scraped the remains of her hash into Boo's bowl after picking out the onions, and set it down for him. The lobby bell pinged, indicating someone was ready to pay their bill, so, letting the matter drop, she went to tend to her guests.

Concerned for her weather-bound guests' despondent confinement to the lobby, she sought the

Clement's advice. "These people are going to be bored to death just sitting inside and watching it rain," she whispered to them as she took their money. "What would you suggest for entertainment tonight? A singalong, perhaps, or get some of the musical folks together and hold a dance? Would that suit better than games and card tables, do you think?"

Molly grinned. "Lovely! A dance is a wonderful idea."

Rio sagged with relief. "I could make punch and bake some cookies. And of course, make sure Turner shows up to tend bar. It might take a little something to get the menfolk out on the dance floor."

"As long as I don't get called out, Molly and I will be here," Dr. Clement said. He grinned at his wife. "Rain or no rain. It's been a while since we took a twirl around a dance floor, Molly."

"Could you take a notice over to the store? And maybe one at the post office?" Rio felt a little surge of anticipation. This would be something she'd never tried before. It could not only prove profitable for the hotel, but it would be a welcome to Win and Beckett.

Did Beckett dance? She didn't know.

"I will," Molly promised. "I just hope it quits raining by then."

Rio and Molly put their heads together and made plans while the doctor stood, a little impatiently, jingling some coins in his pocket.

When Rio waved goodbye, she found Miss White and her maid seated at the largest table in the room glaring at her. All the pleasure she'd felt at making plans with Molly faded to nothing.

No big surprise, Miss White and her maid

devoured the hash with ravenous appetites, disappearing upstairs as soon as they finished. All without saying anything beyond the bounds of ordinary discourse. It was as if Miss White had gotten an overnight shift in personality.

Oddly enough, Rio got the idea that they were waiting for something to happen. Or waiting for someone to arrive. It did not make her feel any easier.

The guests, who'd grown in number to truly fill every room and included two more women, mostly lazed around the lobby, talking and drinking coffee. A fire blazed in the big fireplace, spreading light and warmth to the dismal morning. Rio broached the idea of an evening of dancing, which delighted most of the guests. At least she hadn't heard any complaints.

Shortly after breakfast, Beckett begged the use of one of the hotel rowboats, and he and Win went across to the town. They didn't mention their intentions. A matter for Rio to puzzle over.

Plans for the dance went forward as soon as she heard from a guitar and banjo player, a fiddler, and a woman who was amiable to pounding away on a piano that may have been slightly out of tune. When the Golz ladies arrived, Rio would be free to bake dozens of cookies and concoct a kind of punch suitable for women and children. She'd put a block of ice in the bowl when the time came.

In the afternoon, the sun came out, drying the paths around the hotel. Light danced over the tops of waves blowing in off of Painter's Bay. Loons and mud ducks dived into the depths of the lake while gulls flew squawking overhead. Boats were rented out to fishermen after all, and there was a sort of anticipation in the air. Better yet, dinner reservations came in, giving this evening the best Saturday attendance record since the hotel had reopened. Mention of a dance showed to have gone over well.

Introducing a new entertainment was terrifying. And exhilarating.

———

VESTA WHITE FLUNG the shawl she'd had draped around her shoulders onto the bed and flounced to sit on the one chair. She was scowling, her nostrils flaring.

Bindle, wisely, didn't say anything. She just set about tidying the room, even making the bed, well aware that Vesta wouldn't allow anyone from the hotel into the room, no matter how messy it got. And it would get messy. Vesta was notorious for leaving mayhem in her wake, clothing scattered, bottles left open, spills not wiped up. Especially when she was fretting.

And right now, fretting may not have been a strong enough word. Fuming might've been more accurate.

Best then, to get her talking.

"The food is good here. A surprise." Knowing full well this would bring on an argument, Bindle made the comment sound innocent. That it was true just sent fuel to Vesta's fire.

"Huh. That hash is probably the only thing she knows how to make." The tone scathed.

Bindle, whose first name was Lena although Vesta never called her that, forced a chuckle. "I hope not. I'd hate to eat the same thing every meal."

"You mean like you used to eat boiled beans morn-ing, noon, and night? Uh."

"It wasn't so bad," Bindle said, hiding her glare, but that wasn't true. To this day, she could barely tolerate beans. Why did her employer always have to throw her early years of poverty in her face? Her life before she came to be Vesta's maid and sometime confidante had not ever been easy. Anyway, beans, even morning, noon, and night, would've been good back then. At least her belly would've been full. She wished she'd selected a different subject for conversation.

Thankfully, Vesta beat her to a change, not that it went any better.

"Since he insisted he was coming, I wish David would hurry up and get here." Vesta swung her chair around to face a mirror. She peered into it, smoothing a frown line from between her brows with a forefinger. "I need someone to escort me when I go outside in this wild place. Trees everywhere. Rain."

Yesterday, she'd been hissing like a wildcat when she thought of David getting too close, saying she didn't know why he said he'd be traveling right after them. "Nobody," she'd said, meaning herself, "invited him along."

Looking, no doubt, for another man to sink her claws into, Bindle thought. Just as she'd thought earlier when she saw the fine-looking man seated at the hotel woman's breakfast table. When Vesta got a peek at him, she'd become all soft and womanly, innocent and afraid. In need of protection. And any man who bought her act would be sure to pay the piper.

———

BECKETT FERRIS LEANED into the oars, pushing the boat along at a great rate. Win, on the middle seat, leaned over the side and trailed his fingers in the lake.

"Whew, this water is cold." He flipped his fingers. "I'd hate to capsize."

Beckett laughed. "We're not going to capsize. If I remember correctly, you caulked this boat just a few months ago. It should be good until spring."

"Yeah, well." Win had something else to say. "Why didn't you tell Rio about running for sheriff? You know, how Dr. Clement and Mr. Meadows and...and the grocer—I forget his name—got together and said they'd sponsor you."

"Mr. Lewis. Fred Lewis." Beckett supplied the name as if it were an afterthought.

"Yeah, him. Why didn't you tell her? Her and Wash were agreed, you know. Wash talked to you about it before he got killed."

"I didn't want to remind her of Wash right then." Beckett eyed his brother. "Don't want you to, either. Looks to me like she's got plenty going on here as it is."

Win had to agree. "Hope that White woman she told us about doesn't cause trouble. Do you think she could be related to Rio's half brother?"

Beckett snorted and, pulling hard on the oars, shot them skipping across the chop as they neared the other side of the bay and the dock. "I'd say you can almost count on it."

Mostly, his assumption stemmed from previous circumstances when it came to Rio. Her whole life, all twenty-two years of it, had been fraught with deception, dishonesty, and dishonor. There wasn't anything he could do about that right now. The way his job as a customs agent sent him from place to place was one reason. Or the fact he had no permanent address. Then there was his responsibility to his young brother.

But if he were to be elected sheriff, he'd have time to settle. The thing to do was to wait until after the election. A couple months is all. If all went well, then he'd speak.

The thought sent a ripple through his entire being.

"Hey," Win yelled. "Wake up. We're gonna hit the dock."

They didn't. But just by a frog's whisker.

Three

K eeping the dinner menu as simple as she could justify considering the set prices, Rio hardly had time to wonder where Beckett and Win had gone and when they were coming back. There were musicians to contact, cookies to bake, punch to concoct and chill, guest rooms to tidy, and, feeling the need to make herself presentable, wrinkles to press from her best dress. When she'd taken the office and made a corner of it into her personal living quarters, she'd stuffed her spare belongings from the room upstairs into a trunk and stowed it at the head of her cot, using the flat lid as a table. Fortunately, or unfortunately, as the case may be, she didn't have much in the way of possessions. Nothing that took up much room, at any rate.

The dress looked a sad case, to be sure. Boo, totally bored, watched as Rio set up the ironing board in the kitchen and heated the sad irons on the stovetop. Interruptions kept slowing the process.

"Could be worse." Blanche Golz, studying one of Rio's prized recipes as she prepared a horseradish sauce to accompany the boiled tongue on the menu, laughed as the bell at the lobby desk pinged yet another summons. "Just think if the sun hadn't come out."

She had a point.

Rio released the iron's head from the handle onto the stovetop to keep it hot while she went to answer the bell, huffing a wordless reply.

A gentleman stood at the lobby desk, casting an inquisitive eye at a grouping of ladies seated in armchairs arranged around the fireplace. Miss White and her maid occupied two of the chairs. The woman who'd complained of the noise last night resided in a third, and an elderly woman, who'd come to fish and decided she'd rather gossip, huddled in yet another. Other than that, the room was empty.

As Rio hurried toward the desk, she didn't miss a certain look passing between Miss White and the gentleman. Her first thought was that they knew each other. Her second was to wonder how and why. Her third was to realize the woman didn't look especially pleased. And her fourth knew the maid strained to hide her expression.

Meanwhile, Miss White and the gentleman ignored each other after that first jolt of recognition. The maid looked away, leaning in to seem a part of the other women's talk.

Slipping in behind the tall desk, Rio murmured, "Good afternoon. Welcome to the Painter's Bay Hotel. How may I assist you?"

The man gave a start, as if he hadn't noticed her approach. But he turned to her and smiled.

"How do you do? Yes, I'm seeking a room and trust you have one available."

His smile, though charming, indicated he expected her to accommodate his needs, regardless. Quite a winning smile—provided one was unable to tell it lacked genuine goodwill.

As if she could conjure a room out of nothing. But as it happened, she did have a room. In fact, she had two.

"I do," she said, smiling as brightly and just as falsely as he did. She gave prices and inclusions. He acted pleased, whereupon she passed the register toward him. "Sign here, please."

He did, upon which, she turned the book around and took note of his name. "Mr. Freeman from New York. You've come a long way. Welcome. May I ask what brings you to Painter's Bay?"

His face went blank. A question he hadn't prepared for? Then he had an answer, perhaps because just at that moment a fisherman came in and waggled a stringer of twelve-inch brook trout to show his wife. The fisherman was grinning like a schoolboy.

Mr. Freeman, sans any of the tackle a fisherman needed, let alone attire, stared down at her and said wisely, "Why, I'm here for the fishing. I'm told the... the...fish are plentiful."

"Indeed," Rio murmured. "And will you be wanting to rent a boat? Or a fishing rod, among other things?"

Mr. Freeman appeared completely flummoxed and appalled. He swallowed. "Er...yes. I expect so. Let me get settled in first. I'm quite weary at the moment. It's a long way from New York."

She'd just said that. "Indeed, it is, sir," she said, handing him a door key attached to a metal loop with a small wooden five dangling from it. "Up the stairs. Your room is to the right."

Miss White started to rise from her chair. Catching a slight shake of Freeman's head, she sat down again. He picked up a cardboard suitcase, a piece curiously cheap-looking for a man with the means to travel all the way from New York to fish.

Rio remained standing at the desk, uneasy at what she'd just seen. Although there were several lines at the bottom of the register's page bearing David Freeman's signature, she flipped the page over. Picking up the pen and loading it with ink, she carried the book over to Miss White.

"Madam," she said, cool and calm, quite as if the woman and her maid had never screamed threats at her the previous night. "I'm afraid we've neglected to get you signed into your room. If you could take care of that now for both yourself and your maid, please?"

She'd chosen a good time if Miss White didn't want to make a scene in front of these other women. Scowling, the woman complied, her handwriting quite readable even though it almost seemed as if she deliberately scribbled. The dollar bills she took from her small leather purse were folded and new-looking. "I'll have another night."

Miss Vesta White and maid, Lena Bindle. New York.

Now she knew. *Vesta.* She'd heard her father mention the unusual name to her half brother Eino before he set off on his two-year journey. A family name, Elias had said, bestowed upon a cousin in this generation, or so he'd heard. Rio had no idea how close a cousin or if she was a member of Mr. R.B. White's immediate family.

But what was this cousin doing at the Painter's Bay Hotel? Quinn would've told Mr. White the circumstances of Eino's time here. It should've been a complete break. God knows Rio didn't want and wouldn't tolerate any more involvement in her half brother's life.

No, indeed. And if anyone thought differently, they'd just better take another think.

Closing the cash drawer with a thump, Rio went back to her ironing, sliding the hot iron over wrinkles as if not just to press them away, but to demolish them. And seconds after she left the lobby, she caught sight of Vesta climbing the stairs and turning to the right, although her room was to the left.

———

EVENING WAS DRAWING on when Beckett and Win returned from wherever they'd been. Rio and Blanche had just finished plating meals for the first seating of diners. Beckett, seeing her busy, paused in the kitchen doorway and gave a small salute.

Rio waved back. She had to be satisfied with that for the present. There was no time to speak with him just then, no matter how anxious she was to ask his opinion of why Miss Vesta White had turned up in Painter's Bay. Not that he would know, of course. She knew that. But she needed to confide in somebody. Maybe he'd have an idea why Vesta and this David Freeman were keeping their acquaintance secret. It all struck her as a sign of trouble.

Trouble for her, she meant.

Blanche set a final plate on the serving table and

grinned at Rio. "You're sure glad to see Mr. Ferris. You look livelier than you have since...since he left."

Unable to deny the claim, Rio shrugged. "Oh? Well, I... He and Win, they're good friends."

Blanche snorted. "Friends! Win maybe, but he's just a kid. Beckett, he's more. Don't try to say he's not. I won't believe you."

Left speechless, Rio turned her back.

Meanwhile, Eliza and Marie darted from table to table like hummingbirds at a feeder, transporting heavy plates as if they were nothing. Conversation rose and fell, cutlery clinked on the crockery, laughter pealed high and excited. Every table was filled.

Almost everyone mentioned to Rio that they intended to stay and dance after dinner. Enough to make her think this may have been a good idea, one to consider for another time when she had more time to prepare. She took a moment to peek into the lobby. The room was chock-full of people waiting to eat, mixing with the people who'd already eaten and were staying for the dance. Turner, the bartender, had all he could handle in his small domain. When the third seating was finished, she planned to ask a few of her regular customers if they'd help move the chairs and tables to the side to leave room for dancing. She couldn't help worrying a little. Given the crowd, she knew it would be a crush.

The musicians were already tuning up and testing the acoustics from various spots around the piano. She had put a basket on the old upright that said, "Donations," and left a few coins as seed money. All signs pointed to a profitable evening for them.

By eight thirty, the kitchen, cleaned to what the

Golz women called a lick and a promise, was shut down, the lights dimmed. The Golz sisters had changed into their party dresses, which set even the dignified Blanche to giggling. Rollicking music came from the lobby. Rio, pleased to hear the piano sounded better than she'd feared it might, felt excitement rising in her as she exchanged her plain skirt, blouse, and apron for the dress she'd labored to press. Doing so reminded her of David Freeman and Vesta White. Would they be joining the party? Would the bitter-faced maid?

She shrugged. Not worth thinking about, she told herself, and rubbed a dab of an infusion scented with roses onto her pulse spots. She made the scent from her own flowers. Better, she felt, than always smelling of cooking. Would Beckett like it?

With a final pat to tuck a lock of hair in place, she went to find out. She left her little revolver behind, but made sure to lock the door.

She found Beckett propping up the wall between the dining room and the lobby. Waiting for her, she discovered, with his arms folded across his chest in a casual pose. He smiled, a slow, appreciative smile, when he saw her.

Heart beating faster, Rio started toward him. He looked nice. He'd shaved, put on fresh clothes, and cleaned his boots. The look he gave her showed he liked the picture she made as well. He held his hand out to her. She took it. Maybe he sensed her trembling, for he said, "Don't worry. Your dance party is already a roaring success."

He must've misconstrued the cause of her tension. It wasn't the come-one, come-all dance. It was him.

Rio forced a laugh. "And after my emergency planning, it isn't even raining."

In fact, due to the heat, someone had opened the front door, holding it ajar with a bucket of sand from the beach. Most of the children had claimed the porch to practice their dancing, the boys as eagerly as the girls. Their parents crowded the open area in the lobby, the usual wallflowers—old maids, shy bachelors—standing along the edges.

Swinging her into his arms, Beckett led her around the designated dance floor. Rio, who hadn't much in the way of dance practice, found it fairly easy to follow him, but only because he knew what to do.

"Relax," he whispered to her after she'd stepped on his toes for the second time. He gathered her just a little closer. "I've got you."

He did indeed. Rio felt a tingle everywhere their bodies touched. After a while, she did relax. Enough to ask the question that had gnawed at her ever since he and Win had arrived on her doorstep. Why had they shown up just now? So she asked.

Beckett looked down at her, his expression sober. "Doc Clement sent me a letter." He stopped, acting as if he had more to say, but didn't quite know how to say it.

"Dr. Clement?" She may have missed a step.

"Yes. I'd asked him to let me know when the county opened up nominations for sheriff."

Rio's heart thumped. "And?" It came out as a whisper.

"Which they did last week. He said they started accepting applicants Monday."

"And?" Without noticing, they'd stopped dancing and stood still. Rio no longer heard the music.

"Doc nominated me on the spot. This afternoon, I filled out the forms and threw my name in the pot."

This is what she'd wished for. So why did the thought make her go trembly and breathless? Because the sheriff got put in danger all too often. At least, an honest sheriff did.

After a moment, Beckett gave her a little shake. "Aren't you going to say anything? I thought you'd be glad."

He'd done it for her, she knew. For her and for Win, who needed a settled place to live and school to attend. She'd hoped Beckett would, but all of a sudden, she was having second thoughts. Is it what he wanted to do for his own sake?

"You'll be a good sheriff," she said.

He made a little huff. "Not unless I win the election."

"Do you want to win?" She looked up at him, dark eyes meeting his darker ones. "I'm not glad unless this is truly what you want to do."

He drew her in a little closer, and their feet started moving again. "Are you worried it isn't? Rio, I'm not a man to be a martyr. I guarantee to you that if I didn't want the responsibility, or if I thought I couldn't do the job, I wouldn't run for office. Don't forget I've been a customs agent for several years. Now it's time to settle down in one spot. My choice. This isn't so different. I do want and can do the job. And I know you trust me to do what's right. That means a whole lot to me."

It was like the wind went out of her, and relief

poured in. "You mean it." She let herself lean against him. "You'll be a great sheriff."

He laughed. "Damn right," he said, and swept her back into the dance.

Rio hardly had a moment to greet anyone. Molly and Dr. Clement, who grinned big when they passed in the dance, and Beckett nodded to him. Mr. Meadows, the mortician, as smiling and happy as anyone there. Mr. Burton, the postmaster, and his wife. Fred Lewis, her friend, the grocer. Had they been the ones who got together and nominated Beckett? She rather thought so.

And then, a surprise to see Miss White and Bindle joining the soiree. They were seated at one of the tables, the maid turning down one of the single men, but Vesta accepting the invitation of Bernie Jensen, the banker's assistant, to dance.

He was a little younger than Vesta, but like to like, Rio supposed. Those who considered themselves upper class joined together. But what about David Freeman? She spotted him at the bar with an amber-colored drink in his hand, watching Vesta with a jealous eye. He wore a tortured-looking scowl when Vesta laughed at something Jensen said.

The Golz girls had no problem finding partners. Single men flocked around them, competing for their favor. Even men such as Bernie Jensen, who sidled up to Eliza. Blanche's admirers included young Jess Stokes, whose father leased the sawmill from the Salo estate and who Rio had asked to assume control of the logging operation after Wash Ames was murdered. The elder Stokes had turned the running of the logging crew over to his son.

Rio couldn't help thinking the two of them, Blanche

and Jess, made a good pair if the glow in Blanche's rosy cheeks indicated anything beyond the heat getting to her. The crush of warm bodies in an overcrowded room foretold a problem with the punch holding out.

Before long, it occurred to Rio to open up extra space in the lobby for the sitters and free up more room for the dancers in the dining room. Volunteers saw it done, and the dancing went on. Laughter filled both rooms, rising at times over the music.

But then, in a sharp clash, everything stopped and, to her astonishment, what was apparently an odd sort of campaign for public office began. For sheriff, in plain fact.

Bull French, one of the two blacksmiths in town, started a major kerfuffle. One that ended up on the verge of a riot, and he did it seemingly by intention. Why he chose to intrude on the dance she'd never know since he hadn't attended a dinner service in the restaurant. Not ever. In a nutshell, he should never have been there at all.

He'd been a follower of Thor Donaldson, she remembered, shuddering a little when she first caught sight of him in the doorway. He was a big guy, heavily muscled, with brutal features. Dirt and soot from the forge were ground into his hands and even the wrinkles around his neck. Well-named, too, a bully who'd even tried to push her half brother around. Until their father, Elias, got wind of it and put a stop to the strong-arming. She'd never heard exactly how Elias managed it.

So why had Bull showed up here?

Rio became aware of his arrival as she and Beckett chanced to dance past the open door as he entered the lobby. Entered? Stalked, more like, arrogance in every footstep. And he didn't appear to be interested in dancing. A fight was likely more to his taste as he had a reputation as a brawler.

Which caused her, yet again, to step on Beckett's toes.

At least this time, she had an excuse. Namely, because Beckett had stopped abruptly and given a funny sort of little sigh. And under his breath, a rather rude curse.

"What is it?" Rio looked up at him to see what had stopped the dance. She followed his line of sight to see him eyeing Bull. "Oh, him?"

And if Beckett had a steely gaze fixed on Bull, Bull had one equally as steely fixed on Beckett. Rio would've had to be blind not to see something unpleasant and unresolved going on between them.

The confrontation wasn't long in coming.

Bull had a voice that matched his appearance. Deep, rough, rude, raspy. Untutored. Even the Salo's Chinese logging crew, the ones who spoke English as, she'd recently discovered, many did nowadays, used their words more ably.

Bull clapped his big, dirty paws together loudly enough to draw attention and shouted over the music. "Hush up this racket afore I put a bullet where it'll do the most good."

His fingers went to rest on the butt of a revolver stuffed in the waist of his britches.

The piano was last to stop, seeing that Miss Abrams, a middle-aged spinster who played at the church on Sundays, had her back to the room. She turned on the stool to see what had happened to leave her playing on alone. Her eyes widened at the way Bull glared at her, and she hastily dropped her hands into her lap.

The poor lady turned tomato red. Though in truth, probably no redder than Rio, what with the way her temper took a leap.

Detaching herself from Beckett's grip, she stepped forward. She put her hand in her pocket, forgetting she'd left her pistol in her room. And rueing the silly thought that had said she'd have no need of it tonight.

"What is the meaning of this?" she demanded. "Please leave. I'm sure you'd be more welcome at the saloon in town."

He grinned at her with a show of the broken, stained teeth of a chewer. "I'm shuttin' this here place down. Had complaints saying it's a regular den of inick...inickity and a nuisance. Everybody leave right now—and mind you don't come back."

Rio's back stiffened. "I don't know what you're talking about. I do know I'm looking at the only one who needs to leave. You. Get out. You've no business here. No business and no authority."

There were murmurs from behind her. Agreement.

Beckett stood at her side, his arms free at his sides as if anticipating quick movement might be called for. And he was ready for it.

A little girl came to the door behind Bull just then and started to slip past him. "Mama," she called out just as Bull, evidently sensing movement behind him, struck out with an open hand. His palm caught her on the side of her head. Tumbling to the floor, she screamed.

A scream echoed by the mother rushing forward from Rio's left.

People in the crowd growled a protest. Bull shoved

a hand against the woman's chest, stopping her in her tracks before she reached the child. "You want some a that?" His voice growled. "I ain't opposed to seeing women mind their place." He raised his voice again, loud, hard, and rough. "I told ya to get out. Alla you."

And still louder, he made his announcement. "See, I'm gonna be the sheriff in this here county come next month. You think Thor Donaldson was tough? I'm twice as tough as him. You'll see. What I say will be what happens. As of right here tonight, seeing as how I figure I might as well get started early."

Beside her, Rio felt Beckett stiffen.

Someone, a brave soul, said, "Election ain't for a month. And I ain't voting for you. Not no how."

Bull glared into the crowd. "Oh, I ain't worried about winnin' the election. I got ways. Sides, there ain't anybody fixin' to go against me." His thumb pointed in at his own chest.

Which is when Beckett stepped forward. "That's where you're mistaken. You've got competition. And no authority to lay down demands."

Bull's head turned toward him, slow, much like a beady-eyed grizzly eyes its victim just before it attacks. "Competition? What's that?"

"Means you've got somebody running for sheriff against you," the brave soul answered for Beckett. "I don't care who he is. I'll vote for him."

His bravery, helped no doubt by being hidden at the back of the crowd—and possibly some liquid courage—broke the silence. There was laughter and a chorus of agreement.

Bull's eyes bugged, the muscles in his jaw flexing as if to gnaw somebody's bones. "Hah! Who?"

And Beckett said, "Me. Beckett Ferris." He looked out over the folks pushing forward. "Some of you may remember me from the trouble last June, and then again last month with those unruly folks from back east."

There were nods and a few huzzahs, although a long shiver ran down Rio's back in fear for him at his stated intention. Yes, even though she'd been in favor of him applying right up until two minutes ago. Until before Bull French showed his ugly face.

Four

S hock held Rio in place, right up until Beckett's public announcement. And although Beckett put out a hand to stop her, she found motion again. Striding forward, she darted past Bull and knelt to help the woman gather the sobbing child into her arms and get them out of his reach.

Bull, grinning, ignored her, concentrating instead on outtalking Beckett. That changed when, seeing the woman and her little girl safely moved to be enveloped within a group of other women, Rio stood right in front of him and said, "Get out. Now." The strange part is, her voice came out soft and quiet. And all the more dangerous.

He laughed, raucous and scornful. "You gonna make me?"

Then Beckett was beside her again, saying something and gently pushing her toward someone. Rio couldn't hear what he said over the pounding of her heartbeat in her ears. But she found Win tugging at her. Of course it was Win. She might've known.

Fierce anger raged.

Yes. She was gonna make him. Pulling away from Win, she rushed through the crowd to her room while they looked after her as if they thought she was running away. Only she wasn't. And she didn't pick up the little .32 from the table. No, indeed. She took her father's .45 from the holster she kept in her desk drawer, checked the loads, and carried it back with her into the lobby.

The crowd, seeing the gun in her hand, began whispering.

Turner hurried to catch up. "I can take that," he said.

"It's mine to do." She outpaced him, her stride under her party dress long and sure.

"Miss...Rio...let me help," he said, but she didn't relent.

Then Mr. Meadows, the mortician, of all people, followed her, backing up Turner, while out of the corner of her eye she saw Dr. Clement there too. He had a small pistol pointing at the floor—for the moment, at least. She'd never suspected he even owned a gun, let alone brought it with him to a party.

Bull French, to Rio's everlasting disgust, was still carrying on, making sure his bellow reached throughout the hotel lobby and into the dining room. From the laughter and chatter before he showed up, the silence afterward was shattering. Even the children on the porch had fallen silent.

And Beckett stood easy and let him talk. Bull might be loud and frightening, but he wasn't respected. And everything he said only convinced people he not only wasn't a good choice for sheriff, he should probably have been on the other side of the bars.

But he was intimidating.

So Rio interrupted him in mid-sentence. "Get out." The two words were beginning to feel like an echo. So she added to them. "This is my hotel, my property. I will not allow my friends or my customers to be harassed. If you come here again, you will be considered a trespasser. Do you know what law-abiding citizens do to trespassers? If necessary, they will be shot."

She had his attention now. Seeing the cocked .45 held in her rock steady fist, he finally stopped talking.

His laugh this time almost sounded forced. "You wouldn't dare shoot. Why, you prolly don't know how to aim a gun. I'll bet that one ain't even loaded."

"I'll be glad to show you, if I find it necessary to squeeze the trigger."

Somehow, Rio was aware of Beckett buckling on his revolver, hurrying at it. Win, again, racing into the fray to see his brother went armed.

Bull French hovered, his hand over the butt of his revolver as if undecided. He obviously wanted to draw his own gun, but didn't quite dare. Not now, with Beckett armed. In fact, he ignored Rio and her .45 with his gaze concentrating on Beckett.

Struck by the thought he'd known Beckett had filed for sheriff and that his intention all along had been to scare him out of the running, she had to wonder who put him up to it. A miscalculation on someone's part. Beckett did not scare. Period.

And what Bull didn't know about Rio would've filled a personal diary. Or at least a newspaper column. He'd just made a big mistake.

Although a peaceable settlement seemed a doubtful outcome from the very first, something a little quieter might have happened had the woman with the little girl prevented her twelve-year-old son from taking a hand. Although in truth, Rio doubted it ever occurred to the mother her boy would actually attack a full-grown man, especially one like Bull French, in an attempt to bring him to account.

The boy came from behind a bunch of people standing around, and he was scowling nearly as fiercely as Bull French. The kid didn't say a word of warning. He simply rushed up behind Bull and kicked him hard in the back of the knee. "You slapped my little sister," he shouted then, his voice pitched high and not yet changed to that of a man. "You laid dirty hands on my ma. But you'd better not do it again. Not my ma, not my sister."

It could've been funny, the way Bull dipped and lost his balance when the kick struck a nerve. He went down on one knee. He didn't fall all the way, though, and it wasn't funny at all. Not when Bull recovered and swung around with his fist clenched, thinking to administer a roundhouse blow in payment.

A blow that never landed.

Quick as a star can twinkle, Beckett stepped right into Bull, catching the swinging fist with his right hand and wrenching it up and back, forcing it behind Bull's back. He trapped Bull's leg with his own so any shifting of his feet would throw the bigger man to the ground. And with his left hand, Beckett yanked Bull's little finger backward to a place it was never meant by nature to be. A whisker more and it would've broken.

It all happened fast and smooth, as if maybe Beckett practiced the maneuver every day.

Bull French yipped like a whipped puppy. Beckett,

no weakling himself, had not been gentle. But he had not been lethal.

"Handcuffs," he snapped to his brother, though Win already had them dangling from his back pocket.

It was over, just like that.

If that didn't show the folks of Painter's Bay which man was sheriff material, Rio didn't know what would.

But then the question remained on what should be done with him. The town commissioners, after Thor Donaldson's demise, had talked an older man into being a sort of part-time deputy marshal. Someone whose main job was to see the occasional belligerent drunk locked in a cell to be released the next day when he sobered up. Once, he'd had to keep a cattle thief in jail for three days until a real lawman arrived from the county seat to take him in hand. He hadn't liked it.

The old man was no hero. Everyone knew that. It seemed a bit doubtful the fellow could hold his nerve to face Bull when it came time to turn him loose. Not that anybody would blame him.

Who could possibly forget Washington Ames, who, only a couple of months ago, had been murdered as he released the prisoner? Rio never would.

Most of the men Beckett had met when filing for the election of sheriff had attended the party. It didn't take long for them to get together and decide Bull should be locked up for the night and to appoint Beckett, since he was already involved, to see Bull secured in the jail. Several men volunteered to help. It turned out the men of Painter's Bay did not approve of a widowed woman and her little family being slapped around. Not by anyone.

But after they had gone, a party of four escorting

Bull French and Beckett as they trudged around the point of Painter's Bay to the town, the impromptu dance party wound down earlier than it might otherwise have. Bull French's interruption had stolen the joy from the evening.

In a way, Rio was just as glad. Oh, not for the way it all happened, but she'd had a chance to study her neighbor's reactions to the violence. And watch Vesta White, Bindle the maid, and David Freeman. An odd trio, to be sure. One she couldn't help thinking was up to no good. In what way, she couldn't fathom, but so far, her experience with the White family had not been pleasant. When she thought about it, she realized her efforts to make sure Eino's theft got returned had never received much of an acknowledgment. Odd, because surely Quinn had told them the circumstances. He would, wouldn't he? Unless he'd wanted to grab all the credit.

But then she sighed as she pushed a table into its usual position and dragged two armchairs to sit around it. She didn't really think he'd do that. Not after she'd saved his life.

Win Ferris pitched in alongside the Golz ladies to restore the lobby to order. Turner and a couple of his pals scooted dining room tables into their former positions, and it seemed as if both rooms would be redded up in no time. Rio had set Boo free when the dancers left and the guests retired to their rooms, and he was chasing around, growling at the moving chair legs while finding cookie crumbs to lick up. At last, she stood back and, setting her hands to her hips, stretched her spine.

"Thanks so much, everyone. What do you think? Was this worthwhile? Did you have some fun despite what happened with Bull French?" She couldn't help teasing Blanche just a little. "That Jess Stokes, Blanche. He must be a good dancer, the way you partnered up with him."

Blanche turned red as a garnet as her sisters tittered, but she didn't duck away. "So happens he *is* a good dancer." Throwing her head back, she grinned. "I enjoyed the evening very much."

So... Rio's dark eyes opened wide. The attitude. She thought maybe a lot more had happened tonight than one would've guessed.

And even considering the despicable Bull French, not all of it had been bad.

———

NO MATTER WHAT, a hotelkeeper must be ready to serve his—or her—clients. Six a.m. found Rio in the hotel kitchen with breakfast prepped, plates and cups laid out, and pats of butter on tiny plates. Biscuits were in the oven, sausage gravy stayed warm in a bowl, coffee steamed on the back of the stove, bowls of cinnamon-flavored applesauce awaited a dollop of whipped cream, and buckwheat pancake batter, the leavening foaming and making bubbles, was ready for the griddle.

She went to unlock the lobby door, nodding a greeting to one of the overnight guests as he stumbled down the stairs with his fishing tackle in hand.

"Breakfast is ready, Mr. Cobb. Take any table, and I'll be with you in just a moment."

Mr. Cobb saluted. Through the window beside the door, she saw figures on the porch waiting for her to open.

Unlocking the door, she peeked outside. A light fog

lay between the hotel porch and the dock, blurring the shape of a man stepping out of a boat. Blurred, but didn't obliterate. The figure didn't match Beckett.

"Come on in," she called to the waiting group. "It's chilly out this morning. There's a definite feeling of fall in the air." She waved them inside and told them she'd be there in just a moment, though she paused briefly to look down the trail to town in hope of spotting Beckett there. But although she strained her eyes as if to see through trees, there still was no sign of him.

Looking out over the hillside on the opposite side of the bay, she saw tamarack trees ascending above the fog. Just beginning to glow yellow, they rose above the green of the pines. Bushes made a smudge of red, rust, and gold. One tree stood alone dressed in bright crimson, as if it had been painted with a brush dipped in barn red. The scent of burning wood wafted over all.

Chilly for sure. Soon the fishermen guests would be gone, and hunters would take their places. Profits be damned, Rio dreaded the shift to killing animals. She wouldn't say no to some tender venison steaks or tenderloins, though.

Sighing, she eased the door shut.

Mornings by herself were always hectic. The cooking, the waiting on tables until one of the Golz girls arrived, the cleanup, and minding the till. An hour and a quarter of another passed before Marie arrived, looking as if she hadn't slept her fill.

Win, when he got up, joined Rio in looking worried.

"He'll be all right," she told him. "He knows what he's doing."

"Yeah? Then why are you looking out the door

every two minutes?" Win knew her too well and wasn't taken in by her overly cheery, and utterly false, voice.

Figuring there was no point in trying to convince the boy otherwise—how could she when they apparently felt the same tension—with a change of tactics, she hardly looked up from a griddle full of the buckwheat pancakes starting to bubble on top. "Did Beckett tell you he intended on running for sheriff?" She flipped the pancakes with a deft twist of her wrist.

Win sent her a wise glance. "He didn't have to. I knew when he started tying up all the loose ends in the smuggling investigation. That was six weeks ago."

Rio's dark eyes opened wide. "Six weeks? You didn't warn me. Not in either of your letters."

He shrugged. "Beck wanted to surprise you." He frowned at her. "He thought you'd be pleased."

She had to calm herself. She thought she'd be pleased too. More so than what she was, at any rate. But who would ever have expected a man like Bull French to run for the office of sheriff? She'd bet he was illiterate, for one thing. A joke, almost, except he wasn't. Far from it if last night was anything to go by.

Marie loaded her arms with plates of pancakes and left the kitchen just as the bell at the cash register indicated a customer waiting to pay his bill and depart. Before refilling the griddle with another batch of pancakes, Rio hurried toward the dining room, brushing past someone who reached out to her as she went by.

It wasn't until she headed back to the kitchen from collecting the money that she saw who it had been. Mr. Melvin Carver Sr. For a moment, she hesitated, then, with no other choice, went on.

Mr. Carver wasn't at all shy about claiming her attention.

"Miss Salo," he said, seeming almost to leer—or maybe sneer—at her.

Was it because of her working apron, which, sadly, held more than one stain as proof of her kitchen labors?

Perforce, she stopped. "Yes? May I help you?" She hoped not.

Carver Jr. rose to pull a chair out for her. "Please, sit," he said, looking toward his father. "We have a proposal for you and think you'll be pleased."

Very much aware of not only their so-called proposal from the summer, plus their overheard conversation with the banker a day ago, she knew what he meant. Pleased about was as far from her feelings as it was possible to get.

"I'm sorry." She pushed the chair back under the table to keep it from blocking the area. "I'm very busy just now. Perhaps later, if I have some free time." Free time that would never come if she could help it.

Carver Sr. scowled. "I'm a busy man, miss. I don't like being put off. Sit down."

Rio smiled, the most charming expression she could muster. "And I, sir, am a busy woman," she repeated, and made her escape. Behind her, she heard his breath of aggravation. Her next smile was a real one, even though Carver didn't catch a glimpse of it.

Back in the kitchen, she found Beckett sitting at the kitchen table talking with Win. A plate piled high with buckwheat pancakes and a slab of ham waited in front of him. Her breath escaped in a rush.

"You're alive." The words, ones she'd never meant to say, burst from her.

Beckett looked up at her, his dark eyes glinting, the crook of his lips lightening his face. "Sure I am. You didn't think a character like Bull French could get the best of me, did you?"

Memories of what happened to Wash Ames filled her mind. She found herself shaking. "You're not infallible, you know. He could've taken you by surprise."

Slowly, he shook his head. "No, Rio. He couldn't. A man like Bull, he relies on brute strength. He doesn't think. He'd be a whole lot more dangerous if he did. He just acts, telegraphing his every move ahead of time. You've no need to worry." He turned to his brother. "You either. Got it?"

Win nodded. "Got it." But Rio wasn't so sure. Something about the way he looked indicated he might not be telling her everything.

LAST NIGHT, Beckett's small posse, sure they'd done their civic duty by helping escort Bull French to jail despite his loudly voiced wishes, left seconds after the elderly deputy town marshal rummaged in a desk drawer for keys, and they finally got the job done.

Nervous over this particular prisoner, the old fellow side-eyed Beckett. "Reckon I'll leave you to it. Doubt you'll have any trouble."

Startled, Beckett said, "Wait a minute. Night duty is your job, if I'm not mistaken." He hadn't volunteered to stay the night.

"Nope. Not for him. You fellers brought him here from across the bay. Far as I can tell, this means this here fella ain't a town prisoner. That says he belongs to the county. I hear you're running for sheriff. Guess that puts you in charge."

"The hotel is part of the town of Painter's Bay," Beckett protested. But it was to the deputy's backside as he rushed away into the night.

Bull had already flopped onto the thin mattress on the jail cot and was snoring to beat two of a kind, as he remained for the rest of the night. It was when he woke up in the morning that things got interesting. When he confessed a feller had bought him whiskey and made a suggestion about starting a ruckus. And why it might be in Bull's interest to follow orders.

It got Beckett to wondering.

The commissioners had told Beckett the application period for sheriff closed at the end of this coming week. They hadn't mentioned any other applicants. It surprised him when the old deputy already knew he'd applied. So wouldn't he have known about Bull as well?

Beckett's eyes narrowed as he called to mind the way Bull had acted last night, as if an election wouldn't be necessary for his appointment. As if he'd been promised the job.

French was still belligerent as Beckett worked the lock to set him free. Enough so that Beckett took his time, waiting for him to rid himself of some of that venom.

Beck hadn't forgotten how Washington Ames had died, murdered in this same jail under the same sort of circumstances. He wasn't about to let it happen to him.

Bull's mouth flapped practically non-stop. He talked of the fellow who bought him whiskey and talked about the treasure just lying around, ready to find.

"Treasure? Where?" Beckett asked, but French just laughed.

"Can't fool me," he said. "You want it for yourself, just like they all do. But I'm the one gonna get it."

Bull French talked about Eino Salo, the thieving bastard who, whether he knew it or not, was gonna make someone real rich. The joke'd be on Salo. As long as Bull was the first to find the treasure, that is, and he intended on being first in line. Though, as a matter of fact, he didn't quite trust the fellow who revealed the information. But then, Bull didn't need to trust him. As sheriff, he could force anybody into doing what he said. Just like the old sheriff used to do.

"Yep. Just like ole Thor Donaldson," he said.

Beckett didn't bother to remind him Donaldson's actions were what got him killed.

Five

If Rio thought she could avoid the Carvers and convince them they'd never persuade her to sell, she turned out to be mistaken. As proved when she'd settled into her office to check over the bill from Mr. Lewis, the grocer in town who ordered her supplies along with his own from the distributor in Spokane. She expected to find his account completely honest and accurate. She always did.

In this case, the light tapping on her closed office door gave no indication of an impatient and imperious man who felt entitled to ride roughshod over her.

If he could.

Rio turned in her swivel chair. "Come in," she said, expecting either of the Golz women or maybe, hopefully, Beckett.

What a disappointment.

In they came. Both Carver Sr. and Carver Jr., who closed the door behind them.

Rio's lips tightened. Not only were they in her office, but they were in her bedroom. Although all her belongings were either tidy or put away out of sight, she didn't like the intrusion into her personal space. Not one bit. She let them know it.

"Customers are not allowed in this area. Hence the sign on the door." She'd had to affix one that said, *Private. No entry.* "I'll thank you to confine yourselves to either the dining room or the lobby."

"We've business to discuss." Carver Sr. scanned the small room, searching perhaps, for somewhere to sit. Without success, as it happened.

Rio got up and put her hand in her pocket, in need of the reassurance of the little Iver Johnson revolver residing there.

"I'm the one who decides if I have business to discuss with you." Firm and assured, she moved forward to force them out. "And I've decided I do not. Please leave."

"Now see here. You can't talk to my father like that." Melvin Carver Jr., highly incensed, burst out. "He's an important man."

Rio cast him a look. "Out, the pair of you. You're not only wasting my time, but your own."

The two were shaking their heads with identical, stubborn expressions.

"We intend to finish this transaction here and now," Carver Sr. said. "I'll pay you $450 today. Right now, in fact." He made a motion as if to take out a wallet.

Rio almost laughed. Almost. He'd dropped fifty dollars off the already paltry offer since yesterday. An act of pure aggression, she supposed, which, for a real businessman, made the whole situation absurd.

"Go away. You're making yourselves look and sound ridiculous. I told you before, I'm not interested in selling the hotel." It was true. The thing is, the very fact of their persistence struck her as out of character for the Carvers. Why were they so determined to have her property, a little rural hotel in the middle of wild, and sometimes woolly, eastern Washington state? For people whose base of interest was New York City, no less. It didn't make a lick of sense. Most surely raised her curiosity, though.

"I'm talking cash money," Carver said as if he hadn't heard a word she said. "Right here today."

The repetition raised Rio's annoyance level even higher. It was as if he intended the insult to break her resistance.

His pale eyes glittered. "I give you this nice chunk of money, and you can walk away from the operation just as soon as you can pack your clothes. No more cooking. No more unruly people like that fellow I heard was here last night."

Where had he heard that? From whom? And if Bull's behavior was typical of him, she had to wonder if it had actually been instigated by the Carvers. And where had he and his son stayed last night, since it hadn't been in her hotel? Mr. Masterson's house? Could he be in on some sort of plot to bilk her out of the property?

Carver kept on talking. Something along the lines of, "No more making beds or talking to strangers. Or stacks of dirty dishes, day after day."

He struck a nerve on that last item, but as the business grew, she planned to hire someone to clean up. On the premise that the best way to discover what's what is to ask, she did. And discovered that taking men like this by surprise worked fairly well.

Interrupting Carver's argument of how much better off she'd be when divested of her means of making a living, Rio shook her forefinger at him and asked, "How did you hear of the Painter's Bay Hotel? I've wondered about this ever since you were here in the summer."

As she spoke, a new idea struck. The Carver's first visit had occurred at the same time Eino made his presence known, when several other factions had mixed together. Were they all connected? And now, here was Vesta White, also a connection.

Eino again. Would she never be done with her half brother?

Carver's little piggy eyes opened wider, innocence personified. "Heard about the hotel?"

"If I had to guess," she said as if he hadn't spoken, "I'd figure it has something to do with a certain Mr. R.B. White. Or perhaps Miss Vesta White." Rio glanced at Carver Jr. to find his mouth hanging open. It wasn't an attractive look, though informative. Given the signs, she'd guessed right.

"What about it?" Carver Sr. snapped. "Mr. White and I do business together from time to time. If he isn't interested himself, when he learns of a favorable deal, he will tell me about it. As I will tell him, under the same circumstances. Not that you would know, but businessmen help each other all the time."

"Do they?" She forced a smile. Her father never had. "I find that questionable. But in this case, there is no deal to be made. There never was. Someone, Mr. Carver, has been bamboozling you. And quite successfully, it seems. You've made two trips to Washington without purpose. If I were you, I'd question Mr. White's honesty. Or Miss White's." Rio still had the idea Miss Vesta White was in on this. Why else would she be here? She and Mr. David Freeman, who wasn't particularly good at hiding his interest in Vesta.

Carver Jr. stood stock still and stared at her. "Bamboozled? What does that even mean?"

"It means, Mr. Carver Jr., that you and your father have been made to look foolish. Perhaps you can tell me why. What did they say that so interests you about this place?"

The Carvers, with identical expressions, clamped their mouths shut. Much as she wanted to know, she'd expected that. In truth, she'd learned more than she'd thought she would in this peculiar exchange, all without them having to do anything but deny her claims. Now, if only she knew what it all meant.

"Enough of this." Stepping around them, she went to the door and opened it. An invitation to leave.

"Shoo," she said. "Go away."

Carver Jr. started to speak again until Senior shook his head. Pushing his son ahead of him, her demand worked at last.

"You'll hear from me again," Carver Sr. warned. The door closed behind them.

Waving a hand as if batting at flies, she seated herself again, opened a ledger to a blank page, and picked up her pen. Leaning back, Rio allowed herself to slump. Her hand, she saw, shook like weeds in the wind. Enough to make writing questionable if by chance anyone intended to read it later. Dropping the pen, she closed the ledger and stared blankly at the wall. How she hated confrontations like this. If Melvin Carver only knew, it wasn't cooking or cleaning or even washing dishes she disliked about the hotel business. It was confronting impatient, impolite, or just plain disagreeable people. And there seemed to be far too many of them lately.

Figuring the Carvers had had time to depart, she got up and went looking for Beckett. Maybe he'd have some idea what the men from Chicago wanted badly enough to pester her like this. Not once, but twice. And warned of doing again.

"Beats me," Beckett said when she finally caught up with him later that evening, after the hotel dining room closed.

A few remaining customers had settled in the lobby to enjoy conversation and a post-dinner drink with their neighbors before Rio closed for the night. She and Beckett claimed chairs near the fireplace, enjoying the flames and their own drinks.

A while back, the whiskey salesman had persuaded Turner to buy a bottle of newly popular crème de menthe for a taste trial. He'd already whispered to Rio that next time the man came around, he'd better buy two. Apparently, the ladies had discovered the drink worked wonders for their digestion after dinner.

Rio laughed and asked the bartender to save just a sip for her. He had, and she had it in front of her now, even as Beckett tasted a shot of brandy.

"Tell me everything the Carvers said." He set down the barely touched drink.

She did and earned herself a questioning look out of Beckett's dark eyes.

"What makes you think Eino is involved?" he said. "That's not much to go on."

"I know." Rio touched her tongue to the green liquid in her tiny glass. She liked the sweet mint taste.

Maybe it would help settle her stomach too. "It wasn't only what they said that tipped me off. It was how they looked. For such self-acclaimed successful businessmen, they weren't convincing. The exchange of looks between them if I said something that struck too close, the too fast denials, the general demeanor." She shrugged. "It's possible they didn't consider me capable of homing in on their attitudes and showed more than they would've showed to a man."

He snorted. "I wish I'd met this pair."

"You might yet have the pleasure, if that's what you want to call it. Blanche heard Carver Sr. tell his son they'd discuss this with someone—she didn't quite catch the name—as soon as they got back to town. If that's the case, they will have missed the afternoon train headed east."

"Masterson, do you think?"

"Very likely. Since he owns the Bank of Painter's Bay, an exchange of funds would no doubt go through the bank. And I suspect the Carvers have been staying with him."

Beckett shook his head. "You do get yourself in a pickle, don't you, Miss Salo?"

"Oh, Mr. Ferris, you haven't heard the half of it yet." So saying, Rio tilted her head back, tipped the rest of the green liqueur into her mouth, and swallowed it down, choking a little at the burn. Standing up, she said, "Will you walk with me? Outside?" She spoke a little louder. "Boo needs a walk before retiring."

Beckett's dark eyes flashed his surprise.

From over in the corner, but within earshot, Vesta White huddled with David Freeman. They were drinking from large snifters of cognac, a bottle of which

Turner had scrounged up from somewhere in the cellar. The bottle had been dusty and strewn with cobwebs when he brought it up to show the couple an hour or so ago. To Rio's astonishment, Freeman brushed off the label, read it, and nodded his gratification. Vesta had clapped her hands like a delighted child.

"At last," she said. "Something worth drinking. I wonder who laid it in."

Rio felt sure it must've been her grandfather, Benedict Serrano, when he had owned the hotel, but she didn't say so. She thought she'd know if it had been her father. He hadn't generally been interested in the finer aspects of restaurant drinking and dining. Only the profit.

Turner had simply shrugged when questioned about the cognac's provenance. "Been here a while," he said.

Rio'd had to tend something in the kitchen just then and heard no more. But Turner did. And he passed on to her, word for word, what the pair said next.

Collecting Boo, ecstatic at his release from the confines of the office, Rio and Beckett paused on the porch for her to slip her arms into a sweater. The evenings were rapidly taking on an autumn chill. A single cricket kept singing. Over toward the spring where water was piped to the hotel, an owl called like a lost soul in the darkness. Following Boo, Rio headed that way, Beckett walking close beside her while the dog charged ahead, running in circles around them.

Their hands touched by accident. Then, not at all by accident, Beckett found her cold hand again and wrapped it in his warmth. "What's going on?" he asked.

Her fingers clenched in his, and he stopped. "What is it?"

"I wish I knew."

"Huh. Looks like whatever it is has you worried."

At this, she flashed a look up at him. It was a dark night. Too dark to see him clearly, and she sighed and began to fill in some blank spots.

According to Turner, Rio told him, Vesta had said something that started him wondering. She'd glanced at Freeman and smiled as if someone had just given her a gift. "I wonder what else is in that cellar hiding away," she'd said.

Freeman had laughed. "A mystery."

"And I'm always curious." Vesta laughed with him. "We should investigate."

But at this, Freeman glanced over at Turner, who'd to all appearances gone back to dispensing beer in big glass mugs, and touched his forefinger to his lips in a shushing motion. Vesta raised her eyebrows, but subsided.

Turner lost no time in reporting this odd bit of conversation to Rio. "'Made me wish I hadn't bothered to dig that bottle out,' he told me. 'So happens there's two more just like it down there. I don't suppose your grandpappy figured it was a tipple a bunch of rough loggers, sawmill men, and cowpokes would appreciate. Probably couldn't afford it, either. Believe you me, Miss Rio, I'm gonna charge this pair plenty.'"

Rio was grateful and said so, but what Turner said next started the wheels in her mind spinning, just as it had his.

"What was it?" Beckett asked.

"He said, 'You know, I don't think they were talking

about more pricey liquor hidden away in the cellar. There was something...' His voice faded out then, as if he were thinking back on what he'd heard. 'Something. I dunno what. But you should watch what you say around them, Rio. I don't trust 'em."

She huffed. "He didn't have to tell me twice. But there's another thing." Rio tilted her head to look up at the deep purple sky where stars flicked their light into infinity. "Marie caught a snatch of their conversation at supper as she cleared the table next to theirs. And she couldn't wait to report to me." She smiled a little. "Vesta isn't nearly as smart as she thinks she is. She seems to believe the staff is both stupid and deaf. Especially stupid. I don't think she's ever heard of loyalty, either. And I hope she doesn't learn differently anytime soon. I can use her own words against her if I have to."

At this, Beckett laughed. "You're getting to be a real dangerous lady, you know it?"

Instantly, Rio's nerves tensed. She did know. He was the one who didn't. Not about the man she'd killed right here in the hotel. Or that she and Quinn Callahan had buried him way up on the mountain and never told a soul. The regret she felt didn't stem from her actions, but from the necessity. He'd broken into the hotel and been trying to kill her at the time.

Still.

"Rio?" Beckett peered down at her, concerned by her sudden silence.

"Dangerous?" she asked cautiously. He couldn't know, could he? Not unless Quinn, despite the pact they'd made, had somehow gotten word to him. But no. Quinn wouldn't do that. She trusted him. About this, anyway.

Beckett's amusement faded at her question. "You carry a gun, Rio. You see trouble coming at you from all sides. I know your half brother was about as bad to you as it's possible to be, but don't let your fear overtake your good sense. Just be careful with that gun. You were pretty quick to brandish a weapon the other night at the party."

A gun had already saved her life once. But Beckett spoke like a true lawman, from a lawman's point of view. Correct in a man who wanted to be sheriff, she supposed. Who *she* wanted to be sheriff. She knew that. Even so, her talk with him had lost its momentum. Maybe telling him what Marie had overheard would be better off relegated to another time, even though she knew he was waiting to hear the rest.

The part where Vesta believed treasure was supposedly hidden somewhere on the property.

――――

BECKETT KNEW he'd offended Rio in saying what he had about her drawing the gun at the party. Was he in the wrong? But he'd been right there, already taking a hand in quelling Bull French. If she'd waited just another few seconds, he figured the scene would've ended more peacefully. He couldn't help thinking she'd made a bad enemy out of the man. Maybe made winning the election tougher for him, as well.

The thing is, Bull had let drop an important morsel of information. Something that might play into the trouble Rio was having just now with the Carvers, Miss White and her friend David Freeman, and of course, Bull French.

Treasure lying about somewhere on the Painter's Bay Hotel property.

Did Rio even know?

True or false, the mere whisper of treasure was apt to bring out the worst in people. Everybody wanted to be the one to find it, ill-gotten goods be damned.

When, or if, he became sheriff, he had a feeling he'd be facing big trouble at the first crack out of the box. And Rio Salo would be sitting right in the middle of it.

Six

The next morning began just like the one before it, only with fewer breakfast patrons. Due to the fog hanging over the bay, Rio supposed. Plus, the days were getting shorter as autumn drew on in the mountains surrounding the lake. The hotel guests, there weren't that many of them, slept later, which made for an easy start to her day.

Vesta, not much to Rio's surprise, was one of the late risers. Not the maid, though. Bindle appeared Johnny-on-the-spot for her breakfast. Therefore, the dour woman was not much pleased when, as the lobby door opened and Jess Stokes entered, Rio heard a call from somewhere out on the water.

"Ahoy, the hotel. Can you lead me in to the dock?" Coming through fog grown to the proverbial pea soup consistency, even the voice sounded muffled.

"I think that's Pellow from the livery. Want me to steer him in?" Jess asked, smiling down at her. He topped her by nearly a foot. Nice for Blanche, who was tall, but Rio had to crane her neck.

"Bless you. I'd really appreciate it."

A decision she soon regretted. Well, not the actual doing. Just the necessity. Meanwhile, Bindle had settled at the largest table in the dining room and sat tapping her foot. "I was here first," she said.

Rio refused to apologize. "You were," she acknowledged. "But when a call like that comes in, it takes precedence. You, after all, are in no danger of losing your way and possibly hitting the rocks at the point."

But she was in danger of being dunned for transport on the night she and her boss arrived. From her expression, Rio suspected the duo had indeed neglected to pay Mr. Pellow.

Bindle harrumphed and turned her face into the corner.

Rio had already served the woman her breakfast when Jess finally entered. Mr. Pellow was with him, along with a stranger toting a duffel bag. Someone who'd come to Painter's Bay on the early train, she figured. He headed directly to the check-in desk.

Jess Stokes, who sent inquiring looks toward the kitchen as if looking for Blanche, and Mr. Pellow seated themselves at a table. Jess nodded at the stranger. "Go ahead and tend to him, Miss Salo. Pellow and I will study on the menu. Just a little warning," he added, "he ain't exactly handsome."

Rio had to chuckle. Study on the menu? There was no such thing.

"No matter. This won't take long." Putting a professional smile on her face, she hurried over to the registration desk in the lobby. "Good morning. I take it you're wanting a room?"

A one-eyed man with pasty-white skin turned to

face her. Scars radiated from the eye, the empty socket puckered into a black hollow.

Rio blinked. *Not very handsome?* He had a face to frighten children. And maybe grown women hotel keepers, she had to admit. Nor did he make any effort to lighten the effect he made, even as her smile faltered.

"Yeah," he said. "Ground floor."

She knew a moment of relief—and hope. "I'm so sorry. All the rooms are upstairs." Maybe he'd move on. Go somewhere else. Maybe she could point him to the local dive where the saloon owner sometimes allowed men to stay overnight. She'd dealt with all sorts of men before, the handsome, the smart, the not-so-savory. Some downright outlaws. But this? Good lord, why didn't the man cover his eye with a patch?

Since Beckett and Win were in the one downstairs room—although she'd planned on moving into it herself earlier—right now she was just as glad they had taken it over and she could legitimately turn this fellow down. Stuck in her own little office-bedroom right next door, she'd have hated to have anyone but the Ferris brothers so close.

The man's fearsome scowl showed his dislike of the accommodation. "Upstairs? You sure?"

"Of course I'm sure."

When he moved to take something from the inside pocket of his cheap-looking brown coat, Rio flinched, half expecting him to withdraw a gun. To her surprise, he flashed a badge at her before, in a blur of blue, he just as quickly concealed it again.

"Federal customs officer," he rasped, "here on official business. That gives me a special price on the room, meals included. I'll take one that overlooks the bay. First thing I need to know is who you got staying here."

Rio's right hand slipped beneath her apron and crept to the pocket of her skirt. The feel of the .32 Iver Johnson helped reassure her. Until she thought of Beckett and what he'd said about her gun.

"You must be under some kind of delusion." Proud of the steady, cool tone of her voice, she proceeded to put him right. "There are no special privileges for government workers in this establishment, and I am under no such obligation. Breakfast is included in the room fee only after an overnight stay. Dinners are charged at the regular *table d'hôte* price. No exceptions."

"The regular what price?"

"*Table d'hôte*, a set menu. It means you eat what I'm serving. Be assured, I don't stint. And a guest's privacy is honored. In other words, if you see another guest, you'll have to ask them to introduce themselves. I will not. Take it or leave it." She really, really hoped he left it.

But he didn't. Instead, he laughed, something completely at odds with the look on his face. The part she thought might be capable of actually expressing what he was thinking.

"All right, all right. I'll take the upstairs room." If he thought he sounded jovial, he was mistaken. "You run a hard bargain, lady."

"I'm an honest business owner," she corrected him. "I don't take bribes, and I don't offer bribes."

He didn't like that. Oh, no, he didn't.

She reached for a room key. As it happened, the

end room did overlook the bay, as long as fog didn't close it over.

His name was Merle Pope, or so he wrote in the register in tiny, precise letters that he dawdled over. Rio, certain he took the time to read the names above his, let him have that round. She just wished he'd hurry.

At last, now with a smug set to his mouth as if he'd bested her somehow, he climbed the stairs to deposit his bag in the assigned room.

Rio rushed back to take breakfast orders from Jess Stokes and Mr. Pellow, with another walk-in customer seating himself with them.

Back in the kitchen, she had just flipped one of her famous sourdough hotcakes on the griddle when a new thought struck her. Something important.

In minutes, she stood at the door to room number four. Tapping lightly, she waited. Tapped again. Waited. Tapped harder this time. And this time, the door opened a crack. Beckett's face appeared, his jaw in need of a shave, his dark hair tumbled every which way, as if he'd had a restless night. Or perhaps a short one. She'd had an impression of hearing doors opening and closing during the night.

Seeing who stood there, his eyes flashed. "What's wrong? Is someone hurt?"

"No," she said. "Not hurt—yet. But something is wrong."

At which he gave a little *whoof* of sound and closed the door in her face. Disgruntled, she went back to the stove, turning a skillet full of hash brown potatoes on the edge of burning, and trading her work apron for the more attractive serving apron. Filling cups and taking an order for two

71

poached eggs on toast for a female guest, she was relieved to find Beckett, dressed now with his hair combed, standing over the frying pan with a spatula in his hand.

"Just in time," he said, and handed her the spatula. "Now, what's happened? What's wrong?"

Rio put the spuds in a bowl and set it on the warming shelf above the stove. She took a breath, hoping she wasn't making a fuss about nothing just because she didn't like the looks of a man.

"You told me once that customs officer badges have certain specifications to meet. Things to show whether they're real or fake."

His eyes narrowed as he nodded.

Her voice got quieter. So quiet, Beckett bent toward her in order to catch her words. "A man just arrived under what I believe are false pretenses. He told me he's a customs agent and showed me a badge. It doesn't look anything like yours."

An eyebrow lifted. "What does it look like?"

"Big," she said, "and bright, with a blue enamel center on a brass and silver background. He flashed it at me, so that's all I saw."

Beckett stood up straighter, any look of weariness falling away as he turned toward the dining room. "Show me. There are only a couple men out of the Tacoma office who'd have any business in this neck of the woods. I know them both."

"He took a room and carried up his duffel bag," she said. "He hasn't come back down yet. But I think he will."

"Yeah? Why?"

"Aside from the fact he seems to be looking for someone..." Her smile crooked. "He looked hungry."

Though she neglected to mention it was hard to tell whether she meant hungry for food or for blood.

Just then, the bell at the cash register desk pinged, indicating someone needed her services. Beckett caught her arm before she could escape. "What does he look like?"

"Missing an eye and horribly scarred," she said. "Scary. Believe me, you can't miss him." And with that, she trotted away, finding a short line of people ready to pay their bill. It took her a few minutes. When she passed through the dining room again, she spotted Beckett seated at a small table with a coffee mug in front of him, watching the stairs.

Rio almost laughed when she caught Beckett's expression as the man, Merle Pope, appeared at the top of the stairs and started down to the dining room. But Beckett, not being the kind of man to let much of anything throw him, he schooled his features into a noncommittal expression and sipped his coffee.

Seconds later, she came to take his breakfast order. "Well?"

"Good catch, Rio. I've never seen him before. Bank on it. I'd remember if I had."

The vindication let Rio feel better about her suspicious mind. But it did nothing to relieve her uneasiness. Something out of the ordinary was going on, but what?

Merle Pope spent a great deal of the next two hours sitting in the lobby after he finished his breakfast, which he paid for almost graciously after his third cup of heavily creamed and sugared coffee. Since he was cavernously thin, Rio didn't begrudge him the extra cream and sugar, but she did not care for the way he stared at everyone who entered the hotel. In fact, she counted it a blessing when, around ten o'clock, the fog that had kept people off the lake lifted, and the fishermen either rented all her boats or found places for themselves along the shore.

More than one had whispered to her, "Who is that man? He keeps staring at me." Or, according to the male half of one couple, "He keeps staring at my wife. She's afraid of him. Is there anything you can do?"

There wasn't.

She gave a sigh of relief when Pope went outside, where he circled around the perimeter of the hotel, went down to the barn, searched out her now mostly defunct garden plot, and walked all the way to the rocky point along the shoreline.

Win, always ready to investigate curious behavior, especially when Beckett alerted him there might be something off about the man besides his looks, surreptitiously followed him around. Even so, when they had both returned, Win to make his report, he'd discovered nothing of any importance.

"He just ambled," he said, spreading his hands with a throwaway gesture. "Patted the horses, found his way to the spring and sat a while on one of the stumps, then skipped some rocks at the beach. Like anybody might do. He sure is ugly with that eye, but are you sure he's a wrong one?"

"No," Beckett said, "I'm not. But I'm not sure he isn't either. He shouldn't be telling people he's a customs agent when he isn't."

Win nodded, then turned to Rio with a smile. "Maybe you ought to turn Boo loose on him. See what he thinks."

It wasn't, Rio thought, as silly of an idea as it first

sounded. She'd found her little dog a good judge of character various times in the past.

All that got turned topsy-turvy when Vesta White swanned her way downstairs around noon. David Freeman followed, with Bindle following a respectful two steps behind. Vesta wore a gown Rio privately thought a whole lot fancier than called for in a little out-of-the-way hotel like the Painter's Bay. She couldn't help but wonder if the woman was trying to impress someone. If so, who? Rio figured she could make a good guess. But really, was a shiny, bronze shifting to green taffeta gown the way to do it?

She clearly did make an impression on Merle Pope. That much was easy to see, especially since Rio just happened to be watching him at the time. Furthermore, the impression he showed struck her as not an admiring one. Maybe complacent, as if he'd made a guess about something and turned out to be correct. Or self-satisfied. Yes, that was it.

Vesta had a clear look at Beckett as he stood close to the registration desk, while Rio checked back over the list of visitors during the past week. He'd figured if Pope was up to no good, it might have something to do with one of the guests and asked to check their names for himself.

In Rio's opinion, the most likely person was Vesta White, who minced daintily toward Beckett with her hand outstretched.

"How do you do?" she cooed, gazing up into Beckett's dark eyes as if mesmerized by what she saw there.

No denying Beckett drew the eyes of a great many women, though he seldom paid attention. This time, he did. Anyway, what could decent manners do but compel him to touch her hand with his own?

"Ma'am?" he said.

She drew him away from the desk, a maneuver so practiced Rio felt sure she'd done it before. Taken a man away from another woman just to prove she could.

"I saw you dancing with the proprietress the other night." Vesta looked up at him with rounded eyes radiating admiration. "And then the masterful way you took over when that awful brute of a man barged in. How brave of you. He was very threatening. I think you saved us all."

"I did what I could, ma'am." A flush spread over Beckett's cheekbones. "I wasn't the only one. Others were there to help. It's difficult when a community has no regular law enforcement."

"Oh, yes. I understand. And then, Miss Salo didn't help things when she spoke against him. No tact at all. Looked to me like she made things worse." Vesta had a charming giggle. "Maybe you should've taken her to the jail as well."

"You think so?" Beckett seemed more interested now.

Vesta fluttered. "Well, maybe."

Beckett, though good at concealing his thoughts, wasn't maybe as good as usual just then because Vesta changed tactics.

"I'm Vesta White, by the way. I'm traveling around the country with my maid. We've come all the way from New York City. Well, Manhattan, actually. Have you heard of it? It's the best part of the city." She touched his arm. "I heard you tell the brute that you're running for sheriff. I'd vote for you if I could."

Somehow, and just how Vesta managed it Rio found impossible to say, they'd gotten farther away from her, their voices fading with the distance. Off in the corner, David Freeman sat silently in the company of the dour maid, watching them in the same way Rio tried not to do.

Merle Pope, during all this, had found one of the wingback chairs from which to watch the people. He'd pushed into a dark corner by the fireplace and almost disappeared from view. A blessing, actually. Rio almost forgot about him until, as Vesta put on her act of bonhomie with Beckett, the scarred man regained motion and leaned forward as if to listen to every word.

———

BECKETT SAW Rio's expression when the White woman waylaid him. When he allowed himself to be waylaid. Maybe he should've protested. Put Vesta off until they could meet more privately. But, deciding the chance might not come again with Vesta herself providing the opportunity, although he knew Rio was hurt by his quick agreement to walk with the woman, his instincts told him that discovering why these people were at the hotel at this particular time was more important.

If, by chance, he won the sheriff's position, he needed an advantage and this might be it. He'd make his abrupt departure up to Rio. After all, he was here on her behalf in the first place, and he had no doubt he could talk her around. The simple truth would serve.

He masked the smile he felt at the memory of the sweet, sweet kiss when he and Win arrived the other day. Judging by that, he figured she'd forgive him. He knew Rio wasn't a woman to kiss indiscriminately.

Another thing he knew. Merle Pope wasn't here by accident. If the phony badge he'd flashed at Rio wasn't convincing enough, the way he watched and tried to listen would've done the job. Beckett wondered if the man was actually lipreading, the way his one eye settled on the features of whoever spoke.

As if by accident, Beckett turned his back on the man and moved to place himself between Pope's sight-line to Vesta.

Pope grunted a reaction.

Beckett's smile simply caused Vesta, certain the smile was in response to her charm, to chat even more vivaciously. Taking his arm, she drew him with her, sparkling with animation as she urged him outside, and they walked toward the dock. He didn't struggle.

He didn't see Rio's lips tremble.

———

VESTA PUT all she had into charming Beckett Ferris, under the impression that not only her beauty, but her station in life, put the cook and waitress to shame. And really, she thought, a bubble of laughter rising in her throat, it was no hardship to flirt with a man like Ferris. Those dark eyes of his, for one thing. And he had good teeth, always a plus, especially when one was called upon to put one's words into action with a little romantic follow-up. Some of the men she'd had to kiss almost gagged her. But she'd never had a time when it didn't pay off.

Beckett Ferris would soon fall victim to her charms,

upon which she'd soon know everything he did. He was friendlier with the Salo woman than she liked. Well, in a way. Could be he was just cozying up to her to discover what her brother Evan had told her about the jewels.

Jewels that Vesta intended to have, one way or another.

She stared up into Beckett's eyes, her own wide with assumed admiration, making sure to sweep her eyelashes down every once in a while. Men loved that, she'd discovered.

He looked down at her, his regard admiring. "Miss White," he began.

"Call me Vesta," she cooed and began chatting away, certain his responses would add up when she put them together.

Seven

Though she fought the urge to allow a single thought of Beckett and Vesta together, Rio couldn't stop herself when Beckett's tête-à-tête with Vesta White went on longer than necessary. How long could it take for him to discover what a thoroughly unlikeable character she was and escape her clutches? Even Win, in passing, mentioned his brother's involvement, all innocent of Rio's growing aggravation.

"Why's Beck talking to her for so long?" he whispered to Rio. "She's rude to everyone here. She even pushed me out of the way when I was out on the porch, and swished by like she's the queen of England."

Rio bit her lip and tried to put a good face on her own ire. "People of a certain class *do* think they're entitled to privilege."

"Well, this is America. They ain't."

"Well, they aren't supposed to be." Why not be honest and call what she felt jealousy? Rio didn't try to excuse herself.

It was hard to compete with a woman who dressed

80

like a queen, who poured on charm when it suited her, and who presented a high society image. And especially hard when Rio herself went wrapped in oversized aprons and smelled of onions, garlic, and frying bacon.

When Blanche arrived to begin prepping the evening dinner menu, Rio decided she'd had enough and, checking the pistol in her pocket, donned a sweater and calling to Boo, decided to make an inspection of the grounds around the hotel. That was as good an excuse to get outside and walk off some of her indignation as any.

With the morning fog dissipated, the sun shone. Boo, racing about as if he'd been released from solitary confinement, chased squirrels, leapt at birds, and touched noses with the horses when they began their inspection at the barn. Young Tommy Golz had mucked the stalls, not too onerous a job as the horses spent most of the time until winter outside in the corral. The tack had been cleaned, the feed bins closed tight against varmints, and the chickens had plenty of water and clean straw in their coop.

"That boy does a good job," Rio said to Boo. "I'll give him a bonus this payday. I'd better check with Anna and make sure I'm not working him too hard and that he's keeping up with school." She made a mental note, although she knew very well Anna could, and would, see to her son without help.

They went on to the spring. Rio didn't really care for people visiting the area. She'd always considered it her special space with the soothing burble of the water, the shade of the trees where songbirds sang and fluttered. A few stumps had been left in the ground to use for a spot to sit. She'd relied on the sheltered location for moments of peace when it had been her against her father and half brother, and she still did.

Going by the signs, someone had been there before her this morning. No doubt when she'd been busy with the breakfasts. A man's large footprints sullied the area around the spring where he'd tromped in the mud. Not only that, but she discovered the nasty butt of a chewed cigar at the water's edge and, to her utter disgust, what looked like a puddle of urine nearby not yet absorbed into the ground. Anger caused her to mutter under her breath as she scooted dirt over the wet spot and, nose wrinkling with distaste, picked up the cigar, wrapped it in a leaf, and carried it away with her.

Boo sniffed at the puddle and sneezed.

Rio gritted her teeth. "I'll put up a sign. One that says to stay away from the spring as it's off limits due to health concerns." Health concerns indeed. Though the hotel's water supply was piped from the underground source before it reached the spring's surface, animals drank there. Another mental note added to her collection.

Along the lakeshore, she discovered a vandal had been at work there too, digging through both of the fire pits she allowed on the beach and scattering unburned bits of wood and ash, evidently flinging it about as if in a rage. The debris spoiled the usually pristine area. A rake and shovel would be required to clean it all up again. Her growl sounded remarkably like Boo's at his fiercest.

Crossing from the shoreline to the path between the Salo's logging crew's barracks and the sawmill Jess Stokes's father operated, she started back for the hotel. The sound of the big, steam-powered circular saw cutting through logs followed her. Taking the long way around, she and Boo visited the boat dock and made a circuit around the hotel. There were crushed pine cones on the path—another chore for young Tommy, unless she could hire Win Ferris to help out—but nothing terribly out of place close to the building. Only as she mounted the back porch steps did it occur to her she'd followed the route she'd seen Merle Pope take earlier.

Had he been the one who left the cigar butt and the signs of urination? Who'd despoiled the beach by scattering remains from the fire pits? Who stomped the pine cones littering the path? Why would he?

As she hung her sweater back on a peg, it occurred to her Merle Pope wasn't the only one who'd taken a walk this morning, just as he had the previous day. Followed just about an identical route, as well.

The only difference being that David Freeman seemed too...refined, for lack of a better word, to use the outdoors for a toilet. Although he might *appear* refined, Rio reminded herself, it didn't mean he was. But then, she hadn't seen him puffing on cigars, either, but she'd smelled the smoke on the one-eyed man.

When she turned around, Rio came face to face with the selfsame David Freeman. Boo, a second too late, gave a *whuff* of warning, perhaps because the man had been soundless.

How could that be? She wondered. The old porch boards always creaked under the weight of anyone bigger than Boo. Even her, although having lived here all her life, she knew how to avoid the creaky ones.

"Where are they?" Freeman demanded.

Rio stared at him, her dark eyes rounded. "Where's

who?" she demanded in return, then added, "Or do you mean where's what?"

His air sucked in for an instant, as if she'd taken him by surprise. "I mean Miss White, of course. And that fellow who's running for sheriff. He should be out campaigning for the job instead of taking up Miss White's time." He sniffed. "As if she isn't out of his class."

Some of what he said, Rio agreed with. Such as campaigning for a job and ignoring Vesta. And yes, she was definitely out of Beckett's class, though not pointed in the direction Freeman seemed to imply.

"I have no idea where either of them is," she said tartly. "Why should I? I thought you were her escort. You or the maid. Ask Miss Bindle. She probably knows."

Freeman stamped his foot. "I did. She said she doesn't."

Rio didn't really pay what he said any mind. She was busy looking down at his shoes again. Although from the side they looked as if they had hard leather soles, once again, Freeman had made no sound. It seems obvious they had a sound-silencing substance affixed to the bottom. And the only reason she could think of for anyone to treat shoes like that was if they meant to sneak around with the intention of being somewhere they shouldn't be.

For instance, in the rooms, whether in use or not, of the Painter's Bay Hotel. Perhaps she'd best put a padlock on the door to her office. Who knew? David Freeman might be a yeggman wanting a look in her safe.

Shrugging with careless unconcern, Rio said, "I

guess you'll have to ask Miss White where she's been when she returns. She can reply as she wishes. As far as the maid goes, well, I suppose she follows her employer's demands, not yours." A convoluted way of saying Bindle may have been lying, or that she perhaps needed a larger bribe.

She almost laughed at the look on Freeman's face as the fact dawned on him. Or she would have if it hadn't looked as if he wanted to murder her right now.

Rio lost no time in making her escape to the kitchen to find Blanche dashing here and there like a chicken with its head cut off.

"Finally," Blanche exclaimed. "Where have you been? What are we going to serve for the salad? We're out of fresh greens."

"Then we'll use apples. Apples and cabbage." Setting to work, Rio found a large cabbage, peeled away the outer leaves, and put it in the icebox to chill. A creamy dressing went in to chill beside the cabbage.

A couple of hours before time to prepare potatoes for roasting in the oven, she went to the burlap bag in the pantry only to find a lack of the proper-sized spuds. Grabbing a handy basket, she headed for the cellar where they kept root vegetables in the cool dark.

"We're out of spuds," she called to Blanche, who was combining butter, oatmeal, bread crumbs, sugar, and spices into a mixture as topping for the last rhubarb crumble of the season. "I'm off to the root cellar."

Blanche waved her away. "I'll stir the custard sauce while you're gone."

The steps down into the cellar were not only steep but dark, necessitating the use of two kerosene lanterns. One she left at the top to light the stairs and carried the other with her. She'd passed halfway through the big main room before reaching the root crop storage area when she noticed things blocking the entrance and stopped.

"What the..." Holding the lantern higher, brow crinkling, she gazed around. Broken glass littered the floor in front of some shelves where extra canning jars were stored. Some of them had contained fruit or vegetables. In a dark corner, Rio could see where several wooden crates and boxes had been shifted. Those with lids were open.

Anger flooded through her. What in the world was going on? Why would anyone want to sort through the cellar? A cellar, aside from the boiler used to heat water and the rooms, mostly used for storage of restaurant foodstuffs or discarded items. And bottles of good brandy.

Off to one side was a separate room. Back in the day, when the building had been the logger's barracks, the room had been used to store the workers' possessions. Since many of the workers were Chinese, they had brought artifacts from the old country with them. There was still a section that held items forgotten and left behind. Another section was packed with things overlooked by people who'd stayed in the hotel and, either by design or accident, never repossessed. Rio had always been fascinated by the variety. Surprisingly, there were even a couple worn-out saddles and other pieces of horse tack. A pair of silver spurs, sadly tarnished after all these years, had been left unclaimed. A whole stack of suitcases—most of the cheap variety like the one David Freeman had brought with him—leaned against one of the rock walls. She didn't know if there was anything in them or not. It hadn't taken more than a second for Rio to realize the place, except for this storage room, had been searched. Quite thoroughly and, going by the mayhem, unsuccessfully.

It didn't, Rio realized, take a genius to understand why Mr. Freeman had padded the soles of his shoes. What's more, she suspected that given a bit more time, this room would be searched too. And soon, if she was any judge.

Rio opened her mouth to call Blanche, then changed her mind. The wisest thing to do, she decided, was to keep quiet for now and not to let on that the mess had been noticed.

Best, she further decided, if she were to set some kind of watch and catch whoever had started the process in the act.

Except she'd have to tell Blanche, of course, who also had reason to visit the cellar quite often. Quietly, though. Losing no time in selecting the necessary quantity of potatoes, she dashed back up the stairs.

"Custard is done," Blanche announced.

"Good. Did you add the vanilla?"

Blanche jerked. "No! Thank you for reminding me." Carefully, she measured out the required amount of vanilla. The flavoring was expensive, which meant she took special care. While Rio might use the new artificial stuff in baked goods, the custard required the natural product.

Rio set to scrubbing the baking potatoes and setting them aside to dry. Blanche came to help. While they were close together, speaking almost in a whisper, Rio said, "Have you been in the cellar today?"

87

Blanche looked up, attention caught no doubt by the cautious tone. "No. What about it?"

"Someone has been down there looking for something."

"How do you know?"

Rio rolled her eyes toward the cellar door. "Go see for yourself."

Puzzled, Blanche did. She was gasping when she got back. "Is it what Marie said? You know. What she overheard that woman say about treasure?"

Blanche's understanding was immediate, without need for explanation.

"I imagine so," Rio said. "But there are several people who might have done this. Merle Pope, for one. He told me he's a customs agent, but he's not."

Blanche shuddered. "He's scary. That eye..."

"He is. There's David Freeman, arriving here right behind Miss White. He doesn't seem to have a purpose. Miss White doesn't strike me as being especially fond of him either, although he tries to act as if they're close."

"She doesn't. She's got an eye for all the single men." Blanche had a snippet to add. "Mr. Freeman was hanging around the kitchen last night before I turned the light out on him. He could've been making sure of where the cellar door is."

"He could." Rio told her about the sound blanketing substance on the soles of his shoes.

Blanche's eyes flashed. "Up to no good, that's certain."

"And we mustn't forget Bindle, the maid," Rio added. "I've noticed her creeping up behind several people, listening in to whatever they're discussing. I can't decide if she's out to learn secrets for blackmail or if she's just nosy."

Blanche snorted a laugh. "A combination, perhaps."

Rio smiled too. "Perhaps. And then there's Vesta herself."

"Umm." Blanche thought a moment. "Not that she's above searching the place, but she strikes me as being too squeamish to go down those steps into a dark cellar. I'm a little leery of it myself sometimes. Anyway, I doubt if she's even capable of lighting the lanterns."

Rio tossed the last clean spud into a bushel-sized basket. "We need to set a trap."

At this, Blanche grinned. "Set somebody to guard with a shotgun pointed at the stairs?"

"Might work. As long as nobody actually gets shot. Or scare whoever it is into tripping and breaking their neck. I want him—or her—alive so I can question him or her."

They looked at each other. "We'll figure something out after we close the kitchen tonight." And, with Win and Tommy Golz's help, they did.

———

METICULOUS IN GUARDING HIS REPUTATION—AND Rio's—since a good many folks knew he and his brother were staying at the Painter's Bay Hotel, Beckett had made a point of documenting the cost of living there when he filed paperwork on his financial status with the county commissioners. Since most of them had been aware of Rio's difficult life with her father and half brother and the way her inheritance of the hotel had played out, they were inclined to rely on her honesty.

From the look of things, the commissioners had learned a lesson from dealing with the previous sheriff. This time, they had promised the voting public they'd leave no stone unturned when judging the integrity of the candidates running for office.

One would've thought, Beckett couldn't help thinking, that put Bull French out of the running. Apparently, not so. Although Bull was a rough man of uncertain character, nobody was willing to charge him with any crime worth mentioning. Spending every dime he got hold of wasn't against the law. Yeah, some said, he liked his whiskey a bit too much and was a brawler, but that didn't matter as much as one might think in an area where a great many others were of the same ilk. The loggers were notorious for fighting for the pure joy of it, especially when matched against the sawmill men. "All in good fun," they said.

The womenfolk, many of them looking forward to the day they won the vote, if they ever did, may have taken a different view, but for now, it meant Beckett needed to get out, meet people, and make himself known to the male voters.

In this, he had an advantage of sorts. When the local timber cruiser had been murdered early in the summer, in his job as an undercover customs agent shutting down opium smugglers, Beckett had taken over the murdered man's job and done it well. People who knew were impressed with his credentials.

It all helped because Bull was out there campaigning too.

Which meant Beckett, after escaping Vesta White's

unexpectedly interesting chit chat, saddled the sorrel gelding he'd recently bought and took to wandering the countryside. Some of the folks he visited may have wondered at the questions he asked about Eino Salo. Most of them hadn't seen Salo for two years. As far as they knew, when he showed up a while back, he holed up in the hotel, then when strangers appeared looking for him, took to his heels again. Nobody knew where he'd gone, including Rio. Since he'd been universally despised by the respectable folk, none of the locals gave him another thought. They were just happy he had gone.

Beckett didn't explain his sudden interest.

He didn't intend to tell Rio either. Not yet.

He ended his day of wandering at the low dive where Bull French spent his free time and his money. The time he chose was late afternoon, but before quitting time. Dismounting from the sorrel, he found the saloon open but empty, the bartender an old fellow scrubbing the bar with a fairly clean cloth and glad to have company as he worked.

Beckett bought a beer, peered down into a glass half-filled with foam, and looked up to find the man staring at him.

"You're him, ain't you?" the old fellow said.

Beckett didn't exactly know how to respond. "If you mean to ask if I'm the fellow running for sheriff, yes, I am." He offered his hand. "Beckett Ferris."

The old fellow shook. "Good for you, but what I'm sayin' is, you're the fellow who figured out who kilt Bill Hightower, ain't you? That sumbitch Thor Donaldson."

Beckett huffed. "I guess I am."

"Bill was my nephew. He was a good man."

"So I heard. Glad I could help see some kind of justice done."

It was the right thing to say.

The old fellow, also a Hightower, peered at him through thick-lensed spectacles. "I don't figure you're here for the beer. Truth to tell, it ain't the best quality. You're looking for information. What do you want to know?"

It was a good beginning, Beckett figured. So he asked his questions. And got some surprising answers. A bartender, after all, hears all kinds of stuff. Some of it important, some of it pure BS.

So do older men, those grown too old or too crippled up to work in the woods or sawmills or cattle ranches. Beckett found a trio of them sitting in the sun on a bench outside the hardware.

He nodded to the men and introduced himself. Announced his candidacy for sheriff.

One sage shook his hand. "Heard about you. You're the one finally shut down those damn opium smugglers."

They all had more to say.

Beckett's campaigning led to a satisfying afternoon. And possibly a few votes.

Eight

Win came up with the best ideas for Rio's plot to discover their cellar prowler. Tommy had the nimblest fingers to set it all up. Between the four of them, they considered everything from Rio sitting guard with a shotgun idea to Blanche's more practical tripwire plan.

The tripwire plan, with certain amendments, won the day.

Blanche and Rio smirked at each other as they took several empty tins and put a measure of salt dyed purple with huckleberry juice in each. They'd already put holes in the can tops and strung wire through them. It was up to the boys to attach the whole business from the trip wire, which traveled up the wall and onto the string of cans lightly attached to the ceiling.

Only, instead of starting at the top of the stairs, it was only four steps from the bottom, where the darkest section hid the cans above and the wire below, all ready to trip whoever ventured down.

"Not enough," as Win pointed out, "to kill whoever might fall, but plenty to slow them down and give us a chance to get to the door and lock them inside."

"And cover their shoes with purple salt." Tommy chortled. "It'll grind right into the soles. No way anybody is going to escape all signs of that, even if they did manage to get out."

"They won't," Rio said—a vow.

"Meanwhile," Blanche said, "if nothing happens tonight, it'll be easy enough to detach the wire when we're working and set it up again tomorrow night."

Tommy laughed. "Just don't forget. You two don't want your blonde hair colored purple with salt and huckleberry juice, that's for sure."

Rio smiled too. "We won't forget."

"No. Because the plan is to catch the sneak tonight." Blanche made a show of crossing her fingers.

Rio didn't know if what they were doing was legal, but didn't intend to worry about it. Anyway, as Win told her, "It isn't illegal to set traps for varmints, is it? Bears, coyotes, rats, and such?"

"Big rats," Blanche said dryly.

They all had a chuckle, although Rio didn't really see much amusement in the need for such shenanigans. Win, clever boy, had attached another wire to a bell in her office-bedroom, similar to the setup she'd had when tending to her father, or even the one attached to the hotel's front door. It would be up to her to see that when the can wire tripped and the bell clanged, she got the cellar door locked shut in time to prevent the intruder from escaping.

In theory, she reminded herself amongst the others' euphoria. In theory.

Telling her to mind how she went, Blanche and Tommy headed for home.

Left with Win, Rio had another thought. "Are you going to tell Beckett what we've done?"

He looked at her, wise beyond his years. "Do you want me to?"

She shook her head. "No. If our plan works, and we actually catch whoever was down there, then we can tell him." She sighed. "I expect he'd say we shouldn't do it."

Win shrugged. "Maybe. Or more likely, he'd want to be in charge."

"Yes. Which might be overstepping. Could be the commissioners wouldn't like him acting like a sheriff when he's not."

"He already did with Bull French. The commissioners approved then." Win's dark eyes held a question. "Why do you think they wouldn't approve of this?"

"I don't know. I just don't want to be the cause of Beckett losing his bid for sheriff."

"Ah," Win said. Whatever that meant. Rio wasn't sure herself.

With the trip wire set to go, Rio did her best to keep an eye on the entrance to the cellar until the hotel closed its doors. Though called away twice, once by Vesta White with a complaint about not enough blankets, upon which Rio had to step around to a closet and supply one, she knew nobody tried to get past her as she took it upstairs. A relief, although doing so kept her from observing and listening to the hotel guests' chats. All the rooms had been taken for the night. Soon everyone went upstairs, and after cleaning the bar one last time and making sure the bottles were corked, Turner called goodnight and went out through the back porch.

Rio sat at the kitchen table and waved goodnight to him. She held a pencil in one hand, with a pad of paper in front of her. If he'd asked what she was doing there so late, she would've said, "making a list." But she wasn't, unless one considered standing guard over the cellar door an item on the list.

As soon as Turner had gone, she turned out the lights and locked the front door. Butterflies churned in her belly. Anxiety over what would happen if someone really did try for the cellar to finish what they'd started. But the butterflies weren't only because of that.

Beckett had been conspicuous by his avoidance of her the whole evening. He hadn't once tried to speak with her, instead spending the hour after dinner talking with Vesta, with Bindle, with Pope, and Freeman. And last of all, with Turner.

But not one word with Rio.

She tried not to be hurt. She preferred anger to pain.

———

ALTHOUGH SHE HAD a difficult time going to sleep, sure she'd miss something critical if she did, Rio awakened once along about one o'clock. Sitting up, she held her breath and cocked her head toward the hallway. The hotel was silent, although she was aware of a breeze blowing up outside. It rattled the porch screen door. For several tense moments, she listened. Then, when nothing untoward happened, she decided the rattle had been the fault of the wind and relaxed. Aside from the creak of her cot and Boo whistling slightly through his nose as he slept curled beside her, there was nothing. Shrugging, she lay back and slept again.

At three o'clock, the bell beside her pillow clanged. Clanged harsh and loud. Boo woke up barking. Rio jumped from the cot and promptly sat back down, her head whirling. A second later, she was up even as the bell stopped. Shut off as abruptly as it had started.

Down the corridor, Win burst out of his room wearing a nightshirt and headed for the kitchen. Beckett, one-handedly pulling on his britches while his other hand carried a gun, jumped from foot to foot after him.

"What the hell?" he demanded as he passed Rio's room. She raced along with him, Boo already in the lead into the kitchen.

"Sonofagun! It worked," Win was saying over his shoulder. "I'll be damned. It worked."

Beckett had his britches done up by now. "What worked?" He didn't sound happy.

"We caught him," Win said. "In our trap."

"Caught who? What trap?" Beckett turned to Rio, his gaze traveling from the top of her tumbled blonde hair to her bare legs and feet under a calf-length nightgown.

She blushed, not all because of her attire. And not all because of the questions, either. Right at the moment, she was glad the only light came from the moon shining in through the kitchen window.

The cellar door stood open, although it had been securely closed when Rio went to bed. The stairway itself was a pitch-black tunnel into the depths.

She stopped. "Look." She pointed. "It's open. But how—"

When Win would've plunged right down the dark staircase, Beckett yanked him back. "Stop," he hissed. "Could be somebody waiting to gun down whoever goes first."

Win stopped, looked uncertainly at Rio, then back at Beckett. It was something neither of them had thought of. Boo took matters into his own...paws. With a rush, the little dog skittered past them down the stairs, barking. At the bottom, he paused, his white fur a bouncing beacon to the people waiting above.

After a tense moment where Rio's heartbeat seemed to deafen her it raced so loud and fast, Boo let out a mournful wail.

Otherwise? Silence.

After another few moments, Rio crouched at the top and called down, "Hello? Is anyone down there?"

More silence.

"Boo? Boo, come here."

But he didn't, and though Beckett protested, she snatched the lantern from its peg and struck a match. The flare outlined her as she held it to the lantern's wick. Shaking out the match flame, she held the lantern high and started down.

Beckett, telling Win to stay put and watch their backs, stepped one tread behind her.

At the fourth step from the bottom, Rio stopped. Something had gone wrong with the trap. There was a spillage of purple salt on the step from the one can that had turned onto its side. The salt was mussed, as if someone had stepped in it. Not Boo. The footprint did not belong to a dog. He had evidently jumped over it.

"Hello," Rio said again, then, "Boo?"

Boo appeared at the edge of the light. His tail, she could see, was tucked between his legs, his hackles raised. As he came closer, she saw one of his front feet bore a red stain. Red, not purple.

"Boo!"

Beckett saw these things too and, slipping an arm around her waist, stopped her from going farther into the darkness. "Wait. Let me take the lantern. I'll look."

The lantern shook in her hand, sending light flickering onto the nearest wall. She released the lantern to him and stood still.

Beckett went past her into the storage room. Boo led him toward a tumble of boxes until the light revealed a man's shoe sitting by itself in the middle of the floor. Beckett paused beside it a moment before moving on, going faster now. Then, stopping, he held the lantern higher.

And swore.

Rio gasped.

Boo whined.

"What's going on down there?" Win called from where he stood at the top of the stairs. "Should I come down?"

"No." Beckett sounded as if he were strangling.

Win, quiet as he waited, whirled at a faint sound coming from behind him. "Hey," he called out. "Who's there?"

Rio, still frozen in place on the stairs, came to her senses at Win's question. "Win? What—" But what she heard next was Win yelling.

"Stop. Stop or I'll shoot."

Practically sure he didn't have a gun, she became aware of holding her .32 at her side.

"Win. Wait," she cried out, and ran back up the steps. At the top, she caught sight of Win passing through the dining room and into the lobby where the front door stood open. A figure like a tall, black-cloaked apparition seemed to float ahead of Win, who was a good twenty feet behind him.

A movement of what appeared to be wings tumbled a chair right into Win. Unable to stop, he sprawled over the thing, yelping with pain.

Seeing her coming, he waved Rio on. "I'm okay," he grunted. "Get him."

She tried. In the end, it didn't matter. By the time she got to the door, the cloaked person had leaped from the porch and already reached the band of trees. He was a fast runner, for sure. Stopping, she held her .32 in both hands and fired after him anyway, knowing there was no hope of hitting anything. Not in the dark. And she was shaking.

She'd seen the blood on Boo's foot, a spreading pool surrounding a body collapsed on the cellar floor.

She'd seen it all too well.

No real surprise, the gunshot brought everyone down from the hotel's second floor, most of them rubbing their eyes and complaining of being awakened.

Rio hurried to don a robe over her nightdress, poked up the fire, and started a pot of coffee. Oh, and washed the blood from Boo's foot. She didn't want anyone to see that.

Win, though limping and holding his shoulder at an awkward angle, set the chair upright and got dressed.

Beckett, though Rio figured Vesta would've

preferred him shirtless and barefoot, had also dressed. He carried his gun in plain sight in the shoulder holster he wore over his shirt. His face was stern. He looked every bit the lawman, whether sheriff or customs agent. In fact, he'd pinned his customs agent badge on his shirt for everyone to see. There were a few murmurs.

If Bindle had been the first person down the stairs, Vesta was the last. She'd taken time to arrange her hair, though allowing it to simply tumble down her back. She had powdered her nose and put roses in her cheeks, and wore a lovely silk Chinese robe.

Rio took particular notice of David Freeman, but though she studied him carefully, nothing about him struck her as out of the way. He'd pulled on pants and donned his suit jacket, though rapidly, and it wasn't properly buttoned. She had an idea Turner should've watched Freeman's liquor intake a bit more carefully the previous evening, although it was possible the man had his own bottle. He smelled pungently of last night's alcohol. One thing she knew, the person who fled had not been him.

Other rooms disgorged their occupants, a single from one, and an older married couple from the other. They were merely curious, and as soon as Rio apologized for their inconvenience and told them the shot had been merely to scare off an intruder—"We get one every now and then," she lied—they all turned around and went back to bed. On the other hand, she decided after giving the matter some thought, it hadn't quite been a lie. Her shot had probably done something to chase away not only an intruder, but a killer. They should all be grateful.

Nobody seemed to miss the occupant of the last

room. No one but herself. Anyway, she knew all too well where Merle Pope was.

———

THEY STOOD ON THE PORCH, Rio shivering in the cool of the night. Beckett instructed Rio to put a padlock on the cellar door. They went outside then, where he had her show him where the ghost had entered the trees.

"On the off chance you drew blood," he said. It sounded like a question.

"I doubt I did." Rio shook her head. "Not in the dark."

"You're sure?"

"Yes. That part is easy. The sight of that man disappearing into the woods with his cape or cloak or, I don't know—maybe a cloud of soul dust floating around him? —has been etched into my mind. I'm telling you, Beckett, he looked eerie, to say the least."

"A cloud of soul dust?" He quirked a somewhat annoyed glance at her.

Rio had an idea that he felt compromised by the dead man in the cellar. He probably thought having a man murdered right under his nose wasn't the best way to get votes in the upcoming election. He may have been right.

"We need a trailing dog," he'd said to her, quiet-like, though there was no one else to hear. Unless Win, having followed them out, might have done as he stood nearby. "Too bad that's not Boo's strength."

Rio nodded, saying loyally, "I'll bet he could if he

were taught." And then added, "But I know someone with a trailing dog. He works for Blue Sky Logging Co. and has used his hound to find lost people. We could ask him. I'll pay him something. Would that help?"

"It would. But you shouldn't have to pay." The mention of money was apparently what decided Beckett on getting the commissioners involved in finding the murderer.

"Can't you—" Win began, but Beckett cut him off.

"I can make a start on the investigation." His mouth twitched. "I already have made a start. Thing is, I want real authority, not a fill-in just because there's no one else. Without their okay, I wouldn't be surprised to have Bull French poking his nose into the business."

Rio shuddered. "We don't want that."

"No. We don't. I intend to ask the commissioners to appoint me acting sheriff. Even if I don't win the election later on, I'll do my best to take care of this situation. Whatever it is."

The look he gave her formed a question. One that demanded she say if she knew what the situation was, why it was a problem, and who it benefited.

None of which Rio knew. She did have a strong hunch, and not surprising at all, her half brother Eino's name floated to the top of the list.

They went out into the night. Beckett, his senses on high alert, held the lantern aloft, lighting his and Rio's way to where she'd seen the black-clad person disappear into the thick copse of pines.

"He left a lot of sign getting away," he said, pointing to evidence of a clumsy passage through the thick stand of trees. A limb had been broken from one of the pines as if the ghost held a considerable amount of substance. Bushes, their structure dead-looking with the leaves blown away by the wind, were crushed. Footprints mashed into the damp ground showed proof of a killer who wore regular shoes instead of boots, like most of the working men. Twice, he found bits of black cloth caught on the wild rose bushes. He pulled away from the search then, afraid of destroying the scent trail.

Even Rio could trace the killer's movements. "He seems to have been running blind."

"It's possible he doesn't know the area well."

"Or is not accustomed to the woods."

They went back to the hotel to wait until daylight, when he could row over to the town and talk to the commissioners in a group. He intended to bring Dr. Clement and Mr. Meadows, the mortician, back with him to the hotel. And Mr. Masterson, too, if he would rouse himself that early.

Rio, when the sun finally rose and Beckett left, made sure the padlock was secure on the cellar door and both of the hotel's doors. For all the good the small lock would do now, she thought bitterly. Then, in an act borne of purely disturbed nerves, she went through the routine again—twice. In an effort to fill the time, she baked. Soon, kneading the dough until she was sweating and breathless, bread and cinnamon rolls proofed on the stove's warming shelf. The work didn't stop her mind from spinning the facts round and round in her head like cream in a churn, but it helped.

No. Not facts, she decided. She had so few of those.

Questions. There were plenty of those.

For instance, how had Merle Pope gotten into the

cellar without rousing her or Boo? How had the killer gotten into the building?

Why hadn't Boo barked?

BECKETT, when he got to town, caught up with the mortician first, which served two purposes since Meadows not only took care of the dead, but was one of the commissioners. The mortician heard Beckett out before sending his twin sons to fetch the other two commissioners. Dr. Clement would be easy enough, they figured. The banker, not so much.

"I wish you wasn't mixed up in another murder just before the election." Frowning, the mortician shrugged into his third-best black coat and sent his eldest son to hitch up the mortuary's transport wagon to bring in the body. "Me and Doc, we already decided there ain't nobody with better bonafides than you apt to put their name in the hat for sheriff. Bull French'd be a disaster for this county. But Masterson, he's kinda taken against you for some reason. Now, Doc and me can outvote him, but if he'll go along with us, it'll be best. And he'd be more likely to do that without this feller lying dead in Miss Salo's cellar."

It was a long speech to say what Beckett already knew.

Since Dr. Clement hadn't begun office hours as yet, he hustled right over to Meadows's funeral home upon receipt of the message. Beckett went through the story again.

"So you got no idea who'd do something like that? How'd the killer get in? I know Rio's been locking up pretty tight at night after what happened this summer when those Black Hand people came after her brother."

Dr. Clement, Beckett reflected, didn't know the half of it. He waited until Masterson, who had taken time to eat his breakfast before arriving, settled into a chair and begun picking his teeth.

"What is it now?" he queried irritably. "Something to do with that young woman's hotel, I'll be bound. She seems to be drawing an unsavory element into town lately. We were better off when Elias shut the place down and Thor Donaldson was sheriff." He waved a hand toward Beckett. "I know, I know. According to what you dug up, he was part of the smuggling ring. Guess you can't blame a man for wanting to make money, after all. It was just the Chinese."

Beckett schooled his features, hoping the downright disgust he felt didn't show.

Dr. Clement's face turned white, then red. "It certainly wasn't just the Chinese. I had patients who died because of him and his damn outlaw drugs."

Calmly, Meadows narrowed his eyes and said his bit, too. "That ain't true, and you know it, Eldon. Why're you trying to blame Miss Salo? Wouldn't have anything to do with them Carver fellas come from Chicago, would it? I figure you got your finger in the pie, trying to wrest that hotel from the young lady."

Masterson grinned. "Well, and what of it? I figure she'll go broke soon enough, anyway. She's young. A good cook, but she won't know how to run a business. The Carvers figure to pick the place up cheap and hire a man with experience to run it at a profit. I plan to bankroll them when the time comes."

Beckett's fingers clenched. He had a notion that

squeezing them tight would relieve the pressure he put on them, as long as what he squeezed wasn't Eldon Masterson's fat neck.

The doctor, air rushing in and out of his nostrils like an overworked horse, may have thought the same. "Neither here nor there," he choked out. "I vote we bring Mr. Ferris in as acting sheriff until such time as he wins the election. This murder needs seen to right now."

Meadows nodded. "I second the motion."

The banker shrugged. "Don't know why I even showed up. I figured you two already had it planned." He glanced dismissively at Beckett. "Well, sir, have at it. Do you even know the dead man's name?"

Finding his voice, Beckett forced himself to calm. He'd do Rio no good otherwise. "I do, as long as he didn't lie about it. He told people his name is Merle Pope."

An odd thing happened. Masterson blinked, not once, but several times in succession. The name had meant something to him, and learning of the death was a shock.

"Ah," he said. "Indeed. Another customs agent. But that makes him one of your people."

"Except he wasn't. He lied about that." Beckett eyed the banker's reaction. He could tell the man knew something about Pope. Something that surprised him. Which was it? That Pope had lied about being an agent? Or that Beckett knew?

A man to watch, he decided. And that might include people at the bank, as well. Whatever was going on seemed to include putting Rio out of business. Maybe this wasn't because of Eino. It was a question to ask Rio when he got back to the hotel. Maybe she knew of a connection.

The rest didn't take long. The three commissioners voted two for, one against, appointing him acting sheriff, and Meadows, who had Thor Donaldson's badge kicking around in his desk from when he died, replaced Beckett's customs agent badge with the old sheriff's star. They all shook hands, and that was it. The election was still five weeks away.

Nine

L ate in the morning, as news of the killing spread around the bay and into town, one of the Blue Sky logging outfit, a lugubrious character with a sun-browned and seamed face, brought his hound over to the hotel to see if it could track the killer. The two, man and hound, looked remarkably alike.

Rio, having heard nothing from Beckett, was surprised to see Benjie Akers when he and his famous brindle Plott hound, the only one of its breed in the area, arrived at the back porch. She blinked at him through the door screen. Boo, sticking close to her heels just as he had all morning, growled a little. Warning to the hound, although his tail wagged. The hound ignored him.

"Mr. Akers, it's good to see you. How did you know—"

He had no time for polite talk. "New sheriff sent word you need my dog. We're here. He said there's a body. Where do we start?"

New sheriff? That must mean Beckett had talked his way into the job. At least, Rio hoped so.

Her lips trembled at the thought of going down into the cellar again where the dead man lay. She knew the man noticed, but he said nothing as she lifted the door latch.

"Come in. It...He...is down in the cellar."

His gaze sharpened. "The dog'll need to come."

"Yes. I know. He's fine." She led the way through the kitchen to the cellar, digging the key to the padlock from her pocket as she went.

"Meadows should be here any minute," Akers said. "He said to tell you."

Rio swallowed. "Thank you. The sooner the better."

Blanche stood at the stove, stirring the evening soup offering, made early for the flavors of vegetables in rich beef stock to meld and waft throughout the restaurant. She still looked pale just from hearing about the death, though hadn't wanted to see the result of their plan. A plan gone, through no fault of their own, badly awry. She nodded to the man. "Mr. Akers."

"Miss Golz." He seemed more at ease with her than he had with Rio.

"Do you need me to go down with you?" Blanche asked, her voice fading.

Rio took one look and smiled faintly. "No, my friend. I'll be all right." *I should be used to dead bodies by now*, she chided herself. She had certainly seen plenty of them lately. Had almost been one. But this was the worst.

Pausing to light them each a lantern, Rio proceeded

down the steps ahead of Mr. Akers and his dog, who took the steep steps like a trooper.

They all stepped over the spilled purple salt, the dog as delicately as a fairy, the man frowning. He looked as if he wanted to ask about it, if only he hadn't lacked the words. A few more steps took them close to Merle Pope's body. Rio stood back, staying out of the copious blood, mostly dry by now.

Holding the hound back for the moment while he studied the sight, Benjie Akers had an opinion on what he saw. "Welp, that's a mess." He and the dog made a wide circuit around Pope's body. "Musta had a dull knife unless he was fixin' to cut the man's head off."

Rio gulped and made a little moan.

Akers stared across at her, at the lantern trembling in her hand. "You go on up. Me and Belle can study on this without you. Won't take long."

Grateful beyond words, Rio took him at his word, stumbling a time or two going up the stairs where Blanche caught her at the top.

She led Rio to the table, whispering, "Sit down. Rest. I'm making you a toddy."

Rio buried her face in her hands, although she didn't truly cry. Couldn't. She breathed deeply. "Thank you. Sorry to be such a spectacle."

Blanche patted her on the shoulder. "Guess it's pretty bad."

"Yes."

Then they waited. After a while, Akers and his dog returned, Belle with her nose up scenting the air. Without saying a word, Akers strode past them. The dog, all business, trotted out ahead of him through the kitchen, past the dining room, and on to the front door.

Rio rushed ahead to unlock it even as the hound scratched the door as if to hurry things along. Boo watched, his little black nose twitching. Once unlocked, still silent, dog and handler passed on through, crossed to the trees, and entered exactly at the spot Rio had pointed out to Beckett. The trackers disappeared. Every once in a while, the hound bayed a deep call as if to announce a new discovery.

Shuddering, Rio was still standing on the front porch when Mr. Meadows and his assistant, the same man who'd helped take her dead father away during the summer, came to pick up Pope's body. Beckett, she was relieved to see, rode alongside the wagon, the sun flashing off the badge pinned to his shirt. Behind them, Dr. Clement wheeled along in his natty little green-painted buggy.

Beckett dismounted, smiling faintly as he mounted the steps and touched her hand. "You all right?"

"Yes. Sure." *No*, her brain said in denial. *I'll never be all right.*

Dr. Clement was next. "Rio," he said. "I was hoping I'd never have to make another visit here where my professional services were required."

"Me too," she returned fervently. "In fact, I'm surprised to see you now. There's no doubt Mr. Pope is dead." She took a deep breath. "Mr. Akers could tell you, but he and his dog are following some kind of trail."

Meadows and his helper, each on one end of what looked like a cot with folded legs, crowded onto the porch with the rest of them. Meadows nodded. "Benjie and Belle are a team. They've been a big help a time or two before."

Beckett drew her aside, allowing the other three men, carrying the stretcher between them, to head through the lobby to the kitchen.

"Something is smelling good," Meadows was saying. "Might have to see if the wife and I can make it for supper."

His words made a little something inside Rio give a ping. Apparently, it took more than a grisly death to put the mortician off his food. At least until he got a look at the victim.

Bending toward her, Beckett spoke quietly as he drew from sight beyond the door. "The banker wanted to make a fuss about hiring me. He also acted strange when he heard Pope was the victim. With all three of the commissioners right there, Dr. Clement and Mr. Meadows thought it wisest for them both to come out and take a look at things." The look he fixed on her told volumes, but he spoke plainly anyway. "Mostly for your protection. They didn't want anybody coming back and stirring up a stink on how you must've been involved."

"Me?" It came out a squeak. "Why...that's ridiculous. Why would I? I hadn't ever met Merle Pope until he showed up at the front desk."

"I know." He took a quick look around and moved her even closer to the wall, into the shadows. "And I shouldn't be doing this, either, for fear of muddying the waters."

With that, he bent his head and settled a soft kiss on her upturned mouth.

"Oh," she breathed against his lips. Those butterflies fluttered again. "Beckett." His name was a caress.

"Umm." And without ever coming apart, the kiss deepened, demanded.

Then it ended.

Beckett moved back, smiling down at her rosy cheeks. Cheeks widely different from only a minute ago. "I'd better get in there and tend to business."

Rio nodded.

"We'll talk later," he promised, and something about the way he said it indicated he meant more than talk.

But they didn't. Not that night.

AS IF BY some kind of osmosis, word spread about the mysterious and untimely death at the Painter's Bay Hotel. Oddly enough, at least in Rio's eyes—Blanche's and her sisters too—business was as good, or maybe better, than the previous night. Everybody was curious, asking questions of each other and wanting to know more.

Mr. Meadows, who did bring his wife to supper, turned out to be the man of the hour. His dining table was surrounded by neighbors, all wanting to hear the gory details.

Rio, aware of the patrons pestering Eliza and Marie with questions as they worked, noticed they mostly avoided talking with her. Her feelings were not hurt. She didn't want to talk about the murder. Only the most persistent looked to her, the main reason she had both Golz girls working the dining room while she stayed in the kitchen.

At one point, Blanche glanced over as Rio ducked when a lady hesitated a moment as she passed the kitchen entry on her way to the restroom farther down the hall.

"You're hiding," she said, disapproval in her expression. "Don't. It makes you look like you've done something wrong."

Rio huffed out a sound that may have been a sob. "I did. I got born."

Hands went to Blanche's thin hips. "You stop that."

"I can't." Rio took a cautious glance out the open doorway. "People already think I might've had a hand in it. I heard two women talking when they walked past a few minutes ago. They were quite outspoken."

Blanche spluttered. "Gossips." The word held a nuanced meaning.

Rio smiled, a tiny lift of her lips. "Well, yes. But gossip spreads and sometimes has a measure of truth. And I don't like the way so many locals are talking with Bindle, and every once in a while, even Miss White adds to their conversation. You can be sure she has nothing good to say. Not about me and not about the hotel."

"So? She could always leave. There's nothing holding her here. Everybody must know that."

They went silent for a good many seconds before their eyes, one set bright blue, one set deep brown, met and widened.

"Oh, I think there is," Rio said the words aloud. "Because of Eino. But I don't know why."

Just then, Eliza hustled into the kitchen, a paper pad in her hand. "Table three," she called out. "Four of the leg of mutton and one of T-bone steak, fried rare. They all want the vegetable soup, two desserts of

English Plum pudding, and three of custard pie with raspberry sauce."

Though Rio and Blanche had no time to talk as they prepared the food, Marie had time for a short breather.

"That woman," she announced. She didn't have to say the name. Miss White had earned the designation and they all knew it.

Blanche spared her a glance. "What now?"

"Mr. Masterson and his assistant. What's his name...Jensen? Bernard Jensen?"

"So? What about them? They eat here quite often. I understand Mrs. Masterson doesn't like to cook, and her husband doesn't like what she fixes, anyway. I've heard she's a terror to work for, and she can't find a hired girl that'll stay more than a week." Blanche sounded quite casual, but she sent a meaningful look at Rio.

Rio only wondered why Marie put Masterson, Jensen, and Vesta White together in what was essentially the same sentence, even as the girl sent her a sideways glance.

"Their tables are next to each other," Marie said. "And they're talking."

"About what?" Blanche and Rio asked at exactly the same time.

"About you." Marie paused, her deep blue eyes widening as she looked toward Rio. "About treasure. They both think it's jewels. Rio, what have you got to do with treasure?"

So...*another mention of treasure.* The very idea sent gooseflesh traveling up her arms. "Me? Nothing," she said in surprise. "Why would anybody think otherwise?" She forced a squeak of laughter. "Do I look like someone with chests full of treasure?"

The three women laughed until Marie said, a pensive look on her face, "I don't believe they're thinking you have chests full of jewels, although they do mention the jewels. More likely something in a smaller package. But certainly worth a great deal of money."

Their laughter died. "Worth killing for?" Rio said.

Marie nodded.

Blanche's face twisted. "What did they say?"

"Miss White said, 'I have it on good authority...'"

Rio snorted. "I wish someone would tell me how they all seem to know about these so-called jewels. Or whatever the treasure is supposed to be." Her lips set in a straight line. "I want to know how Miss White became acquainted with Mr. Masterson. I want to know what Merle Pope had to do with it, because I don't believe for one instant he was simply a victim of wrong place, wrong time. His death wouldn't have happened in my cellar if he had been. He must've been down there searching for something. And most of all..." She stopped to take a breath.

"Yes?" Blanche asked.

"Most of all, I want to know who cut his throat. And why."

Blanche nodded wisely. "And who might be next."

Marie sucked in air. "Oooh," she breathed. "Blanche, are you carrying the gun Rio gave us?"

"I wasn't. But from now on, I will."

———

BY TEN O'CLOCK THAT EVENING, the last of the hotel patrons, who'd hung around as if they were waiting for some dramatic event to happen, went home. Turner closed the bar as soon as he delivered David Freeman's final drink of the night, and Vesta and Bindle prepared to follow Freeman as he stumbled up to his room.

Tired to the bone, Rio followed everyone out of the lobby, quenching the lamps as she went. Thankfully, Win had taken Boo out a while ago, letting the dog chase around and work off some energy. It had been a boring afternoon for the dog. And maybe for Win, since he'd also turned in.

Blanche and her sisters had gone home an hour ago, so when Turner left, only Rio, Win, and the guests were left in the hotel. Turner held back a moment, checking behind him to make sure they were alone.

His grizzled face serious, he had a warning for her. "It's that Freeman feller," he said. "Don't you trust him, missy. He was all right yesterday, but today he's got something eating at him."

Rio was almost too tired to think. "Like what?"

"Dunno. But I seen him staring at the White woman when they was eating their supper. Staring at her and watching the banker and his *assistant*. Especially the assistant. And for all them two from New York supposedly being friends, she wasn't paying Freeman any mind at all. Wouldn't even look at him."

If this had been in a book, Rio thought, there would've been quotation marks around the word assistant. Something about the self-effacing young man had struck not only Freeman, but Turner, as wrong.

And who knew what went on between Freeman and Miss White?

Well, she trusted Turner's instincts. They hadn't been wrong yet.

"If they come in again and get together, I'll keep an eye on them," she assured him, and he nodded.

Beckett hadn't returned to the hotel since they took away Pope's body, though she'd waited anxiously all day. His non-appearance left Rio with a sour taste of neglect. So much for the date he'd set with her earlier. As always, she fretted about his absence. What could he be doing that took so much of his time?

Tired though she was, Rio didn't think she'd sleep until she heard what Dr. Clement and Mr. Meadows had to say about the circumstances of Merle Pope's death. And surely Beckett had spoken with Benjie Akers. Having heard nothing to the contrary, she figured Belle must've lost the trail.

In this, she learned the next day, she was correct, though through no fault of the hound. Belle had followed the killer to the edge of the bay. Akers, so he said in his report to Beckett, surmised a boat had been waiting for the ghost there because the trail went cold. Belle could do no more. All in all, only slight progress in the investigation. Or maybe none at all.

———

VESTA PRECEDED Lena Bindle to their room. Ahead of them, David Freeman's door closed. The key in his lock as he turned it was perfectly audible in the silent upstairs.

Vesta nodded that way. "Have you spoken to

David? He was very silent tonight, acting as if he had something serious on his mind. And I didn't like the looks he gave Mr. Masterson or Mr. Jensen."

Bindle shook her head. "I don't know, ma'am. He isn't interested in talking to me."

"Huh. He's a pain in the behind. And he's been no help at all this trip." Vesta wasn't too disturbed by the man's silence. In the end, he always did what she told him to do. And this time, his job was to scout around and discover what Evan Salo had done with the jewels he stole from a certain *very important man* in New York. So far, David had been spectacularly unsuccessful.

It was odd there'd been no word leaked about the theft of jewels. On the other hand, people in a class with the Rockefellers, and especially if they were high up in government circles, wouldn't want it noised around that people could steal from them and not get caught. They were evidently keeping a very close lid on the theft.

Evan, she knew, clever villain that he was, always played it smart. He'd told her about some of his other thefts where he got away free as a bird. Bragged about them, really. He'd told her the profits made it possible for him to travel around and that the sale of these gems would soon allow him to live high on the hog in Europe, or maybe Australia. He had a yen to visit a country of kangaroos. From what he'd said, he intended to hide his loot away until it was safe to come back and get it.

Well, apparently he hadn't yet, as there'd been no word of a jewel collection of the rumored magnitude having hit the market.

Where else would he hide the treasure but at his

family homestead, this bleak little spot on the map in Washington state? Every speck of information she had indicated the jewels were still here. Somewhere.

She giggled, a sound that made Bindle shoot her a curious glance. Wouldn't Evan be just so disappointed when he came back and found the jewels gone? Vesta almost wished she'd be here to see the look on his face.

As long as she was the one to find them first. The Carvers and Mr. Masterson were going to be out of luck. Merle Pope's luck had most certainly run out, and she figured one or the other of them—probably the Carvers—had simply gotten rid of a competitor. But she had better get a move on. Luckily, she had a wild card working for her.

The Pope fellow's murder had made things a little more difficult by all the attention brought to it, but not impossible.

Besides, she was a well-to-do lady. Who would ever suspect her?

Ten

By the next afternoon, Win, restless without something to keep him busy, volunteered to rake pine cones from the path up from the boat dock to the hotel's front porch. Boo helped, giving a little yip at every thrust of the rake.

Rio, looking out an upstairs window as she smoothed the quilt over the bed she'd just freshened for the next occupant of the room, gave a sigh. At least those two were able to pass their time with some sort of mindful activity. Her own work gave too much latitude for her thoughts. For instance, where was Beckett? What was keeping him away for so long?

Those thoughts came to a halt when she saw Win's head shoot up and point toward the trail around the point from town. Boo dashed forward, tail wagging. A sorrel horse broke from the trees. The rider, giving Win a wave, headed for the barn.

Win leaned the rake against a tree and followed the horse, man, and dog at a run.

Rio's innards gave a lurch. Beckett at last.

Wishing she could follow Win and Boo's lead and go meet Beckett, Rio remained mindful of her hotelier duties. She had to finish clearing one more room before she'd be free to make an escape. It made her think longingly, though just for a moment, of how a few months ago, when she'd been tending to her father in his last days, she could've simply dropped everything and gone. Briefly, at least. Her father had kept her close, at his beck and call.

She set to work again, every motion hurried until at last she called to Blanche, already prepping for the evening meal, saying she was going to the barn.

"We could use another dozen eggs as long as you're there," Blanche replied.

Rio could tell Blanche had been able to see her excitement at Beckett's return. Apparently, her face was an open book.

The Ferris brothers turned to greet her as her shadow preceded her into the barn. Beckett was brushing his gelding with smooth, even strokes as the horse munched a handful of oats in the manger at the front of the stall. Win stood with his arms crossed atop the gate. It seemed apparent their discussion had been serious.

Beckett, Rio observed, appeared tired. So did the horse, as if he'd been ridden hard. What had they been doing all day?

"Can we talk now?" she asked, oh, so coolly. She handed the egg basket to Win. "Could you see if you can find a dozen eggs, please?"

The boy glanced at his brother, who nodded. "Sure."

The coop occupied a large stall at the back of the

barn, where a door opened to a strongly fenced area that allowed the hens to hunt and peck for bugs while it kept chicken-stealing varmints away. The distance between the coop and the horse stalls was plenty to allow for privacy.

Rio's brown eyes flashed. "Where have you been? I've been worried sick about you. Not to mention, I don't appreciate being kept in the dark about what concerns my own property." Except that she had just mentioned it. More than mentioned.

"Where shall I start?" Beckett pushed out of the stall and set the brush on a ledge just outside it. Folding his arms across his chest, he leaned against the gate.

"At the beginning," Rio replied, a snap in her voice. "Last thing I know is you rode off following Mr. Akers and his hound."

He sighed. "Seems like days ago."

It had been yesterday, or no, the day before, she thought. More than a whole forty-eight hours. It did seem longer. Had he even gotten any sleep last night?

She forced down her sympathy and waited for his reply.

"Akers and his dog did their best," Beckett said. "Even so, it didn't get us much further ahead. Whoever killed Pope apparently had a boat waiting over near the little cove between here and the sawmill. When Akers and Belle lost the trail there, they went on to town. They went to the landing and tried to pick up scent on the other side, but the dog didn't show any interest. Either the fellow put to shore somewhere else or—" He stopped, brow puckering.

"Or?"

"Or he might've skinned out of whatever he was

wearing and dropped it in the lake. Most likely, he had blood on him."

She nodded, remembering the flowing black cloak. "But he wouldn't have dumped his shoes, would he?"

"His shoes?"

"The blood had been walked in." She swallowed, a convulsive reaction. Thinking of what she'd seen raised her gorge. "And then there was the salt. Purple salt. If he was the one who walked through it, there would've been some clinging to his shoe's soles."

He went silent, then nodded. "Probably means he landed somewhere else, then. Dammit." Stifling a yawn that threatened to break his jaw, Beckett paused a moment to think. "Next thing, it turns out Dr. Clement and Mr. Meadows had already called a meeting to introduce me to some of the people around here. That was early this morning, right there at the jail. Kind of a mix-up as it happened, since Masterson had done the same for Bull French over at the bank lobby."

Rio's eyes opened wide. "Mr. Masterson is backing Bull French?" She could hardly believe it. The two hardly seemed like allies, Bull being barely civilized. If at all. "How did your meeting go?"

He shrugged. "Seemed as if there were plenty of men crowding into the jail. 'Course, that could've been due to the jail not being very big. I don't know about over at the bank. A couple men came by after going there first and said most folks weren't too interested in hobnobbing with Bull." He snorted a laugh. "Which doesn't mean they approve of me, either.

"Then I rode out to a couple of lumber camps, which served a couple purposes at once. Campaigning and questioning some fellows who'd been seen drinking with Pope the night before he was killed."

"With men from the logging crews?" This surprised Rio. Pope had been a city man. A stranger. As a general rule, those kinds of men kept to themselves and made it a point to stay away from the rough men from the woods with their calloused fists and caulked boots.

"Seems he spread a good deal of money around in the brief time he was here, trying to buy goodwill."

"But why?" It made no sense to Rio.

He stared at her, silent for as long as ten heartbeats. "One of the Henderson crew didn't mind talking. And none of the others tried to hush him. He told me Pope'd been asking to talk to the men who knew Eino Salo ever since he got here. In fact, he got kind of pushy about it."

Rio's heart felt like a lead weight in her chest. Eino, again. Somehow, he always managed to figure in the conversation.

"And," Beckett went on, "Pope got pretty aggravated when the men drank the hootch he bought, but laughed behind his back. Seems he finally figured out Eino was the kind of fellow who talked a good story but kept the details secret. And that he has a real penchant for lying."

She had to agree with whoever'd finally spilled the beans. She nodded. "And if anything real slipped out, our father paid to keep it quiet." The bitterness echoed until she said, wailing, "But how did Merle Pope end up murdered in my cellar? That's what I want to know. And why?"

Beckett's dark eyes studied her. "I think he might've asked too many questions of the wrong person."

"Who, for instance?"

His mouth quirked. "If I knew that, I'd be a whole lot closer to making an arrest."

"I'm thinking of closing the hotel." Rio folded her arms across her middle as if to hold in the ache. "Kicking these people out and only running the restaurant. At least until hunting season and then just taking in the regulars." There were certain people who came every season. She'd hate to disappoint them. Plus, she knew they wouldn't cause her any trouble. It was the people from back east—the Carvers, Vesta White, David Freeman, and the late Merle Pope—to blame for this. And Eino. Of course, Eino.

If she'd thought Beckett might try to dissuade her, it turned out she was way off.

"Might not be a bad idea," he said. "But not until I've cleared everyone who was here while Pope was getting himself killed."

———

TALKING with Beckett about the footprint in the purple salt reminded Rio of another smidgeon of information. She wasn't any too certain of its importance, or if it had any importance at all, but she decided to tell him, anyway.

"It's about Mr. Freeman," she said, her eyes wide and serious as the memory surfaced. They were on their way back to the hotel. Rio was carrying the basket of eggs over her arm since Win had gone back to his raking. The sun, warm on her shoulders, seemed to help chase away the collywobbles that kept dogging her. Unless that went to Beckett's credit.

"What about him?" Beckett glanced down at her. "So far, he seems to be keeping his nose clean."

"I don't think he's a brave man." Agreement of sorts. "But I noticed something odd the other day. I saw that he'd glued something over the soles of his shoes to deaden the sound."

Beckett stopped. "He what?"

"He glued something to the soles of his shoes to muffle his footsteps," she repeated. "He didn't make a very tidy job of it either. I think it's a layer of soft leather." Rio made a little scoffing noise. "He'd better be careful, though. He's apt to take a fall if the leather gets wet. Anyway, find a way to get a look at his shoes. If he's the one who stepped in the salt, there's sure to be traces of it stuck in the leather. Huckleberries stain something awful, and salt will stick in any crack."

Beckett got a far-off look on his face. "Doesn't sound like something an innocent man would do." Even so, he shook his head. "But it wasn't him Belle was trailing. If it had been, the hound would've picked up his scent there on the stairs. Instead, she passed through the lobby and followed her prey right into the woods."

Rio didn't know whether to be disappointed or not. If it had been possible to catch a murderer so easily, she would've been breathing a whole lot easier right now. On the other hand, the thought of sheltering a murderer with innocent people—including herself—under the same roof was disquieting, to say the least. The murderer's retreat seemed to indicate he wasn't staying at the hotel. And in a town this size, there weren't many alternate places for a stranger to hide out.

She gave a startled gasp, enough to make Beckett look at her. "What?" he asked.

"What if whoever killed Mr. Pope isn't a stranger?" Her wide brown eyes stared at him. "What if he is someone we know?"

And Beckett, who, after all, was not a resident of Painter's Bay, and had been wondering this same thing, raised his eyebrows. "Such as?"

But this was where Rio came up short. "I don't know. Let me think."

"Someone with access to the hotel? Is there anyone like that?"

Slowly, she shook her head. "Not after hours. How could there be?" Still, the question lodged in her head and refused to go away. "There shouldn't be."

But it was something to set her to wondering.

"What about the Golz boys?" Beckett threw the question out. "Any of them ever been in trouble?"

"No," Rio replied. "Never. I'd as soon suspect myself." And so the conversation ended.

An exceedingly grubby old man came by later, enticing her with a creel full of wriggling crayfish he persuaded her to buy.

"Jambalaya," Rio announced.

Blanche, busy rubbing salt and pepper and dried herbs from the garden onto the surface of a massive baron of beef prior to putting it in a slow oven, looked up with a frown.

"Jam...what?" she asked.

"Jambalaya." Rio was smiling. "A sort of stew, but like none you're apt to find around here. The recipe was one of my grandfather's favorites, made in the Creole fashion with tomatoes, sausage, chicken, and lots of spices." Other things too, but she wasn't about to recite the whole recipe.

Blanche gestured at the crawfish, her nose wrinkling. "Creole? And you put those in the stew and eat them?"

"Indeed, you do. Poor man's lobster. You'll see. It's delicious," Rio said and proceeded to lay out items for the stew. For the first time since finding Merle Pope's body, she felt almost normal as she added spicy sausage, chopped chicken, sun-dried tomatoes, and the mandatory celery, onions, and pepper to the pot. Still, even as she worked, the question Beckett had posed earlier nagged at her. *Access to the hotel?* But still nothing came to her.

In the evening, as Eliza and Marie were placing flatware, water glasses, and napkins on the tables for the first dinner sitting, Mr. Pellow, his face as tired and hangdog as ever, dropped off a tall, thin man wearing a charcoal gray long coat and carrying a small satchel who demanded a room for, as he said, "An indeterminate amount of time."

For Rio, who'd hurried from the kitchen to check him in, it took only seconds to spot the revolver he carried beneath his left arm, mainly because the weapon was big enough that he carried the arm at an odd, sprung angle. Guns, as a rule, didn't disturb her. But something about this fellow raised her hackles.

And Boo, who, against the rules, had followed on her heels into the lobby, growled. Instantly, she made a play of looking through a book beyond the man's sight and said, "I'm sorry. We're booked full for the rest of the week. I only have a room for this one night." Maybe she really would close down the hotel for a while. Until they'd discovered who killed Merle Pope in her cellar, at least. She'd be happy to send the disagreeable Vesta White and her equally disagreeable maid on their way.

The tall man frowned, started to speak, and changed his mind. "That'll be long enough, I expect. One night will do."

Do for what? His comment echoed in her mind. She watched as he wrote down a name, the handwriting scraggly, careless, and nearly unreadable. But not to someone with Rio's experience. "Arnold Heckert, PA? Welcome, sir. I assume you plan on dinner service?"

He, appearing a bit surprised as she repeated his name, raised his nose and sniffed. "Yeah," he said. "Sure. Included?"

"No," she said, crisp and steady. "Dinner is extra. Breakfast in the morning is included."

"Huh," he said, and paid up without protest.

What, she wondered as she handed him a key, did the letters PA stand for?

Rio, taking a moment to survey the crowded dining room just before the first sitting changed over to the second, had a moment of startlement when she discovered the Carvers occupying one of her largest tables. They hadn't been around for a couple days, and she'd believed them gone back to wherever they were from.

Well, she wished they had.

They sat with the banker and his assistant, Mr. Masterson slouching uncomfortably—far from his usual habit. Jensen, the assistant, was notable for the way his eyes shifted from person to person as they talked, although he seemed to be keeping his own thoughts to himself.

Amazing her even more, their dinner companions were Vesta White and David Freeman, with Bindle sitting silently at the edge of the already crowded table like some kind of add-on, her chair an impediment awkward to get around.

Turner, Rio saw, had uncorked a bottle of red wine for them, and brought out some fancy stemmed glasses. Apparently, the wine had hit Vesta hard. Her voice rose in less than mellow tones above the normal clink of utensils on china plates and the soft talk of the other diners. Even the normally unruly loggers knew enough not to shout in the Painter's Bay dining room. It was their connection to polite society, after all.

"Well, Mr. Carver, raise your offer," Vesta was saying, waving a fork laden with rare beef, as if pointing a rapier as dribbles splashed on the tablecloth. "If she's anything like her brother, she'll snatch at it as long as the price is right."

Bindle leaned over and whispered something in Vesta's ear, and Vesta laughed.

"Yes," she said, and repeated, "As Bindle reminded me, keep your eyes open. Evan Salo is not noted for keeping his end of a bargain, and neither is she."

A fire smoldered in Rio's belly. She knew the *she* Vesta meant. None other than Rio Salo. She crooked a finger at Marie, their waitress for the night—poor girl.

In seconds, Marie stood beside her.

"Can you hear what else she's saying?" Rio asked. The direction of her glare was plenty to indicate the *she* she meant.

"She's drunk on the wine," Marie whispered back. "But they were talking about buying the hotel again. So that means..."

Rio finished the sentence. "Means she's talking about me. And Eino."

Marie nodded. "I was trying to ignore her, but I'll pay more attention if you want."

"Yes, please." Rio, on her way back to the kitchen, was beginning to have doubts herself now. Could Eino have managed to steal some sort of valuables, whatever it might be, and hidden it here? Or could he have passed something on to their father before he died, and Elias done the hiding? She wouldn't put it past either of them. But surely Eino would've taken anything of value with him when he left the last time. She believed he'd intended to leave the country—most likely forever.

Or had he?

The fact was, Rio just didn't know.

But she knew one thing well enough. A man had been killed—in her cellar—for Eino's treasure, whether real or imagined. And whoever had done the killing, while trying to steal from a thief, was someone even worse than her half brother. At least he hadn't actually murdered anybody—that she knew of, at any rate.

She'd barely switched her frilly customer-visiting apron for the cooking cover-all when Marie hurried into the kitchen again. "They told me to come fetch you, Rio." The girl looked more than a little worried. And angry.

"Fetch me? Whatever for?" Taking her time, Rio lifted the lid to the pot of jambalaya and gave it a stir, then checked if the fresh batch of rice was tender and fluffy. It was, and she nodded in satisfaction.

Marie looked behind her as if afraid one of them had followed her to the kitchen. "I don't know, but I don't like what they're saying. Is Mr. Ferris—Sheriff Ferris, I mean—here tonight? Because those people are getting unruly. I mean it, Rio. I think you should ignore them. Please. I'll tell them you're too busy. Maybe Mr. Turner can—"

Rio, shaking her head, switched aprons again, smiled faintly at Marie, and shook her head. "My job." Which might be true, but it didn't stop her from wishing for Beckett too.

Blanche, blatantly listening and still holding the sharp knife she'd been using to slice the baron of beef into precise slices, joined them.

"Listen to Marie," she said, taking her sister's part. "You don't want to give them an opening to work against you."

"I don't think I can ignore them, though I'd like to. I'll do my best to prevent a riot," Rio said. And yet, part of her thought just the opposite. A riot might be the best way to excuse shutting the hotel down until these people left her in peace and Beckett found Merle Pope's murderer.

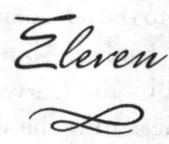

Eleven

B indle, her gaze fixed on the doorway from the kitchen, touched Vesta's shoulder.

But the maid, as Rio saw right away, wasn't the only one at that table on the lookout. Jensen—she'd forgotten his first name at the moment—watched as well, a half-smile on his face.

Or maybe it wasn't a smile at all. Might've been a grimace.

Rio did her best to keep her own features blank as she stopped beside the overcrowded table. She stood beside Mr. Masterson, where she had a clear view of the others.

"Do you have a question about the food?" she said. "Miss Golz said you needed to speak with me? How may I help you?" Her politeness verged on excessive. She knew it. They knew, or sensed it. And they didn't intend to talk about the food. That much was plain.

Carver the younger hooked an empty chair from the table next to them and dragged it over, the scooting legs crossing the floor with a noisy scritch.

"Sit down," Carver the elder said. "We need to talk."

As though she wasn't burning with anger, Rio made a show of quietly restoring the chair to its original position and apologizing to the occupants of the other table.

Masterson, the banker, squirmed in his chair, notably embarrassed by the Carvers' boorish behavior. Rio could see him measuring the way their ill manners would reflect on him and his position in the community. She sent him a narrow-eyed stare. She hoped it did.

Next, fixing her gaze on Carver the elder, she ignored the son. "I can't speak with you at the moment. When you stop at the cashier desk on your way out, I'll try to find a moment to make an appointment. Sometime in the morning might be best. But if your intention is to make another offer for the hotel, you might as well save your breath. You've had my final word and wasted enough of my time."

"Sit down, I said," Carver thundered. He half stood, his round face flushing a violent red.

Vesta giggled.

A hush fell over the entire dining room, faces turning to seek the cause of the angry outburst. Marie, Rio noticed, her hands full of emptied plates, stopped mid-stride, her mouth in a rounded O. The silverware lay on the plate rattling as she trembled. One of the loggers from Blue Sky, a regular Friday night customer, stood up and took a step toward them, his big hands forming fists.

Carver Jr. noticed him first. He sent an alarmed look at his father and jerked a thumb toward the logger. Carver Sr. dropped back into his chair. So...not the bravest of men. Not when faced with a man who cut big timber for a living.

Yet Rio, when she spoke, was almost relieved the Carvers were finally revealed as thoroughly unsavory men, and that perhaps Vesta White, and even Masterson, had finally shown their true colors as well in their association with the easterners.

"Finish your meal, pay your bill, and get out." She maintained an icy calm. One she didn't feel. Not in the least. "And don't come back. Miss White, Miss Bindle, Mr. Freeman, I'll expect you to pack up and leave in the morning. Please be aware I shall inspect your rooms for damage before you go. Mr. Masterson and...and..." She glanced at his assistant and shook her head without saying more.

Vesta's dismayed gasp was probably heard all around the large, silent room. "How...how dare you," she cried. "You can't do that."

"I can. Easily. In the few months since I reopened this hotel, I've been shot. I've been cheated and intimidated. I've had people repeatedly try to kill me or scare me away. Yet here I stand. I intend to remain standing and tending to my business. I will not be frightened off by people who want what belongs to me. No matter what I have to do, I will defend what is mine against all comers. I don't care who they think they are."

Spinning on her heel, Rio went back to the kitchen. Just out of sight of the diners, Blanche clapped her hands in silent applause. Win stood in the hallway grinning. Marie finally got the dirty dishes to the sink, where she set them on a sideboard and gave a gusty sigh.

"Well said." Someone, a man in the dining room

with a loud voice, seemed to be speaking for everyone. "We're with you, Miss Salo," he called out.

But was it well said? Had she finally won this particular little war? Or had she made herself into an even bigger target?

Turner came into the kitchen, shaking his head. "Missy, you've done it now. If that wasn't a dare, then I've never heard one. Them Carvers, they're bad ones. You want to be careful."

His words all too accurately followed her own thoughts. A sinking feeling told her she should've listened to Marie. And Blanche, though both staunchly supported her now.

"Do you think they murdered Mr. Pope?" Suffering from an unaccountable clog in her throat, Rio choked on the words.

"Well, now, I just don't know. Dunno how they would've got into the hotel, let alone the cellar, so I can't say one way or the other. I figure they called you to the table tonight, intending to make threats. Probably figured you wouldn't let out a peep where folks might hear."

She smiled wanly. "Guess they were wrong. Though I probably shouldn't have."

"I don't know about that." He eyed her with a look that said he knew she was strained to the breaking point. "You ain't going out there to deal with them no more tonight. I'll run the cash register. Hell, I handle cash for the bar. Reckon I can do the restaurant for a while. By the time the second seating is ready to pay up, this'll all blow over."

Thinking he might be overly optimistic, she was still grateful and took him up on the offer.

The routine of supplying food to people with hearty appetites while maintaining the ebb and flow of the service allowed the evening to speed past. As Turner had predicted, at the end of the second seating, most of the public had better, more pleasant things to talk about during their evening out.

By the time the restaurant closed, the jambalaya, as it turned out, had been eaten to the last scraping from the pot.

———

RIO, key in hand, had locked the hotel's front door and was on the back porch to secure the rear when she spotted Beckett riding past on his way to the barn. Another whole day had passed with no progress—that she knew of, anyhow—in finding Merle Pope's killer.

The slow clomp of the sorrel's hoofbeats on the grass allowed a surge of relief to sweep over her. She'd been afraid, but she stopped that line of thought before it went any further.

She'd go meet him, she decided, although even the short distance between the hotel and the barn made her see shadows moving in the dark. Wishing for the cheerful chirp of crickets, she missed the sounds of summer. As fall approached with frost and cold, the night was eerily silent.

She had just stepped off the porch steps when something made her stop and go back. Inserting the key in the lock, she gave it a firm twist and heard the click.

Boo saved her from making a fool of herself and doing something so unseemly as running, or calling out, or...Well, she didn't know what else. Unconscious of doing so, she touched the hard steel of the .32 Iver Johnson revolver concealed in her skirt pocket.

"C'mon," she told the little dog, snapping her fingers and striding off toward the barn. Boo led the way. He'd seen Beckett too. And the sorrel. He liked to touch noses with the horses.

Beckett had the lantern lit and was putting his saddle on a wooden rack when she and Boo got to the barn. He dropped the saddle onto the rack and whirled, his face set at the sound of their feet rustling through the straw. A sure sign he was aware of growing jumpy these last few days.

Rio flinched. Maybe she wasn't the only one who wished for eyes in the back of her head.

Boo, unaware of his mistress's tension, dashed forward to greet the man and the sorrel.

"You should've called out." A mere twitch of a smile touched his mouth. "I could've shot you."

Rio had noticed. "Sorry," she murmured. "I didn't think."

He fondled Boo's ears before the dog moved on to the horse, which left him free to look at her. He shook his head. "No reason why you should have to."

He must not have heard what happened here tonight. She sighed. "That might not be entirely true."

Beckett studied her for a moment, then reached out and pulled her into his arms. He settled her against him, a perfect fit. "Tell me."

That was all the encouragement she needed. The story came pouring out, and by the end, Beckett's expression had closed off and gone cool. He didn't release her, but pushed her a few inches away to see her better. His opinion of the encounter echoed Turner's quite accurately.

"I've got to agree with your bartender friend," he said. "What you told them? It did sound like a dare." His eyes, showing a deep black in the weak lantern light, flashed dangerously. "Although it might be one way to draw them out. But not the safest."

She stirred as his arms tightened around her again. "Use me as bait, you mean?"

He shook his head. "A bad idea, one that won't happen. I won't let it."

Rio appreciated his intention to keep her safe. She truly did. But this—what would she call it? An interlude, as she stood with his arms wrapped around her, and hers, she discovered, around him?—was the longest conversation they'd had for a couple of days. Who knows what could've happened in that length of time. Could have, but hadn't.

Beckett had other duties now. She'd asked for his help, and he'd come. But with his run for sheriff of the county official, it meant he had to get out, make himself known to voters, and, by preference, catch Merle Pope's murderer. And not waste too much time doing it, either. The chase took him into deep timber and open country-side, where he, too, would be at risk.

She was well aware she'd have to look after herself, even if he hadn't realized. Or at least, he hadn't let it sink in yet.

Her lips trembled a little as she looked up at him and forced a smile. "I know you don't want to put me in danger. Don't worry. I promise to be careful. For instance, I won't go wandering around outside by myself after dark."

"Which you just did. But don't depend on Boo. I don't consider him a satisfactory guard." His warning teased.

The thing is, it was true. He knew it, she knew it.

His eyes narrowed then, fastening on her up-tilted face and her smile. As if he couldn't help himself, his mouth lowered. Their lips met. Those stars and sparkles that always seemed to surround her when he kissed her lit within, and she forgot everything else. Everything except him. And for the next few minutes, her world came right.

As all good things did, at least in Rio's experience, it didn't take long for the brief respite to end. Which meant when, breathing a little faster than normal, Beckett's arms opened and he backed a few inches away. The sorrel was nuzzling the back of his neck.

"I think he's hungry."

His rueful grin made Rio smile too. A real smile this time. "Then you'd better feed him." She saw where the saddle had ruffled the horse's hair. "And brush him down. He probably itches."

"Yes, ma'am." Beckett put a scoop of oats and a flake of good timothy hay in the manger and set to work with a brush. "Keep me company. I don't want you walking back to the hotel on your own."

Not that she wanted to, but she said, "I'll be all right. I have my .32."

But Beckett shook his head. "Stay. Talk to me. Tell me what's been happening besides this meeting with the Carvers tonight."

It was the opening she'd hoped for. And oddly, Rio found it comforting to sit in the dim light of the lantern as Beckett brushed his horse. Watching the smooth strokes of the brush, she felt as soothed as the horse. And found it easier to talk when he listened and didn't speak much.

First was her idea to close the hotel and evict Vesta, Bindle, and David Freeman. "They're a large part of the problem," she said, turning to watch Boo chase a mouse into the dark. Somewhere at the end of the barn, a couple chickens rustled and squawked a soft sleepy call before quieting again.

"Do you believe you can convince her—assuming Miss White is the ringleader of the group—that your half brother lied?" Under Beckett's hand, the brush swept over the sorrel's rump. "Get rid of the bunch of them?"

"Oh, she's the ringleader, all right." Rio sighed. "But convincing her of anything is doubtful. She wants to believe she's going to get rich." She laughed. "By stealing his stolen treasure, whether it's jewels or something else." A funny situation in a cockeyed way.

"I am going to close the hotel," she said abruptly, her mind made up in the instant. "To everyone but the hunters who come every year, and they're not due for another month or so. They have no interest in the hotel except for a place to stay while getting a big buck or a fine, fat elk. But it isn't just because of her and her friend David Freeman, either."

Beckett stopped brushing. "It isn't?"

"No." She paused, brow creasing. "Merle Pope was an odd one, if you remember, with no obvious reason for coming here. Although I guess we know now." She huffed. "And look what happened to him.

"Another stranger turned up here last night," she went on. "One Boo took a dislike to and growled at. At first, this stranger wanted a room for 'an indeterminate amount of time' to quote what he said. I told him I only had a room open this one night. It was late, you see, and Mr. Pellow just sort of dumped him off. It didn't seem right to turn him down. Not for no real reason."

She had Beckett's attention.

"How did the stranger react?" he asked. "Angry?"

"No. He thought it over and said he'd just stay the night then. But he said something else that struck me as odd."

"What was it?"

"He said, 'One night should be enough.'"

Beckett frowned. "That's all?"

"That's all. Don't you think that was a strange thing to say? What do you suppose he meant? Enough for what? He's still here, by the way, even though I told him the room was only for one night."

A shrug answered, but Beckett had questions of his own. "Did you get his name? Or where he's from? Any idea what his business might be?"

Rio shook her head. "I got his name when he signed the register, although from the scribble, I thought he might be trying to hide it. Arnold Heckert, PA. I don't know what PA means." She included those initials that had, and still did, puzzle her. "He didn't say where he's from—" She stopped when she saw the way Beckett stared at her. "What?"

"Arnold Heckert, PA?"

"Yes." She drew the word out, all the way into a question.

"PA. Pinkerton Agent. I wonder..." He didn't seem happy.

Rio's brows drew into a vee. "A Pinkerton agent?

Why on earth would a Pinkerton come to Painter's Bay? Who hired him?" Then it dawned. "Oh! You think this business about Eino and hidden treasure brought him here? Like it brought Miss White and Mr. Freeman. And Merle Pope? But not any of it is true. I'm sure it's not true." She shook her head. "It can't be. One of Eino's stupid and hurtful jokes."

Beckett stowed the brush and slapped the horse on the rump in parting. "Well, it would seem someone thinks it's true. The Pinkerton. Is he still up?"

"I don't know. All the guests went to their rooms a while ago. Whether they stayed there or not I couldn't say." She was thinking of Vesta and Mr. Freeman. Freeman had indicated they were close, but to Rio's eye, Vesta had other ideas. Vesta would use the man if it came in handy. That's all.

"I think I'll go knock on his door." Beckett grinned. "And Freeman's too, while I'm at it. I've got the weight of the sheriff's office behind me now, and a murder to investigate."

Rio had been thinking. "Maybe the Pinkerton is here because of Mr. Pope. Maybe it's nothing to do with Eino and a supposed treasure."

"Maybe," Beckett said, but she could see he didn't agree.

Blowing out the lantern after Rio recalled Boo from his mouse hunt, Beckett took her hand for the walk back to the hotel. Almost by accident—but maybe not—their fingers intertwined.

"We haven't talked as much about the murder as we should." He looked down at her, his voice quiet. "Win gave me a long-winded explanation about setting up your scheme on the stairs with some purple salt."

She didn't need daylight to read his expression. He found the idea silly. But it hadn't been. There had been the person Akers's dog had managed to track from it. If only the culprit hadn't taken to the water.

"Can you ask to see Mr. Freeman's shoes?"

"It wasn't him the dog tracked," Beckett reminded her.

"No, but those fake soles will tell you if he went down there with Mr. Pope."

"And the killer."

"And the killer," she agreed.

He sighed a little. "I will," he agreed. "When I knock on his door."

It was a start, Rio thought. A sign Beckett wasn't brushing off the things troubling her.

Though they'd walked slowly, they reached the back porch, where the door swung wide open.

Rio gasped and clenched Beckett's hand, her fingernails digging into him. "No!" It came out a moan.

"What?" He jerked her back, although she'd already stopped stock-still.

"The door." She whispered now. "When Boo and I came to meet you, I shut and locked the door. How—"

Beckett didn't ask if she was sure. He knew she was. He motioned her to stay back. Lighting a match, he made a quick appraisal of the latch before standing erect and turning to look at her. "Somebody either has a key or knows how to pick a lock."

This time, her moan was clearly audible.

At which point Boo, bold and brave, scooted into the dark well of the porch without a care in the world. Slower by far, Beckett and Rio followed.

Twelve

"Stay behind me." Beckett carried his revolver leveled before him, leading the way through the porch and on into the kitchen. There, he had Rio light the lantern while he kept watch.

Once lit, though shadows still filled the corners, the lantern helped ease their first concerns of an ambush. The kitchen looked just as she'd left it a half hour ago. Warmth remained in the cooling stove. A few large pots were drying on the counter beside the sink. The room was clean and tidy although she could still smell the potent spices of jambalaya.

Rio went immediately to the cellar door, which, when she twisted the knob, remained locked tight. "Nobody here," she whispered. One tiny fear eased. Only one.

Nodding to her, Beckett went back down the hall. He looked in the bathroom and found it empty. The door to his and Win's room remained locked, although through the thick door they heard loud snores.

Eyes wide, she turned to Beckett. "You have to sleep through that?"

He chuckled.

On then to Rio's office-bedroom, where a quick look around showed things in order.

In order, but it struck her as she was backing out, not quite as she'd left them. The papers on her desk were misaligned, as if quickly scanned and carelessly restacked. The ink pen had been moved and leaked ink onto one corner of the night's receipts. Boo's mat was wadded up and kicked aside. And the bottom sheet on her cot had been pulled from being tucked under the mattress.

"Look." Her voice trembled, more from anger than fright. Slowly, she pointed out the changes. Beckett's mouth clamped shut, and he nodded.

They found the dining room empty, although an uncorked bottle of bourbon stood on Turner's bar. Rio knew it hadn't been there when Turner and the Golz girls left. In the lobby, their intruder had opened the cash register and left the drawer half out. But, according to her custom, Rio had put all the money in her safe, and evidently, whoever had ransacked the place hadn't found it. The front door was still locked. Evidently, the would-be thief had departed the same way he'd entered, through the back.

Provided he'd come and gone at all. What if the open porch had just been a ruse as he came and went via the stairs? Could it be he was tucked in his bed at this moment?

At the bottom of the stairs, Beckett held the lantern high. "Got your .32?"

Rio patted her pocket. "Right here."

"Good." He looked back up the stairs. "I want you to stand down here and wait for me. I suggest you stay in the niche where anyone coming down won't be able to see you. Keep a tight watch. If anybody tries to leave, don't stop them. Call to me and I'll take care of them. I don't want anyone leaving this hotel tonight without me knowing."

She nodded, pressing a forefinger on her bottom lip to keep it from trembling as he lit a lamp for himself.

Smiling a little, Beckett bent and removed the finger, replacing it with a quick kiss. One that seemed almost to burn.

"Don't worry," he said. "You'll be all right. I'll be all right."

And then he went up the steps in a rush, disappearing from her sight. In a moment, she heard him knocking on Freeman's door, the next room on the right beside Vesta's. A minute or so later, she heard murmuring, then nothing.

Stepping backward into the bar niche as he'd directed, she waited. All being quiet, she replaced the cork in the bourbon bottle and put it back on the shelf behind the bar. Overhead, a floorboard creaked as Beckett stopped outside the room of one of the two traveling salesmen staying overnight in the hotel. A quick visit before he went to the next. Rio thought it proved Beckett believed, just as she did, that the people from back east were the source of the murder and the trouble here. When he spoke to the second salesman—she didn't think this one had been in bed since he opened up within seconds—and the conversation lasted less than a minute, she was sure of it.

Going back to the bottom of the stairs, she heard

Beckett tapping on the Pinkerton agent's door. After a bit, he tapped again, harder this time. And then again. She was aware when she heard the wide-awake salesman say something to Beckett, his question loud enough to carry.

"No answer," Beckett replied. "But light is shining beneath his door."

She heard the words "fire" and "smoke," which almost caused her nerves to give way. Then he appeared at the top of the stairs. "The lamp is burning, but Pinkerton doesn't answer. Bring me the master key," he called down to her. "I'm going in."

Rio kept the master key in her office, although room keys hung on a board in back of the lobby desk. Years ago, her mother had given her a small wooden box to keep her pretties in. Her last gift, as a matter of fact. Under the premise that it would never occur to any self-respecting thief to look in a child's trinket box sitting open on a shelf, she hadn't troubled to hide the key further.

Her premise had been wrong. The key was gone.

With no time to contemplate how the thief had known, or guessed, the key's location, she stopped in the kitchen for a screwdriver and fled up the stairs to where Beckett waited. The salesman stood beside him, wide awake and curious. He stopped regularly on his route between some small town on the coast, the Idaho panhandle, and Missoula. Right now, she was glad he was the only one awake. He wouldn't be scared off by what was happening.

Probably.

Beckett, already reaching for the key, got a surprise

when she slapped the screwdriver into his hand instead. "What's this?"

She shook her head in warning, unwilling to discuss the missing key in front of the salesman. "All I could find on short notice. Don't worry. This has happened before. Just undo these screws and the plate will loosen enough for the latch to slip out."

Eino had taught her that once when he'd gotten in trouble for having locked all the doors and then lost the master key. Intending to blame Rio for the ensuing aggravation, he'd told their father she had done it. For the only time she remembered, Elias hadn't bought his story, and she escaped the anticipated beating. No doubt the reason she remembered the incident at all.

Taking her at her word, Beckett bent to the work, and a couple of minutes later the door swung far enough for him to reach in and fully release the latch.

Peering over Beckett's shoulder, the salesman's breath let out in a sudden gush. "Holy..." Choking, he stepped back with his hand over his mouth.

Rio caught a glimpse and didn't breathe at all.

Beckett's expression didn't change.

Arnold Heckert lay sprawled in his bed. Like Merle Pope, the Pinkerton's throat had been cut, the raw red wound like a second mouth below his chin. Blood soaked the bedding and the mattress around him, but beyond that and his half-open, unseeing eyes, he almost seemed undisturbed.

"He didn't fight. He must've been asleep." The words hardly sounded like Rio's voice at all, with her mouth so dry.

"Yes." Beckett swung around, the lantern casting wide, moving shadows. "I'll need more light. Gather a few more lamps and bring them in, please. Mr. Sorenson, will you help her?"

The salesman, as if glad to do something—anything—other than look at the bloody body, nodded. A couple lamps stood on a table at the head of the stairs. Rio got one lit, though it took two matches, and, beckoning Mr. Sorenson to follow her, went down and borrowed more lamps from the dining room.

"What's going on here, Miss Salo?" Sorenson's shaky question followed her.

"I wish I knew, sir," she said. "If I did, I would put a stop to it."

"Yes, ma'am. I'll bet you would."

She avoided looking at the body as they settled lamps on every surface that would hold one. Beckett took pity on her, giving instructions to awaken Win and have him either ride around the point or row a boat over to town and fetch Dr. Clement, as he was also the coroner.

"Then," Beckett said, "I want you to get the women downstairs. They must be awake by now. Seat them in the near corner of the dining room and keep them separated from the men. Have the men gather in the lobby by the bar. I don't want them talking to each other.

"Mr. Sorenson, if you feel up to it, I'd like for you to watch me search the dead man and make a list of his things as I find them. Can you do that?"

Rio bet he wished for a deputy about now. A real, competent deputy, not the old codger who only minded the jail when the occupants didn't seem too dangerous. And he'd especially prefer someone other than his young brother, Rio, or the hotel guest.

"I can do it." Going by his expression, his agreement didn't mean Sorenson was happy about the job.

As for Rio, she nodded grimly and went first to rouse Win, then to knock on Vesta White's door.

Vesta herself opened up. She had shrugged into the fancy Chinese robe again and wore matching slippers. "What is going on?" she demanded. "I just got to sleep and now all this noise has me awake again. I demand a refund. I pay for a decent night of sleep."

Since the woman owed for two nights already, Rio didn't bother to answer. "There's been another murder." No sugarcoating. Not necessary since she didn't think Vesta would be brokenhearted over the man dying. Maybe she already knew.

But she couldn't help but take notice of the way Vesta's eyes flashed and her nostrils flared.

"Another murder? Who?" Vesta demanded.

"Mr. Heckert. The Pinkerton agent." Deliberately, Rio added the man's employer

"Pinkerton agent?" Perhaps Vesta hadn't known the man was a detective as she looked rather alarmed. "Why—" She cut off as Bindle stepped up behind her.

"Why should we be disturbed?" Bindle demanded. "We don't know this man."

"Don't you?" Rio shrugged. "But he indicated he might know you." She watched the maid blink several times. A tell. Bindle didn't like the news.

"In fact..." Rio lied, stating her own suspicions as truth, "He said he was led here to wind up an investigation. His murder forces Sheriff Ferris to take over."

"That's nothing to do with me." Vesta glanced at her maid. "With us."

"But the sheriff doesn't know that, does he?

Because you two and Mr. Freeman are from the very area that interested Mr. Heckert. Cooperate and the sheriff will soon know one way or the other. He's asked for all the guests on this floor to gather downstairs. Ladies, just inside the dining room, if you please. The men will be in the lobby. He asks that you refrain from speaking with one another until he's met with you."

"The nerve." Vesta's flounce might've been more convincing if her tone hadn't been hard as horseshoes.

Beckett had been much more brusque than that. He hadn't asked, he'd told.

Vesta started with a complaint, a denial, and a demand, which came as no surprise. Rio ignored everything, simply requiring compliance. Bindle lagged. Once, she tried to close the door on Rio, who, having expected something of the like, had wedged her body against the jamb.

"No playing games, ladies," she said. "The sheriff needs to get started. Don't bring anything with you. No one cares what you look like. You're wasting time. The sooner this is done, the sooner everyone can retire to bed." Unless, the wicked thought came to her, Beckett discovered one or both of them had just murdered a man. Then their destination would be the jail in town.

She felt the small shape of her .32 in her skirt pocket, only a little reassured.

———

FREEMAN and the other salesman moved faster than the women. Sorenson already had them downstairs when Rio shepherded her charges into the dining room and made certain they were seated far enough apart to make talking difficult without being overheard.

Amused, Beckett took note of their scowls, Rio's included. He figured the women hadn't complied with his directive without argument.

"All set?" he asked.

Rio's short nod answered. She dragged a chair over to where she had a view into both rooms and sat down.

Figuring that for a signal to proceed, he beckoned to Sorenson. "Might as well get the worst over with."

Sorenson nodded. He still looked sick, but fished a notebook from a coat pocket and a pencil from his vest. "I'm ready."

Beckett had examined the lock to Heckert's room when he unscrewed the latch. Nodding for Sorenson to write down his findings, he said, "No visible scratches or signs of forcing on the lock. The killer most likely used a key to unlock, then lock the door back up after the murder. Note the hotel master key is missing."

They entered the room. Beckett pointed. "Stand there, Mr. Sorenson. There's no need for you to look at the body. Watch me and write down what I say. Add your own impressions if you have any, but make sure you keep mine and yours separate. We can compare the comments later."

His face a little pale, Sorenson stood even farther back than warranted.

Looking to the left as they came in, Beckett didn't say anything for a while, allowing for a space to study and absorb his impressions. Then he started.

"The room has been searched, but carefully, leaving only small signs. Most disturbed are the contents of Heckert's satchel, which is standing open. He's got a spare shirt that looks fresh from a laundry. Appears to have been shaken out, then refolded, but not the same as before. There's two pairs of socks, one folded, one stuffed inside the other. No idea who did what, but probably a sign of two people handling them. Shaving things sitting on the commode have been left open."

Sorenson had something to add to this observation. "Fellows who travel around don't ever leave our gear out and open like that. In a strange place, they could get spilled, or dropped and lost. Anyway, we're always ready to move on in a hurry. Hotel fires aren't that uncommon."

Poking further into the satchel, Beckett pulled out a thick paper folder that lay at the bottom of the satchel. It had been invisible at first, until he held the lamp directly over the bag and felt around with his fingertips. "Look at this." His dark eyes lit. "I don't think the killer found this. Might've been what he was looking for though."

Sorenson moved a little closer and peered over the sheriff's shoulder as he opened the folder and read the first line of the top document. "It's a contract. Pretty standard, confirming employment."

Beckett moved his thumb to read the employer's name. His brows lifted as he nodded and closed the folder. "I'll finish with these later. Just mention you saw where I found them." He moved closer to the bed where Heckert's clothes were draped over the back of a chair. "Spray from the man's blood is sprinkled on the jacket, but the clothes appear to have been searched after the murder. Could be killing the man wasn't the first intention. Heckert might've started to wake up and got his throat slashed to prevent him from calling out." He paused. "What do you think, Mr. Sorenson?"

Sorenson finished writing something down. "Dunno. Could be. Could also be whoever done it got mad when he couldn't find what he was looking for."

"Good thinking. A possibility." A small breath of relief escaped Beckett. Sorenson hadn't seen the name of the employer as Beckett had covered over that particular piece of writing. The name, a name even he recognized on the letter of employment, made him all the more eager to read the rest of the papers.

But that came later. He was only half done with the summation.

Heckert's identification as a Pinkerton was tucked into a wallet holding a surprising amount of money. Expenses paid in advance? It was something he might have to check. There was the return half of a train ticket from New York City to Missoula and back again.

New York. Yep. He'd recognized the name, all right.

Two well-worn newspaper clippings from early in the summer gave him pause.

And the likely reason for murder.

Voices rose from downstairs, recognizable as Dr. Clement, Win, and another man. Possibly Mr. Meadows, the mortician, he figured. Dr. Clement had probably called for him. Smart, saving another trip to town for someone.

Or, it occurred to him, his young brother Win might've been the one to think ahead. Win was smart as a whip and always on his toes. Beckett had to admit that if his brother had been older, he would've been his choice for a deputy.

Nodding thanks to his helper, Beckett had

Sorenson sign his name, then collected the notes and filed them away in his shirt pocket. By then, Dr. Clement, speaking heartily to Mr. Meadows and sounding wide awake and alert, rounded the corner into the room.

Stopping short, he observed a drying spray of blood reaching to the ceiling and the pool beneath the dead man's head. His lips curled.

"Doesn't look as if I'm bringing this one back to life," he said.

Beckett shook his head. "Afraid not."

"Well, then," Clement said. "Let's get started."

———

LENA BINDLE, still not asleep considering the need to keep from touching her employer as they lay in the same bed, gave Vesta a shake after hearing first the knock on David Freeman's door, then more knocking and more voices.

Whatever was going on, it seemed certain Vesta would want to know.

Lena slipped out of bed and, looking through a mere crack, peeked into the hall to see the sheriff with one of the salesmen standing with him, tapping repeatedly on the latest resident's door.

There was no answer.

She clicked the door shut just before Beckett, as Vesta had familiarly begun calling him by his first name, walked past. She stood listening then, and wondering, until Beckett and Miss Salo hurried back upstairs.

Soon, there was more commotion. More talking.

She heard only snatches. *Get the doctor. Keep everyone together. Dead.*

Another murder. Had to be. Lena shivered. What in God's name was happening here? She didn't mind some of the shenanigans Vesta and her—usually—male friends pulled. Quite often, they were profitable for her as well. But murder?

At least, she consoled herself as she bent over the bed and poked Vesta's shoulder, she knew her employer hadn't done the killing. Vesta didn't do anything that Lena didn't know about.

"Miss White," Lena whispered. She didn't want anyone to hear her, or to know she or Vesta were awake. She poked again. "Miss White. Wake up."

Vesta stirred. Her eyes opened. "Bindle? What's wrong? This had better—"

Lena held a finger over her lips. "Shh. Somebody is dead. Another murder."

Vesta stared at her. "Murder?" She sat up quickly, the blankets falling away. "Who? David?"

Odd that her employer's thoughts had immediately gone to Freeman, Lena thought. "I don't know." She went to the door and listened a moment, then came back. "They'll want to talk to us too. How do you want to play it?"

Vesta smiled and patted her fingers over what appeared to be a large yawn. "Why, Bindle, we were both asleep, of course. How could we possibly be involved? We're innocent."

For once, she was telling the truth.

Thirteen

T he hotel had gone silent as an Egyptian Pharaoh's tomb when Dr. Clement finished with the corpse and the undertaker had carted it away. It was not, Rio thought, a restful quiet. More like everyone in the second story lay in their beds listening with all their might. Who knows what their imaginations told them the settling creak of the hotel meant. What the breeze scraping a tree branch against the window indicated to them. Was that a real owl's call, or some sort of signal to or from a killer? Could what they heard be the footsteps of someone coming to cut their throat?

Beckett had erected a barricade at the bottom of the stairs and drawn one of the lobby armchairs to the front of it. Taking his revolver from the holster, he placed it on a small table next to the chair. A tired-sounding poof of air escaped him as he sat. If anyone attempted to slip past him, either to mount or descend the steps, they'd most likely trip over the barricade and make a hell of a racket. And fall right on top of him.

"Isn't that a rather dangerous position?" Rio, getting ready to extinguish the lamps, eyed his setup. "What if he comes back?"

"He?"

She made a throwaway gesture. "Whoever killed Mr. Pope and Mr. Heckert. Somehow, I can't imagine a woman did this. Not that I'd put it past either Miss White or Miss Bindle, but I just don't think they did. There was no knife, no blood, no indication in their room. Freeman, either. He strikes me as much too squeamish. And neither Mr. Sorenson nor Mr. Schiller had any reason. Besides, both of them have been on this sales circuit for several years and never make a bit of trouble for the hotel."

"I know."

Struck by how weary Beckett sounded, Rio moved closer. "Do you want me to bring you anything? A pillow? If you're going to sleep there, a blanket? Are you hungry? I can—"

Beckett held up his hand to stop her, then reached out and pulled her closer. A short jerk had her in his lap.

"Oh."

"Hush." He settled her into a more comfortable arrangement, which in this case meant crosswise against his chest. "Relax. I'm not hurting you, am I?"

"No," she said. Far from it. She had the thought that she was just where she ought to be. Not that she relaxed, exactly.

They were silent, drifting until Beckett turned her face to his. His lips touched hers, and after a minute or so, from the change in his breathing, she got the idea she was learning about this kissing stuff quite nicely. A thrill shivered all the way to her toes.

She wanted more, but though she knew it cost him, Beckett stopped kissing her and opened some space between them.

"You should get a few hours of sleep," he whispered to her.

Sleep wasn't what she wanted. She wanted him, and her response to his kisses must tell him so. Still, being a practical woman with little experience in matters of the heart, Rio allowed the distance he'd created. Distance that let her think. And though afraid his answer might hurt, a question erupted.

"Beckett, what are we doing?"

He had no ready reply. And though the light around them was dim, she saw well enough to know he searched for words.

He settled for humor. "Canoodling?"

She punched him in the shoulder. Not hard. Just enough to get his attention. "Why?" Wash Ames had kissed her a couple times, then returned to their former simple friendship. If they had ever been friends, considering he'd betrayed her trust soon after.

Quinn Callahan had also kissed her. More than once, in fact, and she'd kissed him back. Yet, when his job here was done, he left without a backward glance.

Thinking back, Rio knew there'd been no reason for their kisses except just for the pleasant experience.

But Beckett was different. To her, when he touched her, when he kissed her, he felt...he felt like...*forever*.

What did she feel like to him?

"Why?" His dark, dark eyes settled on her down-turned face. He answered with another question.

"Didn't you like the kisses? I thought you did. I know I did." A smile broke through. "You serve out very nice kisses."

Not what she'd been asking. And not what she wanted to hear. It made her sound...What? "Do you have a lot of women to compare me with?"

Dangerous territory. Beckett's realization showed on his face. "No. I don't go around kissing every girl I meet. I thought you knew. Hasn't Win told you?"

Rio blinked, recalling Win had mentioned once that he wished Beckett would settle somewhere so he —Win—would have a home. At least until he was old enough to be on his own. But Beckett had told Win he liked his job, and no woman would put up with a man always on the move, as customs agents often were. Win had lived with an uncle until the old fellow died suddenly, which is when Beckett made provisions for his young brother to be with him. Those concerns were part of the reason Beckett applied for the sheriff's position here, where he'd be home most nights. She knew that. Was Win the only reason?

———

BECKETT COULD'VE TOLD her otherwise. He could've mentioned the main reason had been because of Miss Rio Salo, who'd opened the door to him and Win on that stormy night after Win had been shot. Who'd risked the animosity of the crooked sheriff to keep the pair of them safe and secret, and who'd helped him clean out the dangerous opium smuggling opera-tion the sheriff headed up.

"Win hasn't spoken of your lady friends," she said now, struggling a little to release herself from his grasp.

Though he would've rather not, he let her go, and Rio scrambled to her feet.

"I don't have lady friends," he said, took a breath, and added, "There's only you."

Her hand rose and pressed against her heart. "Only me?"

"Only you." His gaze unwavering, Beckett watched Rio's eyes open wide. Watched the corners of her mouth tilt up in a smile even as it occurred to him she seldom smiled. Professional smiles when greeting customers, but not joyfully on her own behalf, like now.

The smile gave him hope, which grew when she said, "Oh," on a soft gust of air.

———

BLANCHE AND MARIE arrived at the hotel a few minutes early, just as daylight arrived with hints of red splitting the eastern sky. A wind warning, which none of them viewed with any anticipation. Admiration, though, at the glorious sunrise.

They found Rio already at work, grating cooked potatoes with some onion prior to putting hash browns on the breakfast menu.

They'd barely greeted each other when Marie, already with an apron around her middle, started off into the dining room with the tub of flatware destined to be set on the tables.

In minutes, she was back, her blue eyes round as coffee cup saucers. "What is Mr. Ferris doing sleeping in an armchair at the bottom of the stairs?" She whispered the question.

Rio added salt and some pepper to the potatoes, paying attention and being careful not to overdo the seasoning. She looked up and took a deep breath. She knew only one way to say it.

"There was another murder last night."

The pot lid Blanche held slipped from her hand and clattered on the floor. "What? Who's dead? Who did it?"

"Mr. Heckert was murdered in his bed last night." Rio cleared her throat. "We don't know who did it."

Blanche stood, arms akimbo, an expression on her face as if she didn't quite understand what Rio was saying.

"But why is the sheriff sleeping there?" Marie asked.

"He's making sure our other guests remain safe." And didn't make their way downstairs to kill anyone else. But Rio didn't add that.

Blanche nodded. "A little late."

She wasn't wrong. Still... "Not anything we anticipated, I assure you," Rio said.

"See," Marie said, speaking to her sister. "I told you Hans said he saw lights on late at the hotel when he came home. He wondered if something else might have gone wrong."

Hans was one of the Golz older brothers. Blanche had already told Rio he was courting a girl from over on the other side of town.

"Seems it has," Blanche said. "Hans got it right."

Rio sensed something accusatory in the way the girls looked at her. "Beckett is doing everything he can.

It's hard when we don't even know how the person gets in. Or why he's killed these two men. But the sheriff will figure it out. You can count on him."

Blanche's eyes narrowed. "He'd better get up and get at it, then. How does he expect to get elected if he doesn't?" She squinted at Rio. "Why don't you seem more worried? What's going on with you? Why did you smile like that when you said his name?" She interrupted herself. "You and Beckett! That's why."

Rio turned away to hide her hot face. "I don't know what you're talking about." Somehow, and she never was sure how, she managed to keep the Golz ladies occupied until Beckett appeared, sleepy-eyed and rubbing his neck, stiff from sleeping in a chair. Hardly waiting for Rio to pour him a big mug of coffee, he beckoned them into chairs across from him.

It seemed even the Golz women weren't immune from questioning.

With Rio left to manage the breakfasts on her own, she only managed to hear parts of the interchange between Beckett and her employees. For instance, Beckett asking them if they had noticed who Heckert had been speaking with during his short time at the hotel?

Marie glanced at Blanche first, as if asking for corroboration, before answering. "I just noticed him at breakfast yesterday. He sat for a while with Mr. Masterson and Mr. Jensen." She snorted. "Mr. Masterson didn't seem much pleased. I think..." She trailed off, as if losing her focus.

Beckett pounced. "What do you think?"

Marie glanced at Rio's back, rigid as she listened

with pricked ears. Especially when Marie's voice went even lower.

"The Carvers came in. I know Rio told them to stay away from here, but they don't seem to pay any mind to any of us. I think they were looking for Mr. Masterson, and he didn't look comfortable to be found sitting with a Pinkerton agent. Kind of turning away, like it was Mr. Jensen the agent was talking to."

"And was he?"

"Not that I know of, but maybe. They hushed right up when I came to take their order."

Beckett murmured something that sounded like "uh-huh" before asking, "Any reason why that might be?"

Marie shrugged in a "who knows" sort of way.

"Did Heckert talk to anyone else?"

Shaking her head, Marie said, "I don't know. I was busy and had no reason to be listening to them."

She wasn't, in Rio's opinion, wrong.

Beckett must've thought the same because he turned to Blanche. "Did you see anything to make you suspicious? Anything at all that seemed out of line? You've got windows and a view from the back porch. Did you notice anyone out there poking around where they had no reason to be?"

"Such as?" Blanche remained crisp.

Beckett gave her a stern look. "Such as anyone looking to gain entrance to the hotel after the doors are locked at night."

Blanche shook her head. "Not like anyone poking or prying. But I did have a short break and went out front to see if more people were waiting. None were, but Mr. Masterson had gone out to his horse and buggy where he was waiting for Mr. Jensen to bid Mr. Heckert goodbye. Not a meeting. Just a 'so long,' like you'd say to anybody you just had breakfast with."

"Jensen, not Masterson," Beckett said thoughtfully.

"Yes. Now, sheriff, if you don't mind, I need to get back to work."

Beckett nodded. "We're done for now. Go ahead."

Though angry with the Carvers, Rio couldn't find it in herself to call out Marie or Eliza for not refusing service to them. If followed through on, their ban lay at her door, not the girls'. A scene she preferred to dodge, since the pair would most likely make it in front of the hotel guests. What with the murders, she considered it yet another complication she didn't need.

Somehow, word had already gotten out about the Pinkerton's murder. As with the Pope killing, she was surprised when business didn't fall off. Her customers' attitudes with the whole sordid mess struck Rio as more of a thrill to attend a house of crime rather than to avoid a repulsive act fit to turn one's stomach.

Later, as she set a batch of custards in a hot water bath to bake, Rio's mind whirled. She'd never understand people. Reservations indicated she'd have to make a second batch of crème brûlée, which meant the room Heckert had occupied would have to wait for cleansing and repainting. The ceiling above the bed, at any rate. The mattress would have to be burned, and possibly the quilt too. Another good reason to close the hotel.

Meanwhile, after speaking with Blanche and Marie, Beckett went to awaken Win and clean himself up. Before he left for town, he told Rio he intended to pay the banker and his assistant a call and didn't want to appear slovenly in his personal care. Masterson, after all, had a vote on whether to accept his application for the permanent job, and he didn't mean to let the opportunity slip away just because he neglected to shave.

"What about questioning Mr. Masterson? Won't that make it awkward?"

Soberly, Beckett nodded. "It will, but there's no help for it."

Rio, applauding the decision, had to smile. She would've liked to listen in on those particular conversations. Mainly because it concerned the Carvers. They were up to no good. She could feel it in her bones, and by that, she meant something over and above just trying to gain control of her hotel. She knew it. But what? And why?

Eino's supposed treasure.

The answer formed in her mind, but scoffing, she put it away as usual.

His nonexistent treasure. A lie. She knew it. Surely anyone with even a passing acquaintance with Eino knew it too.

Exhausted by her labors and lack of sleep over the last few days, Rio fell onto her bed that night and was asleep almost before her head touched the pillow. Boo had to make his own way onto the cot beside her instead of being lifted. He stuck his nose into the cleft between her chin and shoulder and began snoring.

Rio didn't hear a thing until morning. Utterly relieved there hadn't been anything dreadful happen during the night, she rose stiff as a board, inclined to get on her hands and knees and, like her dog, stretch out each limb one by one. She didn't, though, instead electing to do her stretches standing up as she hurried out to the kitchen fifteen minutes past her normal time.

A face peering in through the back window nearly made her jump out of her skin. Until recognizing the face, she made haste to open up.

"Jess," she exclaimed. Her pulse was racing, but not because he'd caught her swinging her arms in wide circles. "Is everything all right?"

Probably not. Staring at him, she knew even before he shook his head. His black eye gave fair warning.

"Come in," she said. "I'll get the coffee on." It was the first time Jess Stokes had been around like this—like Wash used to do, she reflected—since she handed the running of the Salo Timber Products logging business over to him. He'd been doing a good job, she knew. The Chinese workers liked him. Profits had been normal, on a par as to when Washington Ames had been foreman. There'd been no accidents with anyone hurt, and she'd heard no complaints.

And, she remembered, he'd eaten here a few times and come to see Blanche.

But never with business troubles or complaints.

Today, the swelling and deep purple bruising around his eye hinted at something less positive.

Rio got him seated at the table while she poked up the fire in the cookstove and put water on to heat. It would be faster than the boiler in the cellar. Besides, she dreaded going down there and seeing bloodstains still on the floor. Boo, bless his heart, sniffed Jess and kept him entertained until she settled across from him, coffee and breakfast rolls set in front of them both. She picked up her roll, but then forgot to bite into it.

"Are you here to tell me about that?" she asked, indicating his eye.

Jess didn't look happy. "Guess I better," he said, "seeing it concerns you."

"Me?"

"Yup. You and Beckett Ferris."

She gave him a level look. "Then I'd better see if he is up, so you can tell us both at the same time."

"He's up, all right, and gone," Stokes said. "I met him on my way here. I already told him. He said I should talk to you too."

Fourteen

"**Y**our eye looks like it must hurt." Eyeing Jess, Rio settled back into her chair and took a breath. "First of all, tell me who punched you."

"Sucker-punched me, more like. And it does hurt some. My own fault," Stokes admitted. Shamefaced, he stared down into his coffee. "I didn't expect a city boy like him to have the guts to take me on."

Rio could hardly believe her ears. Jess Stokes had been known as a man who liked a good brawl every now and then when younger. Fortunately, he'd outgrown the propensity of late. Partly, she figured, because of his regard for Blanche, and partly because of the responsibilities of running a logging crew. Still, it would take someone either stupid or unknowing of his reputation to force Jess into a fair fight.

"A city boy?" she repeated, frowning. "A prize-fighter?"

His face reddened. "Not that I know of. It's..." He raised his coffee cup and took a swallow. "I think he set me up."

She motioned him to continue, noticing with some surprise that she still held the untouched roll. She put it back on the plate. "Why?"

"See, that's what I don't know. Got a guess, is all. But I can tell you who punched me."

"Just what I'm waiting to hear," she said dryly.

Jess's fist clenched. "That chubby fellow from New York or some place. The one that's been pestering you to sell the hotel for a quarter of what it's worth."

"Melvin Carver?"

"Yeah, that's him. The young one, not the old one."

Rio'd already figured as much. "Did you return his punch?"

"Didn't get the chance." It came out a growl. "Couple of my friends held me back and said I'd better not. Said, depending on which way the election went, I might be in trouble. See, this Carver fella, practically crying, was already making tracks out of the saloon. Seems he hurt his hand when he hit me and wanted to see the doc."

Rio couldn't help the start of a smile at that. Until Jess said, "And guess who was helping him along?"

She had no idea.

"None other than that sonofa..." He stopped.

Rio knew what he meant to say, but appreciated his restraint. "Who?"

"None other than Bull French."

Her mouth dropped open. "What? Why would Bull French and Melvin Carver be together? How would they even know each other?" She thought a moment. "Where were you when all this happened?"

Jess looked away. "In the Dry Well," he admitted.

Not a place, Rio knew, Blanche would approve, she

being a bit more strait-laced than some and not apt to put up with loose living. Not for long. Which, if Jess intended to get serious, he'd better learn in a hurry. That said, it was a place single men gathered after work and had formed a certain reputation.

She thought a moment. "But why would he, well, either of them, pick on you? Although I suppose Bull figured if you fought back, he could protect the man and get you in trouble. Since the Carvers have been staying with Mr. Masterson, maybe he thought his defense of Masterson's friend would encourage the commissioner to keep backing him for sheriff. That's the kind of thing he likes to do. But how does that lead back to me?"

"Beckett Ferris, of course. They know I'm walking out with Blanche, who works for you, and you and him are...uh..."

Beckett and I are what?

The question shot through Rio's mind. Momentarily, she lost track as to what Jess was saying, registering again when he said, "And most of us fellers want Ferris as sheriff. But he—Carver—said something else too." He turned red again. "Something out of line about you and Ferris. I couldn't stand for that."

Could it really be that convoluted? Rio sighed, swallowed her coffee, cold now, and stood up. "Thank you, Mr. Stokes, from the bottom of my heart. Now, I've got witch hazel to put on that bruise. Let me get a pad, and you can apply it to your black eye. It should take some of the swelling down and ease the pain. Blanche will be here soon. I'm sure she'll want to hear all this from you." She smiled at him. "She'll be proud of you."

At this, Jess, flushing with pleasure, sat back in his

chair with an air of relief. "You think so?" He still held the slightly squashed roll. Sticking it in his mouth, he took a big bite.

"I do."

Rio found the bottle of witch hazel in the small closet in the downstairs bathroom. By the time she'd laid out a basin, pad, gauze, and the witch hazel, Blanche and Eliza were approaching the porch. Boo ran to greet them.

"Oh good," she called to Blanche. "You're just in time. Seems your friend here is in need of care."

"Jess!" Blanche's exclamation had Jess sitting up straighter as she hurried forward. "What are you doing here?"

But then, catching sight of his eye, Blanche matter-of-factly took over the nursing, murmuring, "Oh my. What happened?"

Either unaware—or maybe just uncaring—she ignored the way her sister laughed behind her hand and whispered to Rio.

"You'd think a man never came home from the saloon with a black eye before," Eliza said. "Even Dad, though I wasn't supposed to know how he got it. And Edgar? Whew!" Edgar being yet another of the older Golz brothers.

Rio laughed right along with Eliza, a relief to find amusement in anything after what had been happening. Anyway, she was glad Blanche seemed to have decided to overlook the fact that Jess's black eye had been procured in the Dry Well saloon. If he hadn't been there, she might never have learned of this new twist with Melvin Carver.

What didn't please was the sight of Mr. Meadows,

Melvin Carver the elder—but not the younger—and Mr. Bernie Jensen sliding their backsides onto chairs set around the dining room's centermost table. Almost as if it were a deliberate attempt to ensure their topic of conversation went unheard. Observed, but unheard.

And, something told Rio, perhaps to show they'd somehow gained the upper hand. Well, she'd just see about that. Then she remembered the two men murdered in her hotel.

Eliza snorted. "Don't worry about them, Rio. I've got good ears. I'll pick something up. Look at them, conspiring together. You can bet nothing good will come of it."

Rio couldn't help fretting. Where was Carver Jr.? Why wasn't he here, along with his father and Mr. Meadows? Not that she wanted him to be. His very presence would be an insult. Her only worry was that Jess Stokes's set-to with him had gone further than Jess had let on. And most of all, she wanted to know what Beckett thought about this latest wrinkle. If he'd even tell her.

Her anxiety went unchecked throughout the day, even as clouds formed in the north and a light rain began to fall. Come dinnertime, old-timers gathered around Turner at the bar and made predictions.

"Just you wait," Rio heard a fellow with a grizzled beard announce as she went past them with an armful of loaded plates. "This is just the beginning of a spell of bad weather. Come morning, it'll be fine, but not for long. It's gonna turn on us by tomorrow night."

Some of the others nodded in agreement. A few shook their heads. One went so far as to say, "Too early in the year for that, Bledsoe. This'll pass over. What's a little breeze and a few drops of rain matter, anyway?"

"I seen bad storms before," Bledsoe insisted. "And this 'un is gonna be big. Feel it in my bones, I do. It's one that'll break trees like they was matchsticks. Mark my words."

"Wanna bet a dollar?"

"I'll bet two."

With some amusement, Rio saw money change hands, passed on to Turner to hold until the weather itself declared a winner.

True to Bledsoe's prediction, thunder rumbled during the night, awakening both Boo and Rio. She listened for a while, the silence of the hotel reassuring. And empty. Beckett hadn't returned, and as she rolled over and tried to go back to sleep, Rio felt his absence right down to her core.

Also as Bledsoe had predicted, the morning was fine, once again proving the old fellow a true weather seer. More ominously, a vivid red sky greeted the day. A presage of weather to come.

Although Marie, escorted by her little brother, Tommy, had come to work early, Rio had sole possession of her kitchen, Blanche having a well-earned day off. The breakfast seating went well, the cooking not especially onerous, consisting of a menu of French toast, slices of ham, and a bowl of blackberries plucked, not without hazard, from the wickedly thorn-adorned bushes out by the barn. She dressed the berries with a dollop of sweetened cream.

Marie came into the kitchen bearing a tray of dirty dishes after the departure of the last customer. He'd been digging blackberry seeds out of his teeth as he went, and she was giggling.

Rio, scraping at some ham drippings stuck to the grill plate set atop the stove, looked up. "What's funny?"

Taking a cautious peek behind her to make sure she wouldn't be overheard, Marie set the tray beside the sink and began unloading it. "Miss White and Miss Bindle. You know how they always say the food is terrible?"

Rio sighed. "I do know."

"Remember I came in and said someone wanted a second helping of French toast?"

"Sure."

"Well, guess who it was."

The tone gave a hint. Rio's chocolate brown eyes rounded. "Bindle?"

Marie shook her head. "Take a second guess."

"Not Vesta!"

But Marie nodded this time. "Yes, Vesta. What's more, one of those salesmen who stays here regularly noticed. When he stopped by their table and said, 'An extra good breakfast this morning, ain't it?' she actually said, 'Passable, I daresay.'"

"My word." Rio blinked. "High praise indeed."

She and Marie laughed and laughed. A second laugh in two days.

Having used the stale bread from yesterday's bake for the French toast, Rio set her sponge to rise and went to change sheets and clean the rooms that had been used the previous night. From the second story, she had a good view out to where the sky and the bay met.

Clouds raced, obscuring the sun. A brisk breeze chased dust into the air.

Just as the morning's red sky had given warning— and as Mr. Bledsoe had bet his money on—the storm gathered force in the afternoon. Wind blew the waters of the bay into choppy, white-crowned waves that broke on the shore and caused the boats tied up at the hotel dock to buck like untamed broncs. The tops of tall pines whipped back and forth, dry needles and cones flying every which way.

Someone, Rio thought, would have to get out with a rake after the storm passed. Maybe Win? She'd be glad to pay him.

Gasping a little at what had become more ferocious every passing minute, she went outside to gather an armload of dry wood for the stove. When she came back in, she found Marie bundling up with the intention of hurrying for home.

"Watch out for falling trees," Rio warned her.

"I will." The girl looked a little pale.

Marie's absence made the hotel feel empty and dangerous. Once or twice, Rio heard either Vesta or Bindle cry out when an especially wicked crack of thunder pounded their eardrums. A loose board in the floor of David Freeman's room creaked as he paced. Apparently, he didn't care for storms.

For once, she didn't blame any of them. She never failed to jump either, and Boo hid under the cot in her office, shivering fit to break a bone. Then, just as the clock in the lobby struck two o'clock, quite suddenly, rain fell from the deep gray sky as if poured from buckets, drenching anyone unlucky enough to be caught outside. For instance, Win Ferris.

Rio was peering through a rain-smeared window when she spotted Beckett's young brother break from the slight shelter of the trees and run toward the hotel. He held his hat on his head with one hand, while the other held a couple books close to his side in an attempt to keep them dry. Home from the school in town he'd just begun attending, she assumed someone there must've believed in the same weather signs as Mr. Bledsoe and sent the pupils home early.

He should have stayed in town with Beckett, even if it meant spending a night in the jail, she thought. Except, who knew where Beckett actually was?

Blown by the wind, the porch door slammed on Win's heels as he entered. His face, washed with rainwater, bore a rueful expression as he surveyed his books. "Damn," he said.

She tossed him a towel. "Yes. Damn."

One would have to be insane to venture out in this, she was thinking. And except for Vesta and her maid, and David Freeman, the hotel remained empty as the storm went on and on.

Not a single customer showed up for dinner service. Not that Rio had anticipated any. No one wanted to chance a boat on Painter's Bay, or a falling tree if taking the trail through the woods. Earlier, she'd let the fire die in the big restaurant stove and kept only the smaller cookstove burning. With only the three guests and Win, there didn't appear to be any need. The trail around the point to town was a mud warren, and the bay a frothy spray. In the hotel, the wind blew most of the heat up the chimney.

Rio had quit expecting Beckett. In fact, though she longed for an accounting of Jess Stoke's encounter with

Melvin Carver, she preferred he wait until the weather cleared.

Mr. Bledsoe had won his two-dollar bet, fair and square.

"A dull evening," Vesta mentioned to Rio, who'd been quenching lamps whose flames flickered by gusts of wind finding a way inside.

"Unless one is caught outside," Rio agreed. "I think I heard a tree snap a while ago."

"Was that what that crash was?" Vesta smiled. "We get storms like this in New York when it blows in from the ocean. The trees aren't as big a problem, however, in the city."

"No, I suppose not." It was the most civilized conversation the women had ever had.

By nine o'clock, Vesta White, Bindle, and David Freeman had again retired to their rooms.

No doubt to conspire, Rio figured. And Win, promising to clean up the grounds when the weather allowed, went to his room to study and try to mend his waterlogged books.

With no expectation of interruption, Rio shut off all but one lamp in the kitchen before she went to bed, Boo huddling beside her.

She slept like the proverbial log until nearly one o'clock, only to be awakened by the raucous ringing of the hotel's after-hours bell at the front door.

Fifteen

R io stirred and groaned. "Nooo," she begged. Sadly, there was no getting away from the bell jangling so close to her ear.

Boo peeked his head out from under the covers and growled.

"You called it, Boo. Shall we ignore the racket?" She wanted to. She really wanted to.

The wind and rain still raged outside, she noted, although the thunder and lightning had ceased.

No matter her reluctance, habit and an ingrained sense of duty got Rio up, her feet into slippers, and an extra large barn coat over her nightdress. She was halfway to the door when she remembered her .32. Going back to retrieve it, she allowed Boo to come with her. Something she didn't usually do.

Padding ahead of her, Boo led the way and stood waiting.

Even as she wielded the key to unlock the door, the bell clattered again. It was easy to sense impatience in whoever stood out there.

Gun in hand, she opened the door a crack, only to be shoved aside as a man staggered in.

"Bloody well about time," he snarled in a clipped British accent. "My god, have you no lights in this place? I assume this is the Painter's Bay Hotel."

The sign stating its name was right outside for anyone who could read. He didn't sound impressed.

The cocking of her .32 was perfectly audible over the rushing wind outside. "It is. How did you even get here in this storm? Who are you?" Rio said coolly. Standing at her side, Boo snarled. Combined, the two warning sounds silenced the man, but only for a moment.

"Who I am is none of your business. What I want is a room for the night. And it had better not have bedbugs!" Rainwater dripped from the edge of a hat with much too narrow of a brim to provide shelter, as well as from the hem of his coat. Mud coated his shoes and rose halfway to his knees.

He looked, in fact, like a drowned rat, or maybe a weasel, and was shivering uncontrollably.

It was too bad, Rio thought, studying him as best as possible considering the dark room, his discomfort didn't make him more agreeable. She felt remarkably unsympathetic to anyone so ignorant as to come out in a storm like this one. Ignorant, or, it occurred to her, desperate.

"Well?" he said. "If you're not going to help me, call the manager. I demand service."

Behind her, Rio heard footsteps. Win, come to investigate the disturbance.

His voice came out of the dark. "Want me to light a lamp, Rio?"

"Yes, please. The one on the lobby desk."

Boo went to help, and within seconds, the lamp provided enough light for everyone to better see each other. Win, jaw set in an expression copied from his brother, his hair tousled, and his feet bare, held the porch shotgun in the crook of his arm.

The wayfarer looked more like a weasel—drowned or not—than ever now that she could see him clearly. Small beady eyes the color of an unripe chestnut, a narrow chin sporting a clump of hair along the sides of his jaw, and largish ears that stuck out from his head were part of her first impression. He wasn't much taller than she and rather thin in build. He must've fallen somewhere along the way, she decided, judging by all the mud on his trousers and on the back of his coat. He carried a small suitcase, but at least no visible weapon.

Which didn't mean she put the .32 away. She gestured with it toward the desk. "Leave your coat, hat, and case here. And wipe your feet. That's what the mat you're standing on is for." She made no pretense of being anything but disturbed.

Swiping rainwater from his face, he gave her a sharp glance and did as she bid.

At the desk, without setting the shotgun aside, Win opened the registration ledger. Before proffering a pen, he looked to Rio. "You going to put him up?"

She nodded. "I suppose I'll have to. This isn't a good night for anyone to be out and about."

Win, who no doubt had memories of himself and Beckett also arriving in a bad storm in the middle of the night—with him about to bleed to death—nodded and held out the pen.

The man's hand shook as he took it. He asked no questions.

But Rio had noticed the way his squinted eyes took in the names of guests here before him. He wouldn't get much information from there, she thought, almost snickering. The page had been turned since the dead men had added their names. There wasn't anything to be gained from the present page.

Why did she connect him with Pope and Heckert?

She just did. The small sound almost inaudible, she snorted.

Slowly, he signed the register. Harrison Fields, he wrote. From Virginia, yet with a British accent. True or not, she didn't know, but over the years since she'd begun noticing their guests' origins, only a very few had come to the Painter's Bay from the southeast. Quite a few were from the northern tier. Coincidence? She thought not.

He dropped the pen on the counter, making a splodge. She frowned and nodded to the last key on the hook. It was the poorest room, the coldest, with its windows in the full blast of the wind when it came out of the north. And farthest from the bathroom. But at least there were no bloodstains on the ceiling.

Yet.

"That will be a dollar a night, breakfast included. If you eat dinner here, I charge an extra fifty-five cents."

"I don't suppose—" He started, and she shook her head.

"The kitchen is closed until six in the morning." There was no give to her words.

Apparently beaten, he nodded and went to pick up

his case. Leaving his hat and coat on the rack, he trudged up the stairs to find his room.

Mr. Harrison Fields remained, which soured Rio's thoughts on how she'd handled him, a mystery man.

"He talks funny," Win said.

"From England," she said, explaining everything with the one word.

"What do you suppose he's doing here at this time of night, in this kind of weather? How'd he get here?"

"No idea, but I guarantee he didn't come by boat. Looks like he walked." Finding an old bar towel on the shelf beneath the desk's top, she dabbed at the spilled ink. "He was certainly rude and rather threatening. Tried to be anyway."

Only later did it occur to her that he hadn't answered her question as to how he'd gotten here.

"I noticed," Win said. "You gonna tell Beck about him?"

"I am," and she added, "if he ever gets back long enough to talk to."

"Yeah," Win said, and if she had sounded wistful, so did he.

Rio quenched the lamp, and they both headed back to bed. But not to sleep. At least, she didn't as she tossed and turned, which disturbed Boo into finding a place on the floor where Rio had put a rug for him.

At five a.m., she was in the kitchen, stirring up the fire, having already been to the cellar, like it or not, to start the boiler for hot water, and thence to the barn to gather eggs.

The rain and most of the wind had stopped at last.

BECKETT, though not privy to Mr. Bledsoe's weather prediction, was wise enough to read the same signs and come to the same conclusions. The good Lord knew he'd been out before in bad weather. One example, being a trek across the high desert landscape in the middle of the state, came to mind. Let alone the night Win got shot—and he'd as soon avoid any repeats if possible.

Having at present to share the sheriff's office with the town marshal, he bid the marshal goodnight as the old fellow hurried home. He found a simple pad of paper and a pencil and began laying out the facts of the two murders as he knew them. Something he'd been wanting to do all day. A simple method to clarify his mind, he aimed to put down what he knew about any suspect, and what, if anything, he'd discovered about the victims. There wasn't as much as he would've liked. As for *why* the men had been killed, information was even more scant.

He hadn't done much more to his paper than to divide it into two columns headed up with the men's names. One for Merle Pope, and one for the Pinkerton fellow, Arnold Heckert. He paused to think then, tapping the end of his pencil on the desk. What did he know? What did he guess?

An interruption came as the stout plank door flew open and slammed against the log walls of the jail, nearly pinching a bedraggled old man in the rebound before he could get inside.

Beckett reached for his revolver. "Hold it," he said. Rain, blown inside by the wind, in an instant wetted the floor almost halfway across the room.

The old fellow, smartly, as it happened, ignored the order and fought to close the door. About then Beckett recognized the visitor. Shoving his weapon back in the holster, he rose to help.

"God'll mighty," the man wheezed, breathing like a bellows with a hole in its lung. The door finally closed, he leaned against it and panted. "I ain't seen anything like this since the spring of eighteen and eighty-three. And this is worse."

"What are you doing out on a night like this?" Beckett demanded.

The old fellow hung his head. "Thought Fred might still be here. My name is Charlie."

"I know who you are."

Charlie looked more directly at Beckett. "Sometimes, if the jail ain't filled with drunks, he'll let me use one of the bunks."

The two, Beckett reflected, were much of an age. Probably been friends since the early days when the town first got started as a convenience to the logging companies. He knew a little of Marshal Fred Larkin's history, learned on previous evenings when they'd talked.

He couldn't see any harm in sheltering the man who stood shivering in his wet clothes. Clothes too worn to keep anyone warm on a night like this.

Nodding toward one of the two cells—the other one already staked out for himself—he said, "Strip down, wrap yourself in a blanket, and bring your clothes over to dry by the stove. You don't want to be sleeping in those. You'd be apt to wind up with pneumonia."

Cracking a mostly toothless smile, Charlie hastened

to obey. Passing by the desk with his wet garb ready to hang on wooden pegs knocked into the wall behind the stove, his eyes were caught by the columns on Beckett's pad of paper.

"Say," Charlie said. "Ain't those the names of them two fellows what got murdered over at the hotel? Poor little gal running the place—seems to me she's had about all she can handle lately."

Beckett pulled the paper pad closer. Habit, since there certainly wasn't anything written there worth hiding. "Yes," he said. He could've been acknowledging either of Charlie's statements.

Still wearing his union suit, though securely wrapped in a blanket, Charlie pulled a chair closer to the stove. "I talked to him, some." He pointed a dirty finger toward one of the names on the paper. "I was sitting on the bench out front of the Dry Well one evening after..." He stopped and started again. "Well, I were sitting there, and I heard him asking around about Eino and Elias Salo. And the girl too. Rio, her name is. Pretty name for a pretty girl. Kind. She's fed me more than once when I come to the back door. Used to do it before her pa died, too, though the old fart probably woulda give her hell if he'd knowed. Sometimes I catch crawdads in the creek, and she buys them." He gave a great shiver, and warmth from the stove reached him.

Beckett twitched. The jambalaya Win had told him about came to mind. Made from Charlie's contribution? He wished he'd been able to get back to the hotel tonight before the storm hit. What if a tree fell on the hotel roof? What if somehow the old structure caught fire? What if the murderer was in there, his eye on another victim? What if whoever it was took after Win? He didn't know what he'd do if his young brother was harmed again. Or Rio. Dear God, Rio.

Almost visibly, he came back to what Charlie rambled on about, knowing something had drawn his attention too late. What had he missed? Something important, he thought. Looking over at Charlie, he tuned his ears to really listen. The question being, was the old man reliable?

"Gotta say," Charlie rambled on, "I didn't expect to see him in the saloon. He don't usually associate with folks like us. I figure his boss don't like it. Likes the money we bring in, though."

Evidently, Charlie still considered himself one of the rough-and-ready men who labored in the woods hereabout. Or the farms and ranches. Just as he had done in his younger days.

Eyes narrowing, Beckett made a note on his paper pad. *Charlie*, it said. He didn't know a last name. He'd have to ask.

"Tell me about him, Charlie. About this guy asking all the questions. What did he want to know about the Salo men? Did he sound like a friend?"

"Friend? Naw. I don't think so." Charlie's expression sharpened. "You want me to talk about that one? The Pope feller? Struck me as more like a crook than a pope." He grinned as if he'd made a joke. On second thought, maybe he had. Then he sobered. "I tell you, Sheriff, he seemed downright gobsmacked when I told him it was Miss Rio that owns the hotel. Not her pa and not her half brother. They both did."

Charlie was the first person Beckett had heard refer

to Eino properly, according to Rio, as her half brother. She refused to claim any closer relationship.

"What did he say to that?"

"Said that couldn't be. We had a little argument." The old man chortled. "He says, 'Why would he hide it there, then?' Didn't make a lick of sense to me. I dunno 'zackly what he meant. Hide what? Some other fellers in the bar said he was asking about Eino's treasure he stole." He paused. "That Eino stole." The chortle turned into a cackle. "As if that sonofagun would do anything but spend any money he come across."

"Do you know, Charlie, what Eino spent his money on?" An answer might go a way in figuring out just what he'd stolen.

Another cackle. "Why, booze, women, and a good time, a'course. You know he fancied hisself as a real man-about-town."

Beckett dutifully wrote all this down, word for word as best he could, including, "they both did." His pencil hovered. Dipped hard enough the lead broke.

What had he missed?

"Back up," he said. "Both of who? Who was Pope talking to?"

Later, lying in the other cell on a smelly mattress much thinner than the one in Rio's hotel, Charlie's raucous snores kept him awake. His mind twisted from here to there like a wanderer lost in a maze. Could he believe everything, or anything, the old fellow had told him?

He rolled over, trying to shut out the snoring and the thoughts. Tomorrow.

Tomorrow, he'd have to talk to Rio and probably the

Golz girls, who waited tables again. He'd have to talk to Aaron Black, who owned the Dry Well, and his bartender. Bartenders always heard more than drinking men thought they did. Some of the men who might have seen the men Charlie mentioned together, as well. And while Pope was dead, the other one was very much alive.

Tomorrow. Finally, he slept.

Sixteen

Rio dragged through the next morning. Only five men arrived for an early breakfast, all members of the sawmill crew. Jess Stokes informed Rio he was paying since they'd been on the job all night, attempting to keep the machinery dry and the shed roof from blowing away. His eye, still colorful despite Blanche's fervent ministrations, watered a little.

"Half-price this morning, Mr. Stokes," she said, admiring his loyalty in protecting not only the mill but his workers' jobs."

"No need." He winked at her.

"There is. As far as I know, the mill is still owned by Salo Timber Products, so unless I'm told differently, I figure I have an obligation to see the men are taken care of."

Truthfully, he looked a little relieved as he fished in his pocket for cash and finally found the bills. "Blanche here yet?" he asked hopefully.

Rio felt bad, telling him no.

An hour later, Vesta, Bindle, and Freeman came

downstairs in a noisy group. Vesta, after a quick glance around the empty room, as usual, began her complaint of the bed, the noise, the storm. Most importantly, she demanded to know about the voices she'd heard in the night.

"Don't try to deny it," she said, growing louder as Rio showed a disinclination to speak of the newcomer. "I heard a man's voice. Whose?"

Rio eyed her. "Are you expecting someone?"

"None of your business," Vesta snapped. "Hurry up and bring my coffee. My land, what does it take to receive any service around here? I'm famished."

The woman, after the reasonable interaction last night, was back to her usual disagreeable self.

Bindle didn't say a word, managing to pull out her own chair at the table while Freeman made a production of seating Vesta.

Shaking her head, Rio retreated to the kitchen. She didn't feel like contending with them at this time of the morning. But though the three of them took up space in the dining room until well beyond breakfast service time, Harrison Fields was a no-show. Finally, they went back upstairs.

To plot? Rio wondered.

As soon as they'd retired to their rooms, Fields crept down from his room and peeked into the kitchen. "Excuse me, is there any possibility of something to eat? I...those three...I heard them asking about the disturbance last night when I arrived. And you didn't tell them anything. I thank you. They don't seem like people I want to mix with."

And if that wasn't just about the most peculiar thing Rio had heard in a while, she didn't know what beat it. But the situation had given her a kind of amusement. Almost as good as seeing a play. Or what she thought seeing a play would provide. The only plays she'd ever seen were the little skits put on by school children at Christmas.

"I think the griddle is still hot, Mr. Fields. I hope you like buckwheat pancakes." Her special recipe resulted in light and fluffy, not tough and gritty like some.

"Anything," he said gratefully.

Though they'd gotten off on the wrong foot in the middle of the night, they both had decided to make amends. Rio had remembered something Beckett had mentioned. He'd said as a law enforcement officer, part of his training had included a lesson that showed one learned more by staying on the right side of people. It beat whacking someone around nearly every time, although occasionally that was necessary too. This interaction with Mr. Fields was a change of attitude, and it seemed to work.

The more she thought about the advice, the easier it was to decide Mr. Fields wasn't quite as weaselly appearing as she'd thought at first. Not that he could possibly be described as handsome.

Harrison Fields finished his breakfast—not just pancakes, but an accompaniment of bacon slices and a bowl of oatmeal with raisins and a pitcher of milk. And tea. Yes, Rio had pegged his nationality correctly. Determined to pump him for information, she refilled the teapot and headed back to his table.

He'd selected a spot near a window and stared out to where the bay slowly calmed. Though the boats floated in place, following his gaze, Rio could see every one sat low in the water, in need of being bailed out. She sighed. Continuing on, she set the teapot she carried on the table. "Another cup of tea?"

Looking up, he smiled. "Yes. Thank you."

She poured, and then, to his obvious surprise, sat down opposite him. The .32 Iver Johnson revolver in her pocket bumped gently against her thigh.

"Who are you, Mr. Fields?" she asked directly. "Who, or what, are you looking for here at the Painter's Bay Hotel?"

His eyes narrowed. "I...I...What makes you think I'm looking for someone?"

"Maybe not someone. Maybe something. I'm asking because I don't know. But you're here for a purpose, and I need to know what it is. You may be interested to learn you're not the first person to come here on the same mission. Whatever it is."

Silenced, he stared at her.

Rio pressed her lips together, thinking, then said, "You were rude to me last night. I don't usually have guests arrive in the middle of the night, let alone in the middle of the worst storm of my lifetime, and it caught me off guard. I apologize for my cranky behavior. You certainly wouldn't have been out in it if there weren't a pressing reason. And you reacted to me as if I were an enemy. I wonder why, when you didn't even know who I am."

He blinked. "I knew you were her. And I knew you wouldn't want me here. Plus, you met me at the door with a gun. I'm not much of a hand with guns."

He had a point, she supposed. She decided to be blunt—and honest. "Could be you haven't heard, but two men have been murdered in my hotel in a very short amount of time. I admit to being unnerved by the experience. Believe me, if you were me, you'd answer the door with a gun too." Another thought occurred. What he'd said..."What do you mean, you knew I was her? Her who?"

Fields rose halfway out of his chair before he dropped back. "Two men murdered?"

"Yes. One, a Pinkerton detective. The other was a man who tried to tell us he was from the government. We've since learned he lied, but we don't know why." This man didn't need to know they had an idea. A silly, unfounded idea.

Swallowing as if his throat was dry, he picked up his cup and drank half his tea at one go. His hands shook the least bit. He acted as if he wanted to say more, but worried it might be unwise.

Wishing with all her heart for Beckett to walk in right now, Rio took a breath. Then let it out. What if she said the wrong thing?

Fields blinked at her. "You are Evan Salo's sister, are you not?"

"I am Eino Salo's half sister," she admitted reluctantly. "We had different mothers. Evidently, you know him as Evan. I understand that when he went back east, he introduced himself to new acquaintances that way. Evan is not so old world sounding as Eino, which is his real name."

"Where is he now?" Fields's tone became sterner.

"I have no idea. Possibly in hiding. Possibly in another country running a con on some unsuspecting person. Or possibly dead. The last time I saw him, he was being pursued by a strange little man whose stated intention was to kill him." She looked away. "Good riddance." There it was. Bald and in the open.

She knew her answer shocked him. Fine. She didn't care. Reaching out, she poured the last of the tea into his cup. "Your turn. Who are you, and why are you here?"

He didn't speak right away. Apparently, he was as uncertain as to what he could safely reveal as she had been.

Rio gave him another little nudge. "Those people from rooms two and three that you avoided this morning, do you know them? Vesta White, her maid, Bindle, and someone who insists he's Vesta's special friend, David Freeman."

His mouth compressed. After a moment, he said, "I've heard of them."

She nodded. "Uh-huh. The waitresses here have heard them talk about buried treasure, although they don't come right out and ask. I think that's what the men who were killed were looking for, as well. Treasure." She huffed. "Nobody has told me what this supposed treasure is, or where it came from, or why everyone thinks it's here." She paused. "Do you know?"

Fields sat still as a fly caught in tree sap, though his eyes darted from one corner of the room to another. "I can't say." He spoke in a quiet murmur.

"Or won't."

"Both."

Rio's heart beat faster. At last, someone who might have answers, if only he'd reveal them to her. Beckett...

"You don't want to talk to me. I understand," she said, though really, she didn't. "Would you talk to the sheriff?"

He had to think about it. "Limited information? I think...perhaps."

Progress. She hoped.

———

IN THE MORNING, Charlie was gone from the cell next to the one Beckett had chosen. He'd sneaked out like a thief, probably wanting no more to do with another interrogation by the sheriff.

Or maybe he just hadn't wanted anyone to know they'd spoken at all.

Which was all right with Beckett. He had a whole lot to accomplish today, much of it from information already gleaned from the derelict old man.

Breakfast at the little café next to the general store, not a patch on what Rio provided for her customers, would have to tide him over for the ride out to the Blue Sky logging camp. As they were in direct competition with Salo Timber Products, he figured some of the workers would be willing to spill whatever dirt they might have on Eino Salo to him. And from that, maybe he could work toward learning who might've murdered those men. And why.

He found the Blue Sky encampment five miles out of town. Instead of a barracks like the Salo operation at the point of the bay, the men here slept in sturdy half-log, half-canvas shelters. These had been badly wind-damaged in the storm. His timing couldn't have been better. The men were cleaning up the camp before heading into the woods, while the cook struggled over a campfire to fix breakfast. The canvas sides of the cook shack had given way, and a falling tree knocked down the stovepipe, rendering the cast iron stove inoperable until repaired. Hungry men grumbled as they waited for their late breakfast.

Beckett spoke with the foreman. The man had no objections to the sheriff's inquiries, he said. "Don't know how the men'll feel about it. I can't force anyone to talk."

Beckett nodded. "I know. But if my hunch is right, this won't be anything that reflects on anyone here."

The foreman looked a little relieved. "Fine." He raised his voice and bellowed, "Oscar, need you over here."

"Now?" came a distant reply.

"Now."

The man, Beckett observed, had a set of lungs on him.

Oscar, big and nearly as wide as he was tall, seemed relieved to have a break, especially since he took time to pour himself a cup of coffee before sitting on a stump next to Beckett. Other men in the camp exchanged glances at one another. Not worried, just curious.

"What do you want?" Oscar's cup tilted, sloshing scalding coffee over his hand as he sat. "Damn."

Beckett began slowly. "You've heard about the murders out at the Painter's Bay Hotel."

"Sure." Oscar shook the offended hand. "Word gets around."

"Whoever did it puts everyone who lives or stays there in danger."

"I suppose it do. Sneaky bastard, ain't he? You got any idea who it is?" A shocked look came over his face. "You don't think I—"

Beckett stopped him. "No. I don't think it was you."

He glanced around the encampment. "I don't think it was any of you. But word came to me of a couple men asking you boys questions about Eino and Elias Salo. Pope and another fella. You remember that? I hear he bought you drinks."

Oscar squinted at him. "You think it was him? Pope? That one-eyed polecat? I didn't like him."

"No," Beckett said. "He was one of the murdered men. Had his throat cut. Sliced from ear to ear," he added.

"I'll be!" Scowling, Oscar pondered. It didn't take long before he nodded. "Coulda been the other feller with him. Probably don't take that much if a man has a sharp knife and takes somebody by surprise. And there's something about him. Always has been. I don't like to go in the bank because of him." He grinned again. "So I spend my wages and don't bother with the muckety-mucks there. Bunch of damn shysters if you ask me."

Beckett had a tingle travel up his spine. "The bank?" he said, careful like.

Oscar nodded. "Yep."

Soberly, they studied each other. "But I need proof before I can move on him," Beckett said. "Will you say his name, make sure we're talking about the same man?"

After some thought, Oscar did.

One by one, two other men came forward. They were in agreement with Oscar, having all been treated to a beer by first Pope, then by his mostly silent friend.

If he'd been a friend.

If he hadn't been Pope's murderer.

Beckett's thoughts, his fears, raced ahead. He was one of Rio's most frequent customers and had been chumming up with Vesta White and the Freeman fella. It made sense he'd known both Elias and Eino. Made sense he knew his way around the hotel. Even made some sense to suspect he might have a key to the place and all of its locks.

But Beckett still didn't know why.

———

BECKETT RODE up to the hotel early in the afternoon, his horse's legs gray to its knees with drying mud. He'd come in on the trail opposite the one from town, and the horse looked tired, as if it had put in a lot of miles the last couple of days.

Rio, outside restoring benches overturned by the gale to an upright position, caught sight of them just as they disappeared into the barn. The feeling that rushed over her felt like rubber bands had broken all at once and allowed her squeezed tight insides to return to their proper position.

Shoving the last bench into place, she glanced at the hotel windows to see if anyone might be watching. She intended to speak with Beckett before Mr. Fields started in with him. And exact a promise to repeat Fields's information to her. Hurrying now, she trotted toward the barn, panting when she got there and surprised at having forgotten to breathe.

The barn, dim after the weak sunlight outside, hid Beckett at first, until she heard him talking to the horse. She moved toward the sound.

"I should've ridden you right into the lake," he was saying, matching the swish of the brush sliding over the horse's coat to his words. "Bathed your legs and belly.

And the end of your tail. It's been dragging in the mud. Move over." There was a light slap, evidently giving the sorrel direction.

Rio, avoiding a pile of fresh horse dung, stepped over to the stall gate. "Beckett?"

He turned, a slow smile lighting his tired face. "There you are. I see you and the hotel made it through the storm. Win?"

"He's fine. He's been helping me tidy up the damage. He bailed out my waterlogged boats." She smiled ruefully. "It's a wonder they didn't all sink."

Beckett swiped the brush one last time over the sorrel's back and rump before stepping out of the stall. Reaching behind Rio, he returned the brush to the ledge, and in the same motion, gathered her into his arms and rested his cheek on top of her head. "I'm glad to see you."

"And I, you," she whispered.

And then they didn't talk about anything for a minute or two, their lips too busy doing something else.

Seventeen

To Rio's surprise, when considering the hotel's newly acquired reputation as a murder site, customers turned up for dinner service that night in droves. Oh, not in a celebratory sense. Instead, the seats were filled with people worn out from working hard to replace roofs and stovepipes and remove fallen trees from their buildings. Folks were simply too tired and hungry to fend for themselves this evening and in dire need of sustenance.

In town, someone told her, Mr. Meadows' portico over the entrance to his mortuary had fallen and blocked the way in. There'd been a funeral for old Granny Berson scheduled there today, postponed now until tomorrow or maybe the day after.

The telegraph office had a broken window with no glass in town to fix it.

The awning over the front of the mercantile had blown into parts unknown. Some kids, since the school was closed for the day, had found a corner ripped from the canvas and built a fort out of it. The report was that it looked sturdier than in its original position.

Wind had blown embers in the blacksmith's forge to life and scattered them against the back wall of his shed. The fire had caught, but the deluge of rain put it out before it did more than char a four-foot area. The town had heaved a collective sigh of relief as it had no real firefighting equipment.

Rio managed to get Beckett and Mr. Fields seated together at one of the small, out-of-the-way tables where their talk wouldn't be overheard. Beckett knew of her efforts. Fields only at the last moment.

She found it hard to tell if the Englishman was pleased or not. What she did know, or had a strong guess about, was that Vesta was not at all pleased as she sat all the way across the room.

Every evening when Vesta entered the dining room, according to her whim, she paused at the doorway and surveyed first the seated diners, and then those who were waiting in the lobby.

On the lookout for prey to her feminine wiles, in Rio's estimation. Not only Rio's, for both Eliza and Marie had remarked upon Vesta's boldness. Sometimes with laughter, sometimes with scorn, occasionally with jealousy. A few other ladies present had not seemed pleased either and had gotten a bit more decided in choosing a location to sit.

Tonight, at possibly the most inopportune time, Vesta's gaze settled on Beckett, who sat waiting for his meal. Then, briefly, on Harrison Fields before returning to Beckett. She frowned.

"Sheriff," she caroled, her voice loud enough to carry to Rio in the kitchen and, most certainly, to the other dining room patrons as well. "For shame. Here you are, delegated to a paltry corner table with a stranger. You must come and dine with David and me. The serving girls are aware of my seating requirements."

Serving girls! As if they were serfs obeying their master or mistress's least command. The belittling description of the hardworking Golz women curdled Rio's blood. Enough that Vesta's invitation to Beckett only came second. Not that she blamed the other woman. Or not exactly. Beckett was the most arresting man in the room. Actually, anywhere. Who wouldn't want him as a dinner partner? Or maybe a partner in other things.

She started for the dining room, planning to intervene.

Plenty able to take care of himself, Beckett waved Vesta off. "No thanks, Miss White. I'm fine right where I am."

Plain to see, Vesta didn't like his all too public reply. Her expression mirrored her chagrin. "Oh, but..."

But Eliza, bless her timing, had arrived beside him bearing a large tray of plates of swissed steak along with the trimmings. Slowing her pace as she set their meals before them, with her back turned to Vesta, she winked at him. It allowed him time to cue Fields on changing the timing of their planned talk.

Beckett grinned. "Thanks, Eliza." It wasn't all on account of the food.

"Anytime," she said.

The little set-to made things awkward, curtailing the exchange between the two men. Beckett, aware of Vesta watching him, may have been a little hesitant that an unwarranted slip of the tongue might warn Vesta and her companions that they were under discussion. So he and Fields made small talk.

As for Harrison Fields, as unperturbed as an Eskimo in a snowstorm, he paid no attention to the people at the other tables. When he finished his meal, he headed over to the register in the lobby to pay.

Rio took his money. "That wasn't expected. I'm sorry."

Finally, out of the others' sight, Fields's lips twitched. "We set up another meeting. The sheriff did suggest your presence." He seemed a little uncomfortable at the thought. "I hope you won't be upset."

Giving him a level stare, Rio produced change for his dollar bill. "Anything that has the slightest whiff of my half brother on it upsets me, Mr. Fields. And that goes for most of my life." Her lips twitched. "I've gotten used to it."

"Ah. But murder?"

She made a funny little moue. "There have been attempts on my life as well, Mr. Fields, but here I am, still standing. So yes. Even murder."

He pocketed the change, withholding a dime with instructions to give it to Eliza. "Aside from being a fine waitress, she was most clever in allowing the sheriff and me time to make further plans privately."

"Yes...uh-oh." Rio's eyes widened in warning.

Fields turned to see Vesta bearing down on him, her mouth set in stern lines. Bindle trailed behind like a kite being dragged through the weeds by a child. Meanwhile, David Freeman had stopped off at the bar, buying a snifter of brandy from Turner. He took a stool and waited.

"Sir," Vesta loudly announced as she drew near. Her eyes were on Harrison Fields, eyeing him like a hungry coyote eyes a plump mouse. "I understand the storm waylaid you here. Understandable, of course, but I trust you'll be moving on in the morning."

"Do you? That remains to be seen, doesn't it?" he said, his accent making the terse reply even more stiff.

"On what?" she demanded.

How dare she? The question hit Rio's mind in a fiery flash.

It struck Rio that Mr. Fields seemed almost frail, standing in front of Vesta's authoritative stance. And with Bindle, like a loyal watchdog, hovering in the background.

But Fields didn't flinch. He eyed her levelly. One unruly eyebrow arched up. "Madame? Who might you be? Perhaps you'd care to explain why I should tell you my intentions? I must say, you have aroused my interest."

Vesta's head jerked back. She hadn't expected resistance. "Rude," she said. "I'm just trying to show some curiosity about my fellow hotel residents."

Fields bowed. "Indeed? Misplaced curiosity, I daresay." Turning his back, he walked away, his stride so assured that even Bindle stepped aside for him.

Vesta flounced off then, leaving Rio with a grin so wide her mouth felt likely to split. It wasn't just the way Harrison Fields had spoken to Vesta. It was also that Vesta had been thwarted in just about everything she tried this evening. There was also the way Vesta's too-fancy taffeta gown stretched tightly across her behind, causing a disconcerting wobble as she whirled and stomped away.

Perhaps, Rio thought, Vesta should skip the extra portions she often demanded at dinner. Apparently, in spite of Vesta's incessant complaints, Rio's food appealed enough to make her fat.

———

RIO STARTLED INTO WAKEFULNESS, the side of her face wet. Rolling over, she pushed Boo and his busy tongue away.

"Stop it," she murmured. "It's not time to get up."

But according to Boo, it was.

When she opened one eye, even in the dark, she could see him staring expectantly at her. But he wasn't panting or acting as if he needed to go outside.

His funny little floppy ears pricked. Listening, she realized.

So Rio listened too.

Out on the porch, someone was moving around. She heard the clank of metal on metal. The washtub, she figured. She hadn't felt like taking it down to the cellar, and it had been left to get in the way for the past few days. Whoever was out there had accidentally struck it.

She and Boo, the dog as carefully as she, got out of bed. Rio put on slippers and belted her nightgown so it freed up her legs. She slipped on a coat and picked up her gun. Like two wraiths, they went to her door, listening harder.

Until Boo scratched gently at the door and Rio opened it.

They crept down the hall, reaching the porch just as the outer door closed behind whoever had been inside. Hurrying now, Rio dashed forward and looked out through the window, finally spotting the figure just as he moved into the belt of trees.

She was sure of only two things. The figure did not belong to either Beckett or Win, the only two people she knew she could trust. And he was carrying what appeared at a distance and in the dark, to be a shovel. *Or a club or a rifle or…*

No, it must be a shovel. He must be searching for Eino's so-called treasure.

Excitement bubbled inside her. This was the best chance to catch a killer. But she wasn't stupid. Or fearless.

Running now, Boo with her, she hurried to awaken Beckett.

He'd locked the door on himself and Win. Wise, no doubt, considering past events. Rio knocked, hoping he slept lightly enough that she didn't have to rouse everyone in the hotel.

Boo helped. He scratched and let out a little yip or two. She knocked again, and finally, if she held her ear right up against the door, she heard someone stirring.

"Hurry," she said, her voice low. "Beckett, come on."

After what seemed like ages but was probably only a few seconds, the door clicked open a crack. Then wider when he saw her and Boo.

"Who's dead?"

Rio knew her eyes widened. She hadn't actually thought of another death. How stupid of her. Had the man with the shovel been intending to dig a grave?

She stuttered as she made her report. Beckett, at the end, just nodded.

"Wait here," he said. "Do not go out by yourself. Or with Boo. Understand?"

She nodded. Of course she understood. Why else had she awakened him?

Beckett closed the door in her face, but within a minute or two was back, still strapping his shoulder holster on. He didn't bother to button his coat, most certainly preferring to keep his revolver in ready reach.

"C'mon," he said. "Show me where you saw him last."

They heard nothing as they crossed the yard, going fast. Boo, who'd paused to take care of dog business, caught up before they got into the trees. Groping their way through the dark, branches lashed out at them. Twigs caught in Rio's hair, making her wish she'd thought to pull a cap onto her head. Not only to shield against the elements, but to keep her pale hair from showing.

Although they did their best to avoid making noise, Rio knew they did. So, she soon discovered, did whoever was ahead of them. Worse even for the single man than for the two of them. Three if you counted Boo. Someone not accustomed to finding a way through the woods?

Taking into account where they were at the moment, Rio thought she knew where their prey was headed.

She tugged on Beckett's arm until he stopped and bent down so she could whisper in his ear. "He's going to the spring."

He looked around, taking a fresh view of their surroundings. "I think you're right. That makes it easier. Slow down and be quiet."

She nodded, although he may not have seen. In fact, they went slowly enough that as they reached their destination they heard the thunk of what she now knew was a shovel digging into the wet earth and depositing the soil in a soggy mound beside a hole. The man, she observed, had laid aside his coat and worked in his shirtsleeves. And with every earthy-smelling shovel load of wet soil, he grunted like a hog at the trough. Worse, the hole he dug was close to the lid over the spring itself, threatening to contaminate the water with debris.

Due to an apparent lung affliction that caused his breath to come in stertorous gusts, their approach was totally masked. Until Boo, curious about someone digging a hole—his purview, after all—ran up to investigate. He leapt up on the man's leg as if to ask a question.

Possibly seeing only a white blur, the man gave a shout, swinging the shovel at his attacker even as he slipped on the mud, stuck a foot in the hole, and fell. Boo yipped and darted away.

Gun drawn, Beckett stepped forward. Then Rio.

"What have we here?" Beckett said. "Starting a garden? Looking for gold? Maybe burying a body? I'm sure Miss Salo would prefer that not happen right next to the water supply."

The man glared up at Beckett. He didn't speak.

"Hunting buried treasure, most likely." Rio cut in. "Isn't that right, Mr. Freeman?"

The glare switched over to Rio. "You should know." His face puckered, almost as if he were about to weep. "I suppose you've already found it. I suppose this has all been for nothing."

Beckett cleared his throat. "All of what, Mr. Freeman?" He holstered his pistol and grabbed David

Freeman by the arm to wrest him out of the mud. "The murders of two men? The vandalism to the hotel grounds?"

"Murder? No. No!" Freeman frowned. "Vandalism?"

"Digging holes and endangering the hotel drinking water."

Rio could see the shovel was one of the hotel's that Win had been using earlier to shift more gravel onto the landing in front of the porch leading to the lobby. It helped cut down on tracked-in dirt.

"Using hotel tools without permission. Why, I might've thought the shovel had been stolen. And that would've been against the law." She smiled a little as she said it. It was easy to tell each new idea, silly as they might be, resulted in a more disturbed David Freeman.

He was a weak man. She'd seen that from the beginning. Keep him away from Vesta and he'd soon be spilling everything he knew to Beckett.

"I'll have Win fill in the hole tomorrow," he said to Rio. "For now, Mr. Freeman and I are going to take a little ride."

"A ride? Where? Why?" Freeman's eyes bugged out. "What are you going to do with me?"

Beckett grinned. "Take you to the jail in town where we can have a nice long talk without interruption. We'll make it official. Nothing too much—as long as you give me straight answers. For instance—" Then he stopped and eyed Freeman as if speculating on what this would take.

Rio found it easy to see why he'd been a good and effective customs agent. And why he'd make an equally excellent sheriff.

"Vesta. I must speak with Vesta." A little frantic, as if he might suspect a beating, Freeman did his best to pull away from Beckett. A useless endeavor, as it shortly proved.

"Not now," Beckett said, straightening Freeman's shirt collar for him. "You wouldn't want to interrupt her beauty sleep, would you?"

Upon which, wearing a thoughtful expression, Freeman stopped his resistance. "No," he said. "No, I wouldn't."

Pushing Freeman along ahead as Boo circled around them as if this were a kind of pleasurable game, they ended up at the barn.

"Watch him while I saddle the horses. You know what to do if he tries to get out of line." Beckett's short order to Rio had Freeman trembling in his mud-softened shoes.

Scared or just cold? She had no real idea. Nodding, she stood back.

Before leaving, Beckett pulled her into the stall, hiding them from Freeman's sight. "Watch out for those women," he said softly. "Freeman may think they're his partners, but I find it doubtful. It's entirely possible Vesta has someone else dangling on her line."

"You think she's been using him as a simple flunkey? Someone who is willing—or stupid enough—to do her bidding?"

"I do." He bent and gave her a quick kiss before leading both horses out to the center of the barn. He had to push Freeman up on one. It turned out Vesta's flunkey was no horseman.

Eighteen

To Rio, it felt as if she'd no more than gotten back to bed than once again Boo awakened her, this time by standing on her chest and snuffling.

She sat up, which tossed Boo to the side. "What are you doing, you little wretch?" She rubbed at a damp spot on her nose. The room, with daylight not far away, was bright enough to show the little dog's wounded expression.

A soft scratching sound came from her door. And a low voice with an English accent saying, "Miss Salo. Our meeting."

She fell back against her pillow and groaned. "Oh. Sorry, Boo." She—and Beckett too—had forgotten the meeting planned with the Englishman this morning. And now she'd have to explain. But what would Beckett want her to say? Or should she ask Mr. Fields to put everything off a while longer?

Getting up, she went to the door and opened it a crack. Just enough for one of her chocolate brown eyes to blink at the small man. He still, she decided, looked just a bit like a weasel. Or perhaps, more charitably, a sly fox.

"Shh. I'm sorry, Mr. Fields. There was a...a...an incident during the night. I'm afraid Sheriff Ferris has had to go into town. I'm not sure when he'll be back."

His mouth compressed to the point his lips disappeared. "What do you know about this incident?"

"I know..." She didn't think she had any choice but to tell him the circumstances. But at least she could put him off until she thought what to say. "Hold on. Let me get dressed. I'll meet you in the kitchen in just a few minutes."

He grunted. She yawned in his face.

In a matter of minutes, she'd dressed in her usual outfit of ankle-length skirt, of which every one she owned bore a reinforced pocket for her small revolver, a simple white shirtwaist, and a wide leather belt to help support her back during her day of work. Stopping in the bathroom, she splashed cold water on her face and ran a brush a couple of times through her pale hair.

She found Fields hovering over the cookstove, stirring up the banked embers and shoving small chunks into the rising flames.

"Thank you," she said, rather impressed by his initiative. "I'll just run down to the cellar and get the boiler going. People are going to want hot water, and it takes a while."

He sighed and nodded.

Chills raised goosebumps as she went down the dark, narrow stairs. Finding Merle Pope's body, his throat cut, all that blood...Well, it had left a lasting impression. Shuddering, she hurriedly selected a jar of canned peaches from a shelf, thinking perhaps a nice peach coffee cake would go well at breakfast. Or maybe at dinner. It depended.

By the time she returned upstairs, the teakettle was on, and Mr. Fields had pumped water into the coffeepot. Another pleasant surprise. Taking the coffee grinder, she poured in the roasted beans and turned the crank.

"If you'll excuse me," she said. "I'll keep working." And indeed, the coffee cake was ready to go into the oven the moment it got up to the correct heat, which was about the same time it took for the teakettle to whistle and the coffee to perk. She made tea of a suitable strength for an Englishman, brought the pot along with a cup and saucer to the table. Seating herself, she reached for her coffee.

He poured his tea, added milk, and took a reviving sip. "Now?" he asked, rather dryly.

"Now," she replied. But when she'd finished her story, he sagged.

"I almost hoped it would turn out differently."

"You did?" Her brows drew together. "You mean there is truth to what he's saying? That my half brother stole jewels, and nobody knows where they are. The whole thing sounds nonsensical to me. Besides—" She stopped. Did she really need to repeat the circumstances of the last time she'd seen Eino? Probably, but as little as possible.

"Did you meet him, Mr. Fields? My half brother?"

"I glimpsed him. He was pointed out to me at a party." He had a faraway look in his eyes. "He was dancing with Senator Blackman's daughter. And after that, her stepmother. In fact, he paid particular attention to Mrs. Blackman. Enough for several people to remark on it. She is a good many years younger than the senator, and quite a beauty." He smiled. "A minor scandal."

Rio found it difficult to think Eino would be acceptable at a party where a senator and his family were in attendance. Evidently, the White family had been much better connected than she'd been led to believe. And Eino, when on his best behavior, a much better actor. It also made her wonder how her father had managed to woo and to marry such a woman as Edith White.

"Did she reciprocate? This senator's wife?" Simple curiosity instigated the question. Rio doubted whether she did or not made much difference when it came to stolen jewels. If there actually were any stolen jewels.

But in this, she may have been wrong.

Fields tapped his front teeth in thought, finally looking up at her, his expression suddenly more aware. "Now you mention it, I think she may have. What makes you ask?"

"Women often play a part in Eino's plans. Most of the time, just like him, the women do not have honorable intentions."

"You mean to insinuate Mrs. Blackman might—"

She shrugged. "I mentioned a possibility. Or you said something about a daughter."

Fields shook his head as if casting away a bad dream. "Oh, no. Not Miss Sally. She's so young. A debutante this year. Surely not."

Harrison Fields, in Rio's opinion, didn't seem to be a terribly astute detective, if that was even his job. But she merely said, "Eino always preferred young women to bamboozle. They're easily led."

He groaned.

Rio got up, checked on her cake, and poured herself more coffee. She glanced at the time, then out the window to see if Marie, on shift early this morning, was within sight.

And uncomfortably, she thought of something else to add to what she'd already said regarding Eino. Something, considering his erstwhile wife, Flavia, and now what she suspected of Vesta, that changed the whole of what they knew.

"But oddly enough, he always ended up with an older woman," she finally said. "I'd say he'd rather have older ladies as partners in crime. I suppose they're better about protecting themselves. And him."

An arrested expression froze on Fields's face. His breath gusted from him. "Oh, dear me," he said. "This is bad. Maybe it's bad. Could it be...Oh, dear me."

It was as if he'd been hit by lightning.

The situation had just taken a turn. And whatever it was that made him appear as if he'd just witnessed the white rabbit from the Lewis Carroll tale disappearing down the rabbit hole, it had to be important.

She gawked at him. "What..."

He jumped from his chair, nearly causing it to topple. "What is the fastest way to the telegraph office? That little burg does have a telegraph office, doesn't it?" He didn't wait for her to finish saying that, with the previous storm, the line might be down. He wasn't listening, anyway. "Quickly, quickly. I must speak with Sheriff Ferris. I must get to town. I must get word to Senator Blackman. He will so..."

He stopped, his eyes popping as he stopped before telling her more.

It didn't matter. Rio had heard enough. And she'd never, ever, seen a man in such a panic. All this over some stolen jewels? Some *possibly* stolen jewels? Which, oddly enough, she still didn't think Eino was guilty of stealing. Or at least not guilty of bringing to the hotel. He'd been too occupied in hiding out with the cash he'd taken from the Black Hand. Yes, and avoiding a criminal connected to the woman he'd introduced as his wife. Then there were the bearer bonds, along with a lot of money stolen from R.B. White, who was his own uncle. And Vesta's, hence the connection.

Rio sighed. So many complications.

Harrison Fields, Rio decided, was a man in need of a stiff pick-me-up. She got out the bottle of whiskey she used in recipes requiring a touch—or more—of alcohol and poured a generous shot into his teacup.

Still standing, he stared at it a moment before drinking it down, looking surprised for a moment. "That's good whiskey."

"I use Kentucky bourbon in my cooking. Did you expect rotgut?" she asked, more than a little offended.

The whiskey helped. Fields had snapped back to his normal, collected self by the time Marie actually did arrive, and Rio could give her instructions—somewhat to the girl's horror—on preparing breakfast as well as serving it to the guests.

"There are only four people," she assured Marie. "Unless some extras show up. I doubt they will. I've put the word out that the hotel is closed until the murders are solved. And Mr. Fields is in a tearing hurry to get to Painter's Bay."

Fields's agitation grew, forced as he was to wait long enough for Rio to put on her coat and gather Boo. Getting them all down to the dock and into a boat took only moments.

It had been some time since Rio had worked the oars. Her arms, unaccustomed to the labor, tired quickly as they cut through the storm-churned water. Her breath came faster. Boo didn't help. He seemed to want to jump overboard for a swim.

"Will you kindly hold him?" she said to Fields. At his look of reluctance adding, "We'll go faster if you do."

Boo settled fairly peacefully on the Englishman's lap if one discounted the mandatory licks. In the way of things, within minutes, Boo's presence seemed to settle the man, as well.

Twenty minutes later, she nosed the boat against the Painter's Bay dock with barely a bump, holding it steady for Fields and Boo to disembark. Fields, now so impatient he walked off before she had time to tie the boat to a cleat, stood waiting at the beach and grinding his shoes in the sand. "Which way to the telegraph office? Quickly, Miss Salo. The senator will need the telegram in hand before lunch."

"Painter's Bay isn't so big you can't find it yourself." She wasn't sure she wanted to appear in town, where people might see her anywhere close to him. Just in case he became the next victim. No stretch of the imagination, considering both dead men had been strangers somehow connected to Eino and those supposedly stolen jewels. Fields had better be on the lookout for himself.

She gave him succinct directions and left him to it. He hurried away with an awkward gait that reminded her of a turtle attempting to gallop. Smiling a little, she made her own way to the sheriff's office and pushed open the door.

Beckett was sleeping in the chair. His arms were folded across his chest, legs stretched out in front, with his hat tilted over his eyes. A notepad filled with writing lay on the desk, along with a pencil with broken lead. The result of David Freeman's questioning, she imagined.

Shivering, she noted the fire in the pot-bellied stove had gone out, if it had ever been lit. The room was icy cold.

The door between the office and the cells was closed. She walked over and eased it open. David Freeman huddled in the middle of a rather dirty mattress. She thought he was asleep, but may only have been weary and miserable enough to keep his eyes closed and play possum.

She went back to Beckett and reached down to touch him, only to see his mouth curled in a smile and the one dark eye visible open and looking at her. A light sleeper. Well, she knew that already.

"Sorry," she said. "I'm sorry to awaken you."

He pulled himself upright in the tilting chair. "Please don't tell me Harrison Fields has been murdered, and you're here to report it."

The remark wasn't in the least funny since it's what she'd just been thinking, but she twinkled anyway. "No, but he's the reason I'm here."

Beckett removed the hat and ran fingers through his dark brown hair. "What happened?"

"We were talking. Then I said something, and all of

a sudden, he looked like a dam had burst, and said he had to send a telegram. Send it *right now*."

He grunted. "Interesting."

"Very. So as soon as Marie arrived to take over, I rowed him to town. He's at the telegraph office. He said he'd meet us here as soon as he's able."

"Does that include letting me know who the telegram went to, and what it said? And the reply, if he expects one right away."

"I can tell you who. A certain Senator Blackman. And I can tell you what else we discussed."

He grinned. "Good girl."

He stood up and grasped her hands, holding them between his.

How, she wondered, could he be so warm, considering the room was so terribly cold? But her hands, well, all over really, warmed when he gave her a quick kiss. Not entirely a satisfactory one, but pretty good considering just anyone could've been passing and seen them through the window.

All too soon, he had the fire built up in the stove, had sharpened his pencil with his jackknife, and instructed her to repeat what she and Fields had been talking about that had given him that stricken moment. Beckett had a good many questions. She, not so many answers.

———

RIO, at Beckett's suggestion on the thought that the murderer might somehow have gotten keys to the hotel doors, was on her way to the hardware store to purchase a couple new locks. First, though, she stopped in at Dr. Clement's office. She hadn't seen her friend, the doctor's wife, Molly, for a few weeks and felt in need of the latest tittle-tattle. Molly, after all, was the town's best source of the latest rumors. For current news, she was better than the newspaper, and her commentary was always to the point.

This time, she advised Rio to evict Vesta White and her maid. "Right away, hon, before she causes trouble. Her and her maid. Maids, you know what they say about them."

"No," Rio said. "What?"

Molly laughed, the mirth crinkling her good-natured face. "I don't know either. Not really. I don't have any experience with maids." She sobered. "But I do have some with man-eating women. If only we had alligators in the bay. You could throw her in and let the critters take care of her. I'll bet she can't swim."

Rio smiled, though it could've been a bit weak. "Yes, if only."

Even so, she felt better after the visit despite some truly ill-considered advice.

Having learned Beckett's run for sheriff was prospering among the voters the doctor had spoken with, Rio was still smiling after the meeting. Headed now for the hardware store, it crossed her mind to wonder if she'd brought enough money along to pay for the locks. Looking down, she opened her little purse to check.

The smile lasted until she almost ran into Bernie. Or, as he demanded nowadays, Bernard Jensen. He'd been Bernie when they went to school and in the same class as her half brother. And, as she remembered, he'd been friendly with Eino.

"Oh." She looked up, startled. "I'm sorry. I didn't

see you." Partly, she couldn't help thinking, because it was almost as if he'd waited to emerge from the bank doorway in order to obstruct her.

He'd been to the restaurant quite often since the reopening, usually with Mr. Masterson from the bank, along with the repulsive pair who wanted to run her out and buy the hotel cheaply. *Ugh.* Unsavory company, for a fact.

She stepped around him, but once again, he put himself in her way.

"I've been wanting to speak with you," he said, "but you always are somewhere else when I'm at the restaurant."

Yes, and best I can, I make sure I stay out of sight. The unspoken reply flitted through her mind. "What about?"

"About something you may know."

She cocked a brow. "Me? What might that be?"

"We should go somewhere private and talk." His eyes bored a hole through her.

"Sorry," she said. "Not today. I haven't the time." Nor the inclination. But knowing she needed to keep good community relations, Rio forced a smile. "We've been very busy lately. If you're still advocating for the Carvers, I can tell you it's wasting your time. I will not sell."

Most people with any manners would've let it drop and allowed her to be on her way to the hardware store. Not Jensen. He cocked a brow.

"Are you sure? I wouldn't be surprised if the murders don't drive people away. Right now, they may be merely curious, but that will most likely change. You may regret not selling."

Rio could swear she heard what, if not a true threat, then was at least an ill-wishing in there. "The murders have nothing to do with me. Besides," she gritted her teeth, "Sheriff Ferris will soon search out the killer."

Jensen's ice-blue Nordic eyes glinted. "You think so? The murderer seems rather clever to me. More clever than the sheriff. What if the sheriff is the next victim? Or that young brother of his? What's his name again?"

Win! Now she was certain she heard a threat.

Clutching her tiny purse in her hand tightly enough to make her fingers ache, she met his eyes. "Why don't you talk to the sheriff yourself? Give him the warning. I'm sure he'd be interested in what you have to say. He's right over there in his office."

Pushing past him, she went on toward the hardware, leaving Bernie Jensen chuckling behind her.

"Did I make you mad?" he called softly. "I said nothing more than the truth, you know."

Rage shook her. Once in the hardware store, she could barely remember why she was there. Billy, the clerk, had to ask her twice.

Nineteen

Her business completed with her new door locks wrapped in a brown paper parcel, Rio found Harrison Fields waiting for her at the sheriff's office. He and Beckett were drinking coffee from tin cups much different from the chinaware she'd served his tea in this morning. All seemed amiable between them, but to her pique, they had nothing to say. Not within her hearing.

Their reticence may have been what made her reluctant to report her meeting with Bernie Jensen. Right up until she told herself not to be silly. Win's safety might depend on her personal warning not only to the boy, but to Beckett. Not that she thought Beckett unable to take care of himself. She knew he could. Mostly.

"No," Beckett said in answer to her query. "Jensen hasn't been in to talk to me."

Not a real surprise.

Rio couldn't miss the way Beckett's head cocked to the side, his gaze sharpening.

"Those were his exact words?" he asked. "About my brother?"

"Yes."

He and Fields shared a look, right up until a shout came from the cells. David Freeman, awake and protesting his confinement.

"He's right," Beckett said, smiling ruefully at Rio. "I can't hold him just because we found him digging a hole on your property. Besides..." His voice lowered even further. "We might learn more by turning him loose than holding him here. Just be sure you, Win, and the Golz girls keep an eye out. Hear me?"

Her nose wrinkled. "I suppose that means I'll have to take him back with us."

He nodded. "Afraid so. I'll see you tonight. I promise."

Meanwhile, she thought, *Mr. Fields will manage to keep what he knows to himself, and I shall be in the dark all day. Again.* The disgruntled thoughts were back with her.

"We will talk later," Fields said as Beckett went to the back to free his prisoner. He must have seen how much being put off vexed her.

To her surprise, while David Freeman sat like a lump on the boat's middle seat, Fields apologized for not helping her row on the way back across the bay. "Not something I ever learned," he said. "I'm sorry. I'm not much of an outdoorsman. I've lived in a city all my life."

Freeman shot him a quick look and sniffed, although Rio didn't know why he'd seem disdainful. In this, the men struck her as being two of a kind.

For the second time that morning, by the time they

were three-quarters of the way to the opposite shore, her arms felt ready to fall off even as her lungs worked overtime. Freeman complained about the slowness of the journey.

"Be glad we don't overturn. I doubt you would like the swim," she retorted, and heard Harrison Fields stifle a cough.

Ten minutes later, and exhausted by her efforts, tying up at the dock involved a rebound from a resounding bump.

At least Marie was relieved to see her. "I didn't know what to do about preparing for dinner."

"Don't worry. I've closed the hotel, including the restaurant. The only patrons will be these two, plus Miss White and her maid—unless I can persuade them all to leave. We'll serve a single entrée. If they don't like it, they can go hungry. I don't care. Maybe I'll cook up a pot of pinto beans with ham hocks and see what they all make of that."

She knew. They'd all deem it peasant food.

Marie's eyes about popped out in astonishment. "Beans! My goodness, what will Blanche say?"

This just wasn't one of her better days, Rio decided. A bad joke that proved Marie cared more for her sister's opinion than she did for that of her boss.

The men had already gone to their rooms, although Rio figured Freeman would be reporting to Vesta first thing. It didn't really matter. More aggravating, Fields had escaped talking with her once again. Probably to settle into a nap.

Quite suddenly, it struck Rio that she, too, was tired to the bone. But as always, she couldn't rest. Setting to work, the rooms got cleaned, the lobby and dining rooms aired with the floors swept, the ice in both the big and the small iceboxes renewed, and, more importantly, the drip trays emptied. Then on to dinner prep. Not beans and ham hocks, but *Poulet aux Champignons*. Quick and easy.

Win, the silly boy, laughed when he got home from school and heard Rio's warning about Bernie Jensen. "He's the banker's man, isn't he? He don't look like much. I figure I can handle him if he starts anything."

And nothing Rio could say changed his mind.

So the day passed. At the regular time for the first dinner service, all four hotel guests claimed their seats early. Rio served them a clear soup, and they all began eating. She ducked back into the kitchen to dish up the next course.

That was when the evening went wrong. Wrong? Calling it catastrophic didn't stretch things too far. In Rio's opinion, at least.

Trouble began with the loud and persistent ringing of the after-hours bell summoning Rio to the hotel's locked front door. Putting the service on hold, she rushed through the lobby to the hotel entrance. There, the doorknob, twisted and tried more than once, rattled on its shaft.

And she, rueing the delay when of one of the older Golz boys said he was busy today, though he'd be over tomorrow to fit her new locks, had a decision to make. Behind her, she heard Boo, who was shut up in the office, barking his little head off, agitated by the incessant ringing of the bell. In the dining room, the rattle of spoons and idle talk went silent.

"What's that noise?" Vesta called.

Through the high window, Rio saw Eldon

Masterson standing at the front of three other men. From what Rio could see, he didn't look happy. Not at all. He was talking, although his companions were ignoring him.

"The hotel is closed. I told you I saw the notice posted at the store. We shouldn't be here." He faced the others as he spoke.

"Nonsense, Eldon." Melvin Carver pushed his round belly forward. "It's a hotel. It should be open. Keep ringing the bell." Which is what he did, reaching around Masterson to do so.

Behind him, his son was nodding in agreement. "She'd best get a move on. I'm hungry."

The last man, Bernie Jensen, smiled as if at a great jest. An observer, saying nothing to his boss, and nothing to the Carvers.

Rio opened the door a scant few inches.

Banker Masterson scowled at his companions, then flinched as he turned and caught sight of Rio's set face. For a moment, she wondered if he had been taken hostage by the three.

"We're closed. You'll have to go to the café in town." She'd already begun closing the door.

"What do you mean, closed? I can smell the food." Carver Jr. aimed a strong slap at the door, forcing it open and Rio, to avoid being hit, to step back.

The men, all of them, trooped inside, pushing past her as if she were no more than the hatrack. After a frozen moment, she ran after them.

"Take a table, boys," Carver Sr. said, glee in his voice as he and the others tromped through the lobby to the dining room. "What's on the menu, girl? It'd better be good."

Vesta White looked up from her soup in astonishment at the noisy interruption. Almost invisible at a small corner table by himself, Harrison Fields watched with narrowed eyes.

"I'll have what they're having," Bernie Jensen said, seating himself and pretending not to see the frown his boss gave him. Masterson did not appear happy. Not in the least.

In that, he wasn't alone. Rio, trying to decide if she should draw her pistol and order them out, dithered. She had no one to back her up. She was alone here. Even Turner had taken the night off. Worse, Harrison Fields might need protection. And Win.

Where was Win? Probably in the kitchen helping himself to his own dinner. The best place for him to be, she thought. In the office, Boo continued his clamor. Surely, Win would quiet the dog.

"Somebody shut that damn dog up," Carver Jr. ordered. "Bernie, you got a gun? I'm about ready to shoot the damn thing myself."

Jensen, with a quick glance at his boss, declined to answer.

It was as if she were both there and not there, Rio thought and came to a decision.

"Get up from the table and get out. All of you. I told you the hotel is closed." Her hand went to the pocket of her skirt. She eyed the Carvers. "As for you, you're not welcome here. Not now, not ever."

She didn't expect them to comply peacefully, and they didn't.

Carver Jr.'s face grew very red. He'd just sat down, but now he rose again, fast, the chair sliding back and crashing over. He lashed out at Rio with his fist, catching the forearm she threw up barely in time to block a blow to her head. Even so, she fell to the floor.

At the other table, Vesta and Bindle jumped to their feet.

"Hey," one or the other of them cried.

David Freeman still sat, his eyes popping as if stunned. Harrison Fields stood up and edged toward the kitchen. Rio's adversaries ignored both men.

Rio didn't dare show that the whole of her left arm had been paralyzed by the jolt. A few seconds ticked away as she sprawled there, and Carver glowered down at her.

"I told you I'm hungry," he said, sneering. "Now get up. Jump to and bring us our meal."

His father was nodding approval as he turned to Masterson and spoke pompously. "One is obligated to correct a woman who won't mind her manners."

"Miss Salo..." Eldon Masterson said, which meant exactly nothing. He'd gone pale and may have been in a state of shock.

Rio, taking her time, gathered herself and rose. As if she didn't see the men leering at her, she walked out of the room to the lobby.

One, perhaps Bernie Jensen, called out, "Wrong way, girl. Kitchen is the other direction."

She ignored him. Her father's old .45-caliber Colt was at the lobby desk, a weapon she felt more suitable— more authoritative—for this situation than her little pocket pistol. Besides, the extra seconds it took allowed the feeling in her arm to return. Partially and painfully.

Retrieving the gun, she hid it by her side and stalked back to the dining room to the table. Three of the men had sat back down. Masterson still stood.

The click as she pointed the gun at Carver Jr. and pulled back the hammer seemed overly loud.

"Miss Salo," Masterson held up his hands and began talking again, but she spoke over him. Not shouting—just firm.

She had their attention.

"Enough," she said. "This ends right here. Get out, all of you. Don't come back. Not sneaking around at night and not in the open when you think you can get by with it. I will not serve you. Not now, not ever. I will not sell to you." Her voice rose. "And I am very angry. Don't think for a minute that I won't defend my property or myself. I assure you, I know how to use this gun."

Over at the other table, Bindle cackled. "Give 'em hell, Miss Salo. Give 'em hell." And of all people, Vesta nodded approval. As if that weren't enough, over by the bar, something thumped. Harrison Fields stood there, the shotgun from her porch in his hands. Win stood beside him, carrying a baseball bat and looking grim. The thumping had been him banging the bat on the floor to get their attention.

Win shook his head. "Are you fellas ever going to be sorry when the sheriff hears about this! If I was you, I'd be on the first train out of town."

"Good advice, my boy." Fields nodded approval. "Excellent advice."

Rio's gun barrel pointed at Carver Jr.'s midsection. "You're first."

She knew he wanted to jump her again. She could see it in the way his eyes took on a mad stare. In the way his fists clenched. In the way he balanced on his feet, as if ready to charge.

Carver Sr. put a pudgy hand on his son's arm. "Easy, son. There'll be another time. A better time."

"I sincerely trust not." Finally, Eldon Masterson moved, heading for the door without waiting for his companions. "Jensen, come along. The bank has no further interest in this business. Mr. Carver, I've had enough and will expect you to vacate my spare room as soon as possible. This has been humiliating enough without going further."

Just slowly enough to prove he wasn't intimidated, either by Rio holding a gun on them or Fields with the shotgun, Bernie ambled after his boss.

Their departure apparently decided the Carvers' action. They went, Junior still with that wild-eyed glare. The door slammed behind them, but not soon enough to cut off more loud recriminations.

Slowly, Rio lowered the .45's hammer. "I think that man is insane," she said, not to anyone in particular. Just because it needed to be said.

No one spoke. Not Vesta's group, not Harrison Fields, not Win Ferris. Rio's legs were unsteady, and though she didn't know it, her face drained to white as she walked past everyone, heading for the safety of her kitchen. If, she reminded herself grimly, there was anywhere in this world safe for her.

At the dining room doorway, she paused. "Excuse me, please. I need a minute."

She stumbled to a chair and sat, only to find she couldn't stop shaking. More than a minute passed before her legs felt like they'd support her. Then she got up, went to the cupboard, and brought out her bottle of good Kentucky bourbon. She didn't bother with mixing in coffee or making a toddy. Sloshing some into a glass, she tilted it to her mouth and gulped it down, coughed hard, and drank a little more. The burn as the whiskey made its way to her stomach stiffened her resolve.

In a way, she was almost sorry Carver Jr. hadn't gone at her again. She would've shot, ending his threat once and for all.

He wouldn't be the first man she'd killed, after all, and he'd deserve it. She had the idea set in her mind that he was the one who'd killed two men in her hotel. A ploy to force her into selling? Or was it Eino's treasure that Vesta White and David Freeman kept whispering about?

Not, Rio reminded herself, to discount Bernie Jenson and his veiled threats.

If only she could talk with Beckett.

BECKETT HAD FINISHED his rounds for the evening. Performed one last check of the town and found it quiet, even at the two saloons. He'd donned his hat and shrugged into his jacket for the ride home—and when had he started thinking of the hotel as home?— when a thumping on the stoop outside the office indicated his plans were about to be interrupted.

He eyed the man who tromped into the sheriff's office without pleasure. Not anyone he wanted to see. Not by a long shot. It might depend on just how much hootch his visitor'd had to drink. Plenty, he figured. The powerful aroma reached him from across the room.

As if he were unbuttoning his jacket, he reached in and made sure his revolver was loose in his cross-draw holster.

"Bull French," he said, when the man mumbled something. "What can I do for you?"

He knew what he'd like to do. The old fellow he'd been letting sleep in the jail on cold nights had warned him that Bull had been going around telling folks that Beckett and Rio were shacking up in the hotel. Most people discounted the story. Some did not. Beckett didn't like what the rumor might do to Rio, both personally and to her business.

The trouble is, he almost wished the rumor was true. He wanted her in the worst way, but to love her. Not ruin her.

Bull glowered and clenched his fists. He seemed to be looking for a fight. "You can get outta town," he said. "That's what you can do. Could be you think you got this election sewed up, but you ain't. You ain't gonna win." He cackled like an old hen. "Got it on good authority. A dead man can't be elected."

"Is that so?" Beckett said. "But I'm not dead."

"Yet." The cackle came again. "Thought I'd just give you an idea of what's in store. See, it'll make my election run smoother with you outta the way." His eyes were reddened from the whiskey, and his clothes looked and smelled like they hadn't been changed in the last couple of weeks. He lumbered forward, hands already forming fists.

Why anybody would consider a man like Bull French for sheriff was a puzzle beyond Beckett's solving. A thought occurred. Apparently, someone was behind French's desire to kill him, which would then make him an ineligible candidate for sheriff. With him dead, that would get rid of two problems. The bumbler who knew the killer and the sheriff who intended to put him in prison.

Making a production of sitting in his tilting chair, Beckett propped his feet on his desk. The stance may have looked casual, but it left his hands free for his gun if the meeting came to that.

"This good authority...What is that? Or should I say, who is it? I figure this is some kind of joke, right? Did you make it up or did someone else?"

"It's..." Bull began, but then shut his mouth fast. He seemed bewildered by Beckett's disregard of his threat. "It ain't no joke, I guarantee. I ain't dis...disclosing my sources. Resources." He frowned. "Sources."

Easy to tell he was repeating someone else's remarks. Beckett doubted Bull had phrases like that at work in his own brain. So...who did?

A loud halloo from out in the street stopped Bull in his tracks. Bull stood for a moment as if undecided what to do next, then turned and, without another word, left.

Much, admittedly, to Beckett's astonishment as he watched him go. The whole meeting left a huge question in Beckett's mind, along with a big sense of unease.

Bull's intent to brag had managed to go off course. He'd realized it too, in letting Beckett know someone else was involved. A mistake easy for a drunk to make. One Beckett would now have to investigate. Sighing, because he'd wanted to have his supper with Win and Rio at the hotel, he locked the jail and set out to visit the bars where he'd listen to men talk.

It was long past the dinner hour before he finally set out for the hotel, an uncomfortable ride under the trees and along a dark road. More than once, his sorrel stumbled in ruts grown deeper since the storm, and after each jolt, he worried someone was out there drawing a bead on his back.

But his time at the saloons hadn't been for nothing. He had a handle on the men Bull had been seen talking to. Two struck him as unusual, one of which pointed in a not unexpected direction. For the second time, he remembered. He needed more information.

Twenty

R io had the kitchen cleaned after the dinner service when she noticed the black bruise that had spread along her arm. Carver Jr.'s blow, while stopping short of breaking the bone, had damaged the muscles and put a damper on her work. She could barely lift her large cooking pots with it.

Win, seeing the pain on her face, stepped up to help. The only problem is that he fretted out loud over Beckett's lateness, which caused Rio's own worries to swell. As if she weren't already stewing over being shut out of whatever he and Harrison Fields had discussed, the boy's apprehension made her own tension ten times worse.

"I thought Miss White and that Carver guy were conniving together," Win said as he hung a wet dish towel to dry on a rack near the stove. "They had dinner together a few times. At least"—he frowned a little— "they ate at the same table. Do you think they had a falling out?"

"I don't know," she replied. "Sounded like it."

"We should tell Beckett," he said. "If he ever gets here."

Rio's heart thumped. "He promised he'd get here. He'll be all right. You can tell him about tonight when you see him."

"I don't know why he's so late."

"I don't either." But, she thought, it must've been something important to keep him away.

Boo, who'd been getting underfoot while the work went on and been sent to his rug near the stove, jumped up and padded to the doorway, where he turned toward the porch. He gave a couple of happy-sounding little yips.

"He's here." Win spun to watch the door. "Look at Boo. It must be Beck."

It was. Most of the time, Rio left the porch open for him. Tonight, he'd been locked out. He set to tapping a light tattoo, causing Boo to prance in place. Afraid Carver would be back on his own, Rio had secured the premises the moment the unwelcome guests left.

Win hurried to open the door for him and promptly relocked it as soon as Beckett stepped inside.

"What's happened?" Beckett's dark gaze went over both Rio and his young brother, came back and, as if clairvoyant, settled on Rio. "You're hurt. What happened?"

Rio started to shake her head, but Win got in before she could speak. "Yeah, she's hurt. That damn Carver guy who's been pestering her showed up tonight and got rough. Bunged up her arm and knocked her to the floor."

Beckett went stone cold. "Melvin Carver? The old one or the young one?"

"Young one." Win grinned then. "You should've seen her, Beck. Rio made it to her feet without saying a word, went off and got the .45, and held it on them. She told 'em all to get out. Steady as a rock." He huffed. "They were smart enough to believe her too. The banker went first. I don't think he was expecting anything like that to happen when they got here. He didn't like it. But the others, they acted like they were putting on a show. Oh, and can you believe it? The witch from upstairs clapped her hands."

The way Beckett's jaw set made Rio think of granite. He turned to her. "Let me see."

She shook her head. "It's nothing." A lie.

"I'll decide. You may need the doc."

The bruise was both darker and larger than before she'd begun the dishes, running from just above her wrist to just below her elbow. She thought perhaps having her hands in hot water while doing the dishes had added to the discoloration.

Beckett didn't try to prod the bruise. The swollen flesh told him enough. "It's not broken?" he asked.

"No." Rio found her voice at last. "But Beckett..." Tears welled in her eyes, which is when, little brother or no little brother, Beckett gathered her up and held her close.

She didn't weep. Not really. Oh, a few tears may have fallen, but not enough to qualify as a full-blown crying spree.

But there they were, Beckett asking Win if there were any leftovers from the dinner service, and Rio sitting still when he let her go, trying to compose herself.

Since Win had become quite handy in the hotel kitchen during his recovery from the shooting in the summer, he took over. It left a little time for Beckett to talk with Rio without interruption.

"They were so awful," she said, a catch in her voice. "But I don't know why they came here at all. Mr. Masterson had told them the restaurant was closed, but evidently, they figured to just force their way in. Which they did," she added, her anger rising again as the ache in her arm grew. "But it doesn't make sense. Unless—"

Beckett breathed out. "Unless the idea was to force you into doing what they said. Three men against one little lady, and with the hotel closed, fewer witnesses. Worthless pieces of—" He stopped.

"Four men," she corrected.

"Four?" His brows drew together. "Name them."

"The Carvers, both of them. Mr. Masterson, from the bank. Bernie Jensen, Masterson's assistant."

"Jensen and Carver Jr." He repeated her words.

"Yes. Although Mr. Masterson did make an attempt to stop them."

"Not hard enough, that's clear."

She looked down at the table. "No. Pretty weak." A small smile lifted her lips. "You will be glad to know both Mr. Fields and Win came to my rescue. Mr. Fields took up the porch shotgun, and Win had his ball bat." The smile grew. "They were formidable."

"Good."

"I made it clear to them all I wasn't selling. Clear enough even people like them should finally understand."

At this, he hesitated. "I don't think this is about selling the hotel. I think that is an excuse for staying around."

Rio went so still she almost quit breathing. "Then what is it about?" She knew. Damnation. She knew it could only be one other thing.

"Treasure," Beckett said, confirming her suspicion. "They all want it. As does Miss White and David Freeman. They think Eino had it when he was here, and that he hid it somewhere on the property. They think you know where it is."

Damn her half brother and that horrible woman he'd called his wife. Damn Eino's thieving ways. Softly, she said, "So did Merle Pope and Arnold Heckert."

He nodded. "Yes. And Harrison Fields."

She buried her face in her hands. "I thought as much. I just didn't want to be right."

Win had just finished setting a heaping plate of warmed-over *Poulet aux Champignons* in front of his brother when she looked up again. She hadn't been crying, just trying to shut herself off from everything that had happened.

"I think Mr. Fields knows exactly what these people are looking for. If he would only tell us what it is, maybe we could help him find it." Rio didn't trouble to hide her dejection from Beckett or Win. "Can't you persuade him, Beckett?" A thought struck. "Or has he already told you?"

He stabbed a piece of chicken breast floating in thick creamy mushroom sauce and put it in his mouth.

An excuse, Rio believed, to keep from answering. But finally, he had no choice as she waited expectantly.

"What if the treasure doesn't belong to him, either? Or to the man he works for?"

"I don't care who it belongs to as long as it isn't on my property. That's provided there is anything here in the first place. I don't believe there is. Eino and Flavia were on the run. They hid in their room like moles, and then they made their separate escapes. I doubt there was a time when either of them had a chance to hide anything other than the stolen money in the cook shack before they even showed up at the hotel. They did that together, and it's all they were concentrating on."

"Somebody has stolen something else," Beckett said. "And that something must be worth thousands. I can't see there being at least four separate parties trying to put their hands on it otherwise, can you?"

Win, who'd been silent, had his piece to add. "Worth enough to kill for. Two already. Who's next?"

Rio had the feeling it might be her.

———

HE SHOULDN'T HAVE GIVEN his word to Fields, saying he'd keep the secretive nature of this treasure business quiet, Beckett thought, cursing himself. It wasn't right when the site of contention belonged to Rio. She should've been the first one told—provided there was any truth to the matter at all. She doubted the rumor saying Eino had buried treasure here, and he believed her. More so after hearing what Fields had to say. The telling had been insincere and left a bad taste in his mouth.

Unlike the chicken dinner he was eating at the

moment. He waved his fork. "This is good. One of your mother's recipes?"

"Originally my grandfather Serrano's," she replied, her brow set in furrows. It seemed clear she wasn't thinking about *Poulet aux Champignons*, though she stared right at it. "How in the world am I supposed to convince these people there is no treasure? I can't dig up every square inch of the place to show them. Neither can they, even if they had permission. Which they don't, and I'm not giving."

Beckett, laying his knife and fork neatly on the side of his plate, pushed it away and studied her. "Will you tell me something, Rio?"

"Sure, if I can. What do you want to know?"

"The truth. Just how bad is your arm? Are you sure it's not broken?"

She hesitated. "I'm sure."

She sounded doubtful. Beckett had seen the way she ran her fingers lightly over her bruise and knew it for a sign the arm ached worse than she wanted him to know.

"With the hotel closed for a few days, will you let the Golz ladies run the place? With just these few guests, you should let that arm rest. And have Doc Clement take a look at it." Then he sealed the deal. "If Doc gives the go ahead, we'll take some rides through the woods close by the hotel. That gives you a chance to check around. See for yourself if there's anywhere Eino might've buried anything, even if it's just his trash."

Rio leapt at the offer. It was what she'd wanted to do all along, and he knew it. "All right. We can row over in the morning. You can row, I mean." She smiled. "It will be good to do something besides sit here and worry." Not that she'd been sitting.

He wasn't so sure. A killer might be looking for his next victim, and targeting Rio was the most likely, especially if she seemed to be doing something out of the ordinary. This small act could put her in danger. But if Rio knew anything that might help put this trouble to rest, he needed to know what it was. And most of all, he needed to keep her safe.

———

THE NEXT MORNING turned out to be cool and crisp, with a clear sky. The smell of pine and fresh lake water was enough for Rio to mount her pinto with a sense of euphoria. She patted the horse's neck and told it good morning. Boo, intent on going along, pranced around the horse's feet, eager to get underway.

A basket had been fitted onto the back of Rio's saddle. Beckett pointed at it. "Lunch? I don't think we'll be gone that long. I figured on three or four hours."

Rio laughed. "No lunch. It's for Boo. He's little. When he gets tired, I put him in the basket and let him ride."

Beckett gave her a level look. "Some kids are less pampered than your dog."

"Some kids are less deserving than this dog," she retorted.

The exchange put a bit of a damper on the day. Without waiting for Beckett's help, Rio put her foot in the stirrup and swung aboard, using her legs for propulsion to keep from putting pressure on her arm. Beckett, though he'd been on his way to help her, stopped and shrugged. She'd been Doc Clements's first patient this morning, and he'd given the all clear.

"A bad bruise," he'd said. "Just hold off working too hard and allow the muscles to heal."

Working too hard, Beckett reflected as he mounted his sorrel, hadn't been the problem.

Riding a little ahead on the narrow trail, he looked over his shoulder, just catching a wince as her pinto stumbled a little on a deep rut. Hard to blame her for being cranky this morning, he decided. But time to get past it. "If you were to suspect Eino of burying any kind of treasure, where do you think he might choose?" he called to her.

Of mutual agreement—or some kind of telepathy—they'd headed out toward the high country, both considering the area around the hotel as the least likely possibility. It hadn't taken long for them to decide if anything had been concealed nearby, as many people had been poking into a possible hiding spot would've found it by now.

They'd been riding an hour when Rio, uneasy with the stiffness between them, spoke up.

"These people, the Carvers, Mr. Pope, Mr. Heckert, Vesta, Freeman, and even Bindle." She named them off. "If you remember, they weren't the first ones looking for something Eino might've hidden. Others were here before them. I think the first people last summer were more thorough than these. They had more time, for one thing. But they didn't find anything." Rio was musing aloud. "Anyway, why wouldn't Eino have concealed everything in the same place? The cook shack was close, the cupboard invisible, the catch tricky. When the time came to retrieve his stuff, wouldn't it make sense to only

have one place to go? Especially if he was in a hurry."
She thought a moment. "And he was."

She had another point to add. "Besides, some of
them arrived and began looking around before Eino and
Flavia got here. Doesn't that prove this is pointless?"

Beckett reined the sorrel in. "Would seem so."

"Then what are we doing?"

He grinned. "Getting you away from the hotel, if
only for a few hours. You need some sunshine and fresh
air, Rio. And a rest from the whole situation. A change
of scenery will do you good. I know you like riding, and
you like the woods. And this is the first time you've
been away from the hotel in weeks. Am I right?"

"Oh!" He'd been thinking of her. The realization
struck her with a warm glow. He was right. She did feel
better with the sun over her head, the quiet nature of
the susurrus of pines, the swish of her pinto's tail
flicking at lethargic flies, slowed now by the cooler
weather.

They rode a little farther, bushes and trees over-
hanging the trail and deadening the sound of their talk.
A small creek, one that dried to a trickle in the summer,
ran nearby. The water was high right now, a leftover
from the big storm. She could tell by the sound of the
flow as it tumbled over rocks and around corners,
although the creek was still out of sight.

"Stop," Rio said to Beckett. "Over here." She
pointed to a barely visible deer trail that would take
them to the creek. Boo was already sniffing the trail, no
doubt intrigued by the odor of the small pellets of dung
showing deer had recently passed on their way to water.
But that wasn't all. A horse had come this way too.
Recently.

She led the way. A hundred yards brought them to the creek bank. There was a granite outcropping here, and huge boulders piled up around it. The horse had stopped, and a rider dismounted. A man, according to the footprints left in the mostly dried mud, had picked up a fallen tree branch and used it to poke around the base of a few of the boulders. The branch, its tip still flaking mud, had been cast away when he left. It seemed clear he hadn't found anything of interest.

From atop her pinto, Rio gazed down at the softened earth as if puzzled. "A townsman. Look at the prints."

Beckett dismounted for a closer look. "Wearing shoes, not the boots you'd expect of anyone with any business here. A heavy man, according to the depth of the prints, but one with small feet."

Rio huffed. "This is part of Salo property. Nobody has business here. Not even Jess Stokes. This part of the property isn't being logged just now."

Beckett cast an experienced glance around at their surroundings. "Looks like it'll be another ten years before this is ready for cutting. If then."

"Yes. It was the first area my father logged when he took up land here." She dismounted too, her legs stiff after only an hour in the saddle. Boo, his front paws and muzzle wet from a drink in the creek, plopped down in the sun atop one of the boulders.

"I've been thinking," she said, as if it were something new to her. "As much as I'd rather not, about Eino."

He came to stand beside her. "Come to any conclusions?"

Tilting her face to the sun, her hair lifted under a

soft breeze, the light-colored locks making a halo around her head. "Yes." She chuckled. "This is typical Eino. Typical of everyone else too."

"What do you mean?"

"I mean, he's getting a last laugh on all of us." Rio knew she'd taken Beckett by surprise. "For one thing, there is no treasure. Or if, somehow, there is treasure missing, it isn't Eino's doing. For once," she added. "And for another thing, if he had this supposed treasure, it wouldn't be buried. Eino didn't care much for shovel work. He complained like a baby deprived of his toy when our father put one in his hands and told him to dig. They were working on clearing the spring. You should've heard him."

She paused, another giggle rising. "What Eino would've done is to have found a hiding place that didn't require shovels or digging. There's a place like that here. I don't know how he found out about it, but apparently, someone else knows about it too. I think it's worth the trouble to check." She looked around.

Beckett, not so amused, went still. "Me too."

"I thought you might. Follow me."

Leading the way, she stepped between a couple of mammoth-sized boulders that always made her wonder how they'd come to rest here since there were no other rocks of the same type anywhere around. Boo bounded up from his nap and darted in front of her, up to the top of the outcropping where a lone lightning struck tree stood slowly disintegrating. A hole in the tree showed where the wood was rotting from the inside out.

Thrusting her hand into the hole, she came out with a handful of pine nuts, some grains of grass, a few dried-up specks she thought were fruits, possibly taken from her own bushes. Looking over her shoulder at Beckett, she shook her head. "A squirrel sanctuary. But at one time, Eino hid a gun he stole in here."

"He stole a gun? Didn't his father—"

"Father provided him with several guns over the years. Usually, Eino would sell them to cover gambling losses and tell Father somebody stole them. I'm sure he knew better, but this was Eino. He said he stole this one because the man who owned it had cheated him at cards." Her nose wrinkled. "He said that a lot. I think he's the one who cheated at cards."

Beckett surveyed the contents she'd dug out and the size of the hollowed area. "This is old. Too old for what we're looking for."

Another shrug answered. "It's the only place that I know about. Like I said, if Eino has any idea of what is happening here now, I'd wager he's laughing his head off."

Gesturing to the hollow in the tree, Beckett eyed her, a half-smile on his lips. "How did you learn about this? About Eino hiding the pistol here? Did he tell you?"

"Heavens, no. But he was always careless. I followed him one day, that's all. And he didn't have the least idea I was there."

Going down the hill to the horses, Beckett went first. Their route was steep, and Rio's sore arm made her awkward. Loose gravel slid underfoot. A drift of pine needles covered a ditch made by the recent rains. That's all it took for her feet to go out from under her.

A little squeak warned Beckett in time for him to spin, catching her around the waist as she fell. Trouble came from his boots not having good purchase either, and they both went sprawling. Luckily for Rio, she landed on top. Flat on top, breast to chest, face to face, only inches away.

A little dazed, she blinked at him. And forever afterward, she never knew if what happened next was because she kissed him, or if he kissed her first. But she did know that for the next several minutes, time was suspended, and he became her whole world.

Twenty-One

They came for her in the night.

Rio had no warning, although later, when her mind cleared enough to think about the sequence of events, it seemed Boo had done his best. The little dog had stirred as he lay beside her, sitting up as if in question. But she, exhausted after nights with not enough sleep and a day on horseback, had put out her hand to still him. She thought she heard him growl once after that. Then snuffle.

She forgot Boo in the next fraught seconds—or minutes, she wasn't sure which—in the awareness of a sickly sweet smelling rag being pressed across her nose and of her head being held in a vice. She thought she was dying, and though she fought against it, fought with all her might, she was aware of her strength fading... fading.

Black dropped over her vision. Her limbs refused to obey her commands. Commands she forgot, even as she thought them.

And then it was nothing. She didn't know about the

quilt being jerked from her bed and wrapped around her. Nothing about Boo being unceremoniously dumped from the cot onto the floor as he, poor mite as unconscious as his mistress, got stepped on in the process.

Being transported to wherever she found herself next forever remained a mystery. When Rio awakened, she had no idea what had happened, where she was, or who had taken her. She only knew that although nausea racked her, she was alive and damn well determined to stay that way.

All this was done in silence as Sheriff Beckett Ferris slept the sleep of the just. But not in the room next door to Rio's. He slept in the spare cell in the jail across Painter's Bay, watching over Bull French, whom he had arrested for being drunk and disorderly in the Dry Well Saloon while trying to beat up a gambler who'd won all his money. Not exactly proper behavior for a man aiming to become sheriff.

———

EARLY MORNING BROUGHT Eliza to the porch door of the Painter's Bay Hotel. To her surprise and dismay, she found the door unlocked. In plain fact, she found it standing wide open. Which, it didn't take long for the thought to cross her mind, wasn't at all like Rio's usual operation. Certainly not at this early hour of the morning, and especially now, after two men had been murdered in the hotel. She very well knew Rio had been meticulous with safety procedures, determined that no more murders occur on the premises.

Eliza's worried glance went back to her own passage

over the frost-covered ground. Her footprints showed up clearly, sharp and dark against the white frost. And they were the only prints visible.

Good or bad? She didn't know.

Once inside, she found the porch freezing cold, as if the door had stood open most of the night. And worse, the door between the porch and hallway leading into the building hadn't been fully closed either, so the rest of the hotel was nearly as cold as the outside. So much so, Eliza was surprised there weren't people up and complaining.

She hesitated before entering, pausing to peer down the hall, still dark since dawn had barely broken. No sound of activity broke an eerie silence.

"Rio?" she called softly. "Are you here?" She thought herself stupid, even as she spoke. Clearly, Rio was *not* here. So where was she?

Slowly, she closed the outer door behind her and went the kitchen. Also dark, quiet, cold, the fire in the stove retained barely a touch of warmth from embers nicely banked last night.

First, a light. She struck a match and got a lantern burning. Then the fire built up. But still no sign of Rio. Eliza hoped her boss wasn't sick.

Or dead.

Eliza couldn't stop the thought from consuming her. She went back into the hall, glancing toward the room next to Rio's. The one where Sheriff Ferris and his young brother, Win, stayed. She paused outside the room, listening, but heard no one stirring. Next, she went to Rio's room, the office-bedroom, all the space Rio claimed for her own use nowadays.

She tapped. Not hard. Not hard enough to cause

the door to open, but it did, swinging on silent hinges to reveal an empty bed. The sheets were rumpled, the quilt, a pinwheel design in pretty colors, was missing, a pillow lay on the floor. Eliza gasped, her hands covering her mouth. That wasn't all.

"Boo!" The little dog lay unmoving beside the bed, his eyes half-open. Eliza rushed forward and dropped to her knees beside him. "Oh my god. Boo."

He was dead. She knew it. And what about Rio? Where was she?

Rising, she rushed next door again, pounding with both fists on the heavy panels. "Sheriff," she cried. "Sheriff Ferris. Come quick. Rio is missing."

From inside came the first sounds of someone stirring.

"Hurry," she called. "Please hurry."

The door opened.

But it wasn't the sheriff. Win stood there, looking bewildered. Then alarm spread across his face. "Eliza? What's happened? Where's Rio?"

"I don't know. Where's your brother?" Eliza, breathing hard, clutched the jamb as if to hold herself up. "I think...I think she's been kidnapped. And...and... Boo. I think he's dead."

Win turned white. "Beckett had to keep watch at the jail last night." He seemed able to process only one thing at a time. "Why do you think Rio is..." He couldn't finish. "Maybe she's outside. Maybe...maybe..."

Eliza, already shaking her head, said, "No. And Boo..."

Everybody who worked there—or stayed there, for that matter—knew Rio would never abandon her little dog to lie dead on the cold floor. Never.

257

So Win, completely disregarding the fact he was in his BVDs and barefoot, plunged past Eliza into Rio's room. He didn't bother looking around, simply zeroed in on the dog's form and rushed over. He looked back over his shoulder. "Get that Fields fellow up," he told Eliza. "Quick. He's gonna have to help us."

Eliza, glad to have someone, even if it was only a boy in his teens, telling her what to do, nodded and hurried to the stairs.

WIN COULD NO LONGER HOLD back his tears and with no witnesses, he ignored them and sank down beside Boo. His hand shook as he reached out to stroke the dog. "Ah, hell," he muttered sorrowfully. For a moment, he just sat there, his hand resting on the dog's warm fur.

Warm.

He sat there a long moment, unsure of what this meant. Right up until he felt Boo's rib cage move. A slight rise, a slight fall. And then a whimper.

"Boo," he said and finally dashed his arm across his face to wipe away the wet. "You're alive." He started to pick the dog up, but stopped, took another look, and cursed every bit as vigorously as he'd occasionally heard his brother do after a particularly unsettling event.

He saw that Boo had a broken leg, and God only knew what other injuries. Shifting the pillow to lay right beside the dog, Win eased him onto it. "There, that should be better. Warmer, softer."

Boo acted like he wanted to stand, but Win told him to stay put. By then, he heard Eliza coming back.

She appeared in the doorway. "Mr. Fields is on his way. He'll be here in a minute." She noticed then what Win had done. "That's nice. Rio wouldn't want her dog to—" She broke off as Boo raised his head.

"He's alive!" There was joy in her exclamation.

"Got a busted leg. I know that much. Mr. Fields better bring the doctor back with him and Beck."

Eliza stared at him. "Doctor Clement is a people doctor."

Win's jaw set. "If he can set a kid's leg, I'll bet he can set a dog's too."

Harrison Fields, wearing a robe over pajamas, stood in the doorway. "Have you touched anything except the dog?" he asked sharply. "That pillow?"

He meant the one Boo lay on.

Win shook his head. "It was already on the floor. I just moved it close enough to set Boo on. Otherwise, I haven't moved anything." He glared a little. "I know not to disturb a room."

Fields turned to Eliza. "Did you? Disturb the contents of the room?"

She stared at him. "No. I only came to the door." Being a quick-thinking woman, she had more to say. "I tapped, and the door opened by itself. It wasn't closed. Rio would never leave her door open."

He raised his hand to his mouth. "And yet, it was." He bent to examine the latch plate, a lengthy process, considering, before standing erect again. "Someone has a key."

Almost as if he were in agony, Win rose to his feet, leaving Boo on the pillow. "We'd best get dressed. Will you fetch my brother, Mr. Fields? And the doctor?"

But at this, Fields acquired a helpless stance. "I

don't know how to row a boat. You'll have to do it, and much more efficiently than I. I'll keep watch here and question the tenants as they come downstairs." He turned to Eliza. "I don't care who it is, but if anyone comes to the door, do not let them in. Understand?"

She glared at him. "What about Rio? Somebody needs to look for her."

"The sheriff's job when he gets here," Fields said and turned to Win. "Hustle, young man. The sooner we can get started, the sooner we'll find wherever Miss Salo has gone."

"Been taken," Win said sharply, and Eliza nodded in quick agreement.

"Yes," Fields said. "Taken."

Within three minutes, Win pushed off from the dock and bent to his oars. He'd never rowed so hard in his life, the boat skimming over the choppy waters of the bay. A fast tie-up at the town dock, and he ran all the way to the sheriff's office, bursting in as if blown by gale-force winds.

———

BECKETT, in the process of setting the filled coffeepot on the pot-bellied stove to percolate, hesitated when he heard boots thunking on the boardwalk outside the sheriff's office. Thunking hard. Stiff. Hurried. He spun, just in time to see his young brother push inside. The door slammed behind him.

Win was pretty much out of breath, but managed the core of his message. "Rio's gone. Kidnapped."

The coffeepot landed on the stovetop, water splashing from under the lid.

"What?"

Win drew a deep breath. "Rio's missing. Somebody broke into the hotel last night. He got into her room, hurt Boo, and took her."

"Who?"

"Don't know. All I can tell you is what I just did."

Beckett took note of his brother's white face, breathless condition, and trembling hands. "Sit down," he said. "Catch your breath." He dipped a ladle of drinking water from a bucket and handed it to Win. "Drink."

Win did, though he didn't seem much revived.

Beckett was already putting on his coat. "When did you—"

He didn't have to finish the question. Win already had the answer. "Rio was gone when Eliza got to the hotel a while ago. She found all the doors standing open. She looked for Rio, found Boo. He'd been knocked out and has a busted leg. I'm gonna get the doc." He started up from the chair he'd just sat on.

Beckett held his voice steady. "Any blood?"

"No."

Nodding, Beckett said, "Go get Doc, then. I'll meet you at the boat." He removed the coffeepot from the stove as he spoke and snatched a key from a peg. "I'll let French out."

Win, still panting from his efforts, had yet to move.

"Go," Beckett repeated.

Win went.

Mind racing, Beckett holstered his revolver, leaving his coat open for faster retrieval should it become necessary. He didn't trust Bull French not to jump him if he got the chance. A chance Beckett didn't intend to give.

But he did intend to question Bull before he met Win and Doc—provided the doctor was available—at the boat.

And, he thought, the thoughts as grim as the situation, Bull had better have the answers.

A closed-off area separated the jail cells from the sheriff's office, the log walls a sort of insulation that blocked out normal conversation. Beckett went through, trusting his prisoner had heard nothing of what Win had told him.

Bull, according to appearances still asleep, lay on his back on the cot, the one Charlie used on nights it was available to him. He wasn't snoring.

Keeping his eyes open in case sleep was a ruse, Beckett unlocked the cell and called Bull's name. Twice.

Snorting, Bull twitched around, sat up, and put his feet on the floor. "Whut?" he demanded in a barely awake mumble.

"Time to rise and shine. Pay your fine right now, and you can get out of jail." Beckett figured this would cause an argument, and he was right. Also, right in that he'd correctly believed Bull had drunk up every cent he possessed last night.

Bull stood up and made a show of going through his pockets. He grinned. "Somebody musta robbed me. You?"

Beckett didn't bother with a reply. Just waited.

Pretty soon, Bull found something else to say. "I ain't payin' a fine anyhow. I didn't do anything wrong."

"That's not what Aaron Black says, or the man you accused of cheating. I have to be gone for a while—hard telling how long—but I guess you can make it all right. Might get cold. And hungry. Your choice."

Bull's temper had already risen several degrees. "You can't do that. You gotta take care of me. Best just turn me loose."

Totally feigned sorrow on Beckett's part made Bull even more angry as Beckett said, "Not without paying your fine. Guess that means you'd better huddle on down." He turned as if to leave, shaking the set of cell keys in his hand.

Alarm lit in Bull's face. "Wait. I gotta piss. Let me outta here. I gotta..."

Beckett stared at him. "There might be a way I could turn you loose. That's if you cooperate."

"Yeah?"

"Yeah. For instance..." Beckett hesitated. "Aw, I don't know as I should make a deal like that."

It was as if he talked to himself even as Bull came forward, pressed against the bars, and said, "What?"

"Who paid for you to go on a toot last night?"

"Huh?"

"You heard me." Beckett was certain that if he knew this, then he'd know who had taken Rio.

"What makes you think anybody paid? Anybody but me, I mean." The belligerence came through strong.

Beckett shook his head. "It's Tuesday. You were drunk last Saturday night, and it's not payday until this Friday. That means somebody paid for your spree. Who was it?"

Bull remained silent.

"Who?" Beckett repeated, then, after as long as he thought expedient, he turned away. "Hope it doesn't get too cold in here. Or you don't get too hungry. There's a bucket. You can do your business in that." He was almost to the door when Bull relented.

"Awright," he shouted, cheeks red with anger above a scraggly two-week beard. "Awright. I'll tell you. It was Carver. Carver Jr., him and a sidekick."

Beckett thought the Carvers had gone back to wherever they came from. If not, they'd been hiding out. "A sidekick?"

"Yeah. Him and..." The name Bull came up with didn't surprise Beckett. Not one bit. Saying nothing more, he unlocked the cell, tossed Bull his lowly possessions and walked out, leaving the prisoner to make his own way to where he wanted to go.

"Hey," Bull called after him. "What about my breakfast?"

Beckett ignored him, jogging off to the boat dock where he found Doc and Win waiting.

Twenty-Two

Rio awoke slowly, her head pounding, her body racked with pain and sickness roiling in her stomach. And cold. So awfully cold, her bare feet like frozen stumps. Shivers ran through her body like the eddies in the bay spread when the waves hit the shore. It hurt. She hurt. What had happened to her? Was she ill?

No. Rio knew she wasn't ill, well, except for the nausea. This was something different. She'd been in her own bed, and now she wasn't. And Boo...

Though she tried to call out, she couldn't. For the first time, she realized something had been tied around her mouth. Frantic suddenly, she thrashed about, feeling as if she couldn't breathe. Feeling as though she were suffocating little by little. Her heart pounded. Black edged at the backs of her eyes, and she wasn't sure if they were open or closed.

She blinked, found things better when they were closed.

What's happening? Where am I? Where is Boo?

She had no answers. The last thing she remembered was Boo sitting up and...no. There were no *ands*. Then came nothing.

Wait. There was something she remembered after all, and it seeped into her mind that she'd been drugged and ripped from her bed.

If I scream, will anybody hear? Who? Do I want them to hear?

Think, Rio. Think.

Rio was a strong woman. She'd been through hell most of her life, usually from pain both mental and physical, caused by her nearest relatives. Her father murdered her mother. Her half brother wanted to murder her. And due to their machinations, there'd been whole groups—it seemed in an endless procession —who wanted her dead due to their influence.

Oddly enough, running all this over in her mind helped the panic to recede. Not all the way gone, but the impending hysteria calmed enough for her to start thinking.

What did she know? Well, she knew she was alone in a room that stunk of stale food, cheap whiskey, and unwashed men. She had the sense of lying on a floor, cold and hard, which creaked when she moved as if the boards might be rotten. Also, she was trapped as if in a tightly rolled cocoon. Luckily, her hands were bound in front of her. Whoever had done the binding had been rough. Her bruised forearm ached fiercely.

A flap of the wrapping lay across her face. It was that, she thought, making her feel as if she were suffocating, and answered as to why she couldn't see anything. Hard as she could, she flipped her head back and forth. When that didn't work, she turned her head to one side and scrubbed it against the floor.

The action worked better than expected, shifting the rag around her mouth the slightest bit and easing the tightness. Invigorated by the success, she scrubbed harder. She had to get rid of the gag before it choked her. And do it no matter how much skin she lost in the process. Up and down. Up and down. Side to side. Finally, an end came loose and slipped from mouth to jaw. With one final and very painful scrape, it fell away from her mouth.

Rio took a moment, maybe even several moments, to just breathe. After a bit, she raised her head enough to look around the room and reflect upon what she wouldn't give for a drink of her good spring water.

What should she do next? Pray, perhaps, that they hadn't tied the wrapping around her. If they had, she didn't know how she'd get free. But if they hadn't, perhaps she stood a chance.

The first direction she rolled only seemed to tighten the cocoon. Rolling the other way meant she'd have to crush the sore arm under her body. So be it, she told herself, and gritting her teeth, she rolled the other way, using every bit of her will to propel herself hard and fast.

It didn't work. Or not entirely. Had there, perhaps, been a slight loosening? She couldn't tell. Not for certain. All she knew was that the pain in her arm grew and grew until she screamed out loud and cried a little. Just a little.

Panting, she lay still then, hoping for the pain to lessen and that she could bring herself to try again. And again, if that's what it took.

Which it did.

Light had crept into the cabin through a window before the last of the wrapping came loose. It left her sprawled in the cold, wearing only her thin nightdress. Her feet were bare, her hands still tied, and though she strained, she couldn't break the cloth he...they...had used to bind her. Rio trembled, shaking hard enough that little drifts of dirt fell between cracks in the floor planks.

Cold beyond saying, she drew the wrapping up around herself again, only now realizing the growing light showed it to be the pretty quilt that had been on her bed. Not so pretty now, she saw. Filthy and with more than one tear from snagging on the rough floor, and possibly, she reflected, if her guess was right, on the bed of some old wagon. Whatever they'd used to bring her here. After a while, she managed to sit up, her head whirling from the effort.

Where was she? Discovering this came next. Or no. Her hands. They were next. She had to find a way to loosen and remove those bonds. Gazing down to see what kind of knot she'd have to unravel, it struck her that her captor had not been fully prepared. She was tied with the strings cut from one of her own aprons. Fortunately, from one of the frilly ones, not the canvas she used when cooking.

The discovery gave her renewed hope. She could do this. She could. But first, she'd have to get up.

Rising to one's feet with not only bound hands but suffering the aftermath of chloroform-induced unconsciousness and, she suspected, at least one blow to the head, proved harder than expected. Hadn't everything, she asked herself ruefully?

But at last, she rose to her feet, swaying and curling her toes against the cold. Lifting the quilt around her shoulders, she began a close survey of the building, first trying the rickety door. But for all its fragile shape, it held firm. Probably, she figured, secured with a padlock on the outside.

The one window, so filthy a gray film covered the single pane and rendered it almost opaque, was set in the wall opposite the door. Using a corner of the quilt, Rio swiped at a spot and put her eye to the cleaner area.

There wasn't much to see. Wherever her captor had stashed her, she guessed it was some old homesteader cabin that hadn't been kept up. Trees surrounded the place. A fallen-down shed, basically a mishmash of old lumber, sat just in front of some second-growth trees. From here, that was all she could see. Not especially encouraging when the lay of the sunshine indicated it wasn't morning as she'd thought, but afternoon. She'd been unconscious a long time.

She must free her hands and find a way out of here. Quickly. Before whoever had taken her came back.

"A nail would be good," she said. The sound of her voice, scratchy with dryness, startled her. She hadn't thought to speak out loud. "Or even a good, strong splinter. Or better yet, a knife." She didn't really expect to find a knife. A nail, though. A nail should be possible given the state of the cabin.

Not a nail, but the edge of the windowsill proved most useful. Over the years of abandonment, weather had crept in, wetting, then drying the wood until the grain rose up in rough layers. It meant Rio had to stand in place, her arms raised, and scrub the apron string in a see-saw motion until the fabric frayed and raveled apart. More than one splinter became embedded in her wrists. Blood blended into the fabric, until at last her arms, left first, then the right, dropped to her sides. It felt as if she'd never be able to lift them again.

She gave herself as long as fifteen minutes. Until the bleeding stopped and some kind of strength returned, even though her fingers remained swollen and clumsy.

Shadows were coming into the single-room cabin now. Afternoon advanced, and it seemed likely her captor would be paying her a visit at anytime. She had to be ready for him.

Unless he'd left her here to die.

She wouldn't. The vow swept through her in a hot wave. She'd find a way out.

Another circuit of the room, hands free, wrapped again in the quilt, and her feet gone quite numb with cold. She wished she had shoes. Or slippers. Her moccasins would help, especially the ones with rabbit fur lining.

How could she get away without shoes? Something to worry about later.

She wished there was a stove. And matches.

Coming to a stop, she looked up. There had been a stove here at one time. A hole in the ceiling showed where the stovepipe had been. There was still a metal flashing up there, hanging loose no more than two or three feet above her head. And from the flashing, she saw it. A big, beautiful ten-penny nail. A little rusty, she noticed. But a nail. Just dangling there, a temptation.

In the end, though she first leaped upward from a standing start, and next, from a running jump, she was unable to reach the nail. A sob escaped. Frustration made her angry.

Think, Rio.

What to do? Flipping the quilt around her shoulders again, dust rose from the floor. And then she had it. Taking the quilt, she folded it the long way, stood back, and waved it up and hard through the air. As the quilt came down, so did the flashing—and the ten-penny nail.

A weapon. Even if she couldn't get away, she could fight.

She'd no more than collected the nail when she heard movement outside. A horse whickered. A man uttered a curse.

Rio hurried to the spot where she'd been lying when she awakened earlier. Rolling loosely into the quilt, she flipped a corner over her face. Enough to conceal her face from him, but leaving herself a clear sightline, not enough to conceal him from her. Gripping the nail between fingers clenched into a fist, she listened impatiently as he, whoever he was, removed the padlock from the door.

Her heartbeat quickened, the sound like a drumbeat in her ears.

The door opened.

A floorboard creaked under the person's weight. So he—she thought the person must be male—was probably quite heavy. A man came to mind. A man who'd already hurt her. Carver Jr. She'd bet on it.

Rio closed her eyes as he approached and stood over her. He waited there for a moment, then nudged her with the toe of his shoe. Though it cost her, she didn't move, bearing the pain. She wanted him to reach down to her.

"Wake up," he said. "We didn't give you that much dope. He'll be here soon, you know. And then we'll all three have a nice talk, and one way or another, you'll tell us what your dear brother did with the jewels. But first..." He drew the last part out, dripping with anticipation.

His voice was easily recognizable. And then what he said struck her. He? We three? So while that meant there were more involved than just him, for now, Melvin Carver Jr. was alone.

This would probably be her only chance to get away. Before his partner joined him.

His partner. Why didn't he just say the name?

Carver reached down and grabbed the quilt at neck level, jerked her up about knee-high, then let her drop.

"But first," he continued, "I'm going to have some fun with you. I haven't forgiven you for holding us up like we were common country bumpkins."

No choice. With no way to catch herself, she fell back, head bouncing on the slight cushioning of a layer of quilt fabric. Blackness almost overcame her. Almost lost her precious nail. But not quite.

And although she did her best to act unaware, a moan escaped.

"Hah." He sounded triumphant. Proud. "I knew a little thump on the noggin would get your attention. Good. It's time you showed us where your brother hid the treasure. I, for one, am tired of waiting. I hate this benighted country. City lights for me. The good life, as long as one has money."

But again, she feigned near unconsciousness. *Come on. Come closer, you—*

The nail was in position. All he had to do was be

close enough. An arm's length. That's all she asked. He would need to unwrap her first. The second he did, and the quilt came free when he reached to drag her up, she'd strike. She'd aim for his face. His eyes, if she could. People always flinched when their eyes were in danger. And she'd have to be fast. Fast enough to get past him before he recovered, get out the door, and put the padlock back on, holding him in his own prison.

But of course, it didn't work out according to plan. Not by a long shot.

First of all, instead of using his hands, he used his foot to dislodge the quilt from around her. Then he struck with another of those jabs in the ribs with his toe.

Rio couldn't help herself. She grunted with the pain, opening her eyes to find him grinning down at her. He seemed to be salivating in anticipation of seeing her pain. He laughed. "I killed your damn dog. Did you know that? No, I suppose you didn't."

Rage filled her. Gave her strength. But she wouldn't think of Boo now. She couldn't. Best if she only thought of one thing. Saving herself. The stupid man apparently didn't even notice her hands were unbound. Or that she held a rusty ten-penny nail clamped between her middle and forefingers, pointed end out.

She and Carver stared at each other for a long moment. Finally, he bent, hand extended to grasp the neckline of her nightdress. Rio knew what he intended to do. And he was still watching her face as he lifted her closer, roughly tugging as if to pull the nightdress off. She let him, for a long moment that seemed to stretch into forever.

When he was close enough, distracted enough, she struck. But even as she did, he sensed something in her expression that warned him and let his grip loosen. She swung her arm upward, anyway. Swung with every ounce of strength she had in her. And missed.

Missed his face, but drove the nail into the side of his neck.

He screamed and jerked back, his eyes widening. "You little bitch," he gritted out. "What have you done?" His hand rose to pluck at the nail.

She scooted away, her bottom dragging against the rough floor. "Refused to let you kill me like you did those two men in my hotel." The words were a whisper.

"Not me. Him. He did it." Carver's eyelids quivered as his heartbeat flailed.

"Him? Who?" she said.

"What have you done?" he said again, and with a jerk, tore the nail from his neck, ripping the flesh around it.

To Rio's horror, blood spurted with the next beat of his heart. Onto her. Onto her pretty quilt. Painted everything it touched bright red until he fell to the floor and bled until he was empty.

Twenty-Three

Beckett took the oars on the way across Painter's Bay. Every pull shot them forward, jolting across the water and dropping the bow with every stroke. Right up until Dr. Clement, holding for dear life onto the gunwales, murmured, "Easy, Sheriff. It won't help to exhaust yourself."

He was in no danger of exhaustion, Beckett thought, scorn disputing the opinion. Doc just didn't like the boat's up and down movement. Still, he knew the doctor was right. He'd let his anger drive him to the point of carelessness. Capsize the boat and not only Clement's, but Win's life would be put in jeopardy. Let alone his own. What use would he be to Rio then?

He eased off.

Win, who had a death grip on the edge of the board seat he sat on, was ghost-white and looked miserable. "Did I do right?" he asked Beckett. "When I left Mr. Fields with Eliza and the rest?"

"Don't know what else you could've done," Beckett said. He bent to the oars again. "I'd like to get to the hotel before the others get up, just in case one of them thinks to disturb the site."

The doctor glanced sharply at Beckett. "You think they would?"

"Wouldn't put it past them. Tell me," Beckett said, glancing over his shoulder at Win, "exactly what you saw when Eliza got you up. What did she say?"

So Win repeated what he knew. What little he knew, as he was aware, as the details weren't much. Then, some of what he guessed. "It's that Carver guy, isn't it? He's the one who hurt her arm. He should've been in jail."

Beckett, guilt showing in his face, nodded agreement. "He should've. I should've seen to it. I should've been there for Rio."

Doc played advocate again with a simple statement. "It's hard to be in two places at once, Sheriff. Remember that."

Beckett knew the logic to be true, the trouble being he didn't *feel* as if it were. Silently, he was cursing himself.

At the hotel, he held out his arm to stop them when both Clement and Win would've dashed across the yard and into the building. At first glance, there was nothing to see. The frost had melted, wiping out any tracks there might have been. An examination of the porch door showed no disturbance. But then he bent closer, noticing something else. He pointed to it.

"I told Rio to buy new locks. Why didn't she?"

Win, standing next to him, had the answer. "She did. But the Golz brother who intends on doing it put the job off. He says he hasn't had time yet. He said he'd do it Sunday."

An explosive curse erupted, a product of Beckett's temper and sense of guilt. "I should've seen it done right away myself. My fault again."

But they all knew it wasn't. As the doctor said, he couldn't be in two—or even three—places at once.

"What does this suggest to you?" the doctor asked, a little puzzled. "Why do new locks matter so much?"

Beckett stood erect, his jaw set. "Because someone is either the best at picking locks that I've ever seen, or he has a key to the old ones."

"Good lord," Clement said.

"Does that suggest anything to you? I've been told no one had a key except Rio, and I haven't figured out where he got one. How anyone else got a key. Is there any way..." Attention caught, he watched the doctor.

Clement's eyes darted side to side, an unconscious indication of distress.

"It does," Beckett answered himself. "What? Is there someone else you know of who might?"

"Yes."

"Who?" He would've liked to shake the answer out of the doctor, so slow the answer was in coming.

But at last, it did.

"At the bank." Dr. Clement said. "From when the hotel was going through probate and Masterson thought the bank might have a claim."

"Did it?"

"No."

———

THE WAIT for Win to get back with his brother and the doctor dragged on and on. Eliza sat at the kitchen table with a cup of heavily sugared coffee in front of her. Her hands twisted on her lap.

Bindle, of all people, had brought the hot drink to her when the maid, coming downstairs to fetch Vesta's morning tea, found Eliza alone and weeping.

"What's the matter with you?" Bindle had demanded brusquely. Almost as if she really wanted to know.

Eliza had turned away, unsure of how much to say. But Harrison Fields, who'd heard her speaking, came running to keep watch on the two of them and judge the maid's reaction to the news.

"Go ahead. Tell her," he said.

"It's Rio," Eliza said brokenly. "Miss Salo. She's been taken."

"Taken?" Bindle's mouth dropped open. "Is she dead? Or do you mean kidnapped?"

"Kidnapped. And her little dog. We thought at first he was dead."

"The dog?"

"Turns out the dog isn't dead," Fields answered. "Nor is Miss Salo."

"That we know of," Eliza said, and promptly began crying again. "She's gone. Somebody took her. We don't know where. We don't even know when."

"Or who?" Bindle said, but the two words sounded suspiciously as if she might have a good guess.

She wasn't the only one. "It's that evil fat man. I'm sure of it," Eliza said. "The one who keeps pestering her." Her voice rose. "The one who knocked her down and hurt her arm. I know it."

"You don't know it. None of us knows anything

yet." Fields made the contradiction even as Bindle nodded her head, the two women in agreement.

Bindle, who'd been thoughtful enough to keep the distressed Eliza company, rose back to her feet. "Miss White will be needing her tea by now. Can you..." She asked Eliza as if concerned for her employer, although it seemed more likely she just wanted to give Vesta the news. Watch her reaction. And possibly to ask what she thought of this new development.

Apparently glad of something to do besides sit and cry, Eliza finished her coffee and stood. "I'll get it."

"Oolong?" Bindle said, as if hopeful.

Eliza shrugged. "I dunno. Whatever we've got, I guess." But as a small peace offering, since there was no oolong to be found, she put two small shortbread wafers on a plate along with the pot of plain old orange pekoe.

Fields's thoughtful gaze followed Bindle as she carried the tea tray up the stairs. "I hope that was wise," he said to no one in particular. His meaning wasn't clear.

Minutes later, Beckett, Dr. Clement, and Win arrived at last. Beckett scowled, shaking his head when Fields admitted to telling Bindle about events. "I would've preferred to see Vesta's reaction firsthand," he said, and got to work.

The day wore on. Beckett went over every square inch of Rio's room. He found exactly nothing to point to whoever had stolen Rio away during the night. He talked to Vesta, who declared she'd been in bed and sleeping soundly.

"You heard nothing? You saw nothing?"

"No. How would I?" she demanded, nose lifted, petulant at his questions.

David Freeman said almost exactly the same, except he admitted to imbibing a bit more brandy after dinner than he should have. "The waitress girl. She served me. She can tell you."

Perhaps the only thing Beckett learned conclusively was the timing. Eliza swore there'd been no footprints, no horse prints, no sign of wagon wheels in the yard when she arrived. She'd only seen signs of her own passage, which set the time of abduction to before the early-morning frost settled in.

Which meant Rio had been gone a long time before anyone knew. Boo had lain hurting for hours before being found. And Beckett's expression grew harder with every passing hour.

Dr. Clement could—and did—get the fragile little bone in Boo's leg set. Win helped, finding just the right sticks to use as splints, then sanding them smooth and to the exact height needed. Afterward, Boo refused food but drank water and slept.

Doc told everyone the dog would be fine, although Beckett noticed him crossing his fingers behind his back and admitting he'd had to guess at the treatment. "There should be a veterinarian in this town," he announced angrily. "I can't be expected to take care of the people *and* their animals."

Beckett, seeing his brother in a sad state, figured the best thing for him was to keep busy. First to return the doctor to town, then to find Benjie Ackers and his Plott hound, Belle, and ask again for their help. That one chore took all the morning, Ackers being out in the woods several miles from town, so it was nearly noon before the tracking dog arrived.

By that time, Eliza was frantic. Anna and Blanche

arrived to help, and Jess Stokes pulled his crew of Chinese loggers off the job with instructions to stand by. They'd start a search as soon as Beckett gave the go-ahead if it became necessary. Apparently, he expected the dog to be led to the edge of the bay and the trail lost.

———

MELVIN CARVER JR.'S body twitched a time or two, even after Rio thought surely he must be dead. It seemed to her that it took a long time for him to die, though she may have been wrong because when she looked at the position of the muted sunshine coming in through the dirty window, the shadow's angle didn't appear to have moved.

She hadn't moved either. After a while, she moaned, forcing her reluctant body into motion. First to sit, then to stand.

He would be here soon, she remembered Carver saying. Which meant she must be gone before whoever the *he* was got there.

Gathering her quilt, she wrapped it, the bloody end trailing around her shoulders, and went outside. Oddly, she couldn't even feel her feet anymore, and though she felt near to freezing, she didn't think it was cold enough to give frostbite. Not with the afternoon sun warming the clearing in which the cabin sat.

The horse Melvin Carver had ridden, one she recognized as coming from Pellow's livery stable, stood patiently hipshot while hitched to a nearby tree limb. A patient old fellow, he shied only a little when he caught the scent of blood on Rio's quilt and nightdress.

And on her body too. She could feel Carver's blood

turning sticky as it dried. Setting her jaw to keep her teeth from chattering, she gathered the horse's reins and climbed into the saddle. There was no spring left in her legs. She had to pull herself up using the saddle horn and cantle.

Then she sat, not knowing where she was. But she saw evidence of the horse and where earlier, more hoof-prints had beaten down grass and trampled pine cones. From when they'd brought her here, she surmised. But not in a wagon. On horseback. All she had to do was backtrack. Clicking her tongue, she turned the horse in that direction. Certain the horse would take her to his home barn if she turned him loose, she slumped and let him have his head.

Time got away. An hour, perhaps. Maybe less, maybe more. Rio had no real way of knowing because of the way the trees overhung the narrow path, blocking the daylight and making it hard to judge. Almost without her knowing, they'd entered a narrow area that meandered between walls rising as much as twelve to twenty feet overhead.

With a sense of relief, Rio recognized the place. They were in the only real canyon in this area. Pyrite Canyon, named after the fool's gold that had drawn fortune seekers here forty years earlier, only to be disappointed when they discovered the truth of the mother lode.

The horse plodded on. There was no other word for the old gelding's weary gait. Every once in a while, he dipped his head and snatched a bite of grass, teeth working around the bit as they walked along. She had neither the strength nor the will to stop him. What did it matter, anyway, as long as when she drummed her bare heels in his side, he picked up the pace? At least for a few minutes. And by then her head hurt so much she was glad for him to slow again.

At one such short break, things changed. The sound of someone whistling came to her ears from not too far away. Her first inclination was to shout out and call for help. She even sat up in the saddle, took a breath, and opened her mouth to yell. Until something, perhaps a sixth sense, perhaps a sense of self-preservation, sent a sour warning coursing through her nerves. A reminder of before, when Carver had said "we." He hadn't been alone last night. Perhaps, when his clear intention had been to rape her, he'd thought of it as a way to kill time while waiting for his partner to appear.

Maybe this so-cheerful whistler wasn't help at all. More than likely, he was the partner.

She drew back on the reins. The horse stood. She needed to take shelter. To hide until she saw who it was.

The whistle grew louder by the moment. She bit her lip, undecided. She didn't want to dismount. If she had to make a run for it, mounting again might be beyond her. And her feet. How could she run without shoes? Yet this poor old horse at his best didn't seem much of a runner. The only thing she could do was hide. But where?

Frantic, she looked around. Her gaze settled on another of those huge boulders that broke out of the ground in this part of the woods. No one seemed to know how they'd gotten here, but this one loomed up only a few yards away. The one possibility, as far as she could see.

A kick got the horse going. A touch of reins along

his neck guided him off the trail, around some trees, and then behind the boulder. Not a single boulder, but a grouping of three, along with some smaller ones. The canyon wall loomed behind them.

She tucked them in behind the largest of the stones and reached to pat the horse's neck. "You be quiet now," she whispered, spotting movement as a lone rider came into sight on the trail between the trees. The rider she'd been expecting all along.

And she didn't call out.

"Dammit it all." She hadn't wanted to be right.

And then, not her old plodder of a horse, but the friskier one Bernie Jensen was riding, raised his head and whinnied. His ears pricked, indicating interest in the stones where Rio hid.

Her horse, good old Plodder, moved beneath her as if intending to go out and join his stablemate. And before she even thought, she jerked the reins, stopping him before he broke from cover. Not a wise move. In consequence, the bit in his mouth clanked, and his hooves rattled on the stones.

Please, she was thinking. *Make him a little deaf. He's not much of a horseman. Make him pay no attention. Please, please.*

But, of course, her pleas counted for nothing.

"Oho." Jensen's call rang out. "What have we here?" His head cocked to one side. "Hello? Melvin? Is that you?"

Rio froze in place. So, fortunately, did her horse. If they remained silent, he'd think he was mistaken and ride on, she told herself. He had no reason to think she might've gotten away from Carver. Inconceivable, right? The noise had been a simple rattle of stones loosened by the ferocious storm a few days ago. That's all.

Go away. Ride on. Don't look.

But the gods were not on her side this day.

He kicked the horse in the ribs, gouging deep with his heels while at the same time slapping its rump with the trailing reins. Startled, the horse leaped ahead. Right toward Rio's hiding place.

Jensen had caught the sound and direction of Rio's location all too well.

And she had no place to run.

Twenty-Four

B enjie Akers and his dog showed up within a couple of hours, the man's face sad. He greeted Beckett and nodded to Anna Golz and her daughters as they stood by, trying for composure.

"Look at it thisaway, Sheriff," Benjie said to Beckett. "Belle and me, we ain't trackin' a dead body. Miss Salo ain't dead, far as we know. We're gonna find her and bring her home."

Beckett wasn't any too sure the man's speech did anything to cheer people up, but he had to agree. Rio wasn't dead. Couldn't be. He gripped Win on the shoulder when he heard the boy gasp and gave him a little shake.

"Believe it," he murmured, and Win nodded.

"Where we startin' from?" Benjie demanded. "And where's that little varmint dog of Miss Salo's?" He had Belle on a leash, ready to turn the hound loose as soon as she got a good whiff of Rio's scent.

Win led the way to Rio's room. Boo lay on the floor, still on the pillow where Win, who'd taken it upon himself to be the dog's caregiver, had placed him after the doctor finished setting the broken leg.

Belle went over to sniff Boo first thing. He raised his head, took a look, and lay back on the pillow. "Well, hell," Benjie said, then called to Belle, telling her they were here on business.

"That's Rio's bed. Guess that's where you want to start," Win said.

"Maybe. Sheriff..." Benjie looked to Beckett. "You said the dog was drugged. I suspect the girl was too. That likely means whoever has her got their smell mixed with hers on the bed. Might could be confusing to the dog. How about something she was wearing yesterday? That her shirt?" He pointed at the shirtwaist Rio had worn yesterday, hanging neatly on a hook along one wall.

Eliza answered. "Yes."

It wasn't long before man and dog were satisfied they knew who they were looking for. Belle pranced, eager to be at the job, and finally, Benjie gave her the go-ahead. "Search, Belle."

The hound shot out the porch door without a backward look. Benjie, still with the leash in hand, perforce followed at a run. Beckett was only a step behind. And after a couple of seconds of delay, Jess Stokes and a couple of his men. The men mounted horses. Benjie slipped the leash from Belle, and they were off.

Belle's trail song rose as she disappeared into the woods.

———

THERE WAS nothing Rio could do. Straightening her back, she gathered the horse's reins and held him steady, vowing the whole time not to let Jensen see she was frightened. Except she couldn't seem to stop her hands from shaking. Maybe he wouldn't see.

He rounded the pile of boulders and pulled his horse to a stop. He was one of those people who showed power in every way possible, at least when someone weaker was watching. This time, power over the horse. He yanked cruelly on the reins, the bit cutting into the horse's mouth.

The wide grin splashed across his face struck her as unnatural. He was not as tickled about meeting her as he wanted her to think. He must know it meant something in his plan had gone wrong.

"Why, Miss Salo. Imagine meeting you here? Where is Melvin, by the way? Isn't that his horse?"

She didn't answer, and presently, he shrugged as if it were of no importance.

"Although..." His grin turned into a frown. "I can't say as I approve of your attire. Rather provocative, don't you think?" He gouged the horse, forcing it right into poor old Plodder, and plucked at her quilt. "What's this? Blood? My, my. Does it hurt much?"

He seemed to be under the impression the blood was hers.

She didn't answer, her stare at him almost as if she looked right through him.

He didn't like it. That much was clear. "You should've listened to me." And, as her eyes moved toward him, he added at her puzzled expression, "In the street the other day. You know, when I told you the sheriff's brother might be the next victim? That was my intention, actually. Sort of kill two birds with one stone. But then I changed my mind. Things are heating up, what with your meddling and infernal stubbornness about selling to the Carvers. They don't care a whit about the business, you know. They just want the treasure."

Rio heard him, but her brain was having a hard time processing the words. Her head plain hurt too much to bother.

"So," Jensen said, smiling, "I decided to go right to the fount of knowledge. You, my dear girl."

She still didn't say anything. Couldn't think of anything to say.

Jensen sighed. Her lack of reaction seemed to unsettle him. "Get off the horse."

At this, she shook her head. Not wise. Even in her befuddled state, she knew as much.

"Get down," he said again, but she merely eyed him blankly. The eerie smile he'd worn slipped away, changing into something harder, more evil, and after a moment, he dismounted and shook his head. "Don't say I didn't warn you."

Jensen held poor old Plodder's bit in one hand and yanked at the quilt, as by now, it lay slack around Rio's shoulders. He dragged it away from her and flung it aside, wriggling his fingers in a downward motion. "Off the horse."

Even if she'd been so inclined, she hadn't the time. Grabbing her arm, he wrenched her from the saddle and pushed her up against the tallest rock. The horses, startled by the move and Rio's involuntary cry, trotted away.

"You should have listened. But I'm glad you

didn't." He put a hand on each of her shoulders and forced her hard against the rock wall. "Oh, I won't kill you right away. What would be the fun in that? I have all the time in the world to get an answer from you. In fact, make it hard for me, why don't you? No need to spoil the pleasure." He wagged a finger. "The truth now. Just tell the truth. It will all be over sooner that way."

He contradicted himself practically in the same breath. Did he feel her shaking? she wondered. Inside and out, great tremors went through her body in waves.

"The truth about what?" she said.

"You know very well. Where is the treasure hidden? Come on, now. Speak up. Where did he hide the jewels?"

"You too?" She swallowed, welcoming the rage growing inside her. Better than fear. Oh, by far better than fear. "Are you speaking of Eino? I don't know anything about any jewels. You must know we didn't get along. Why would you think he would tell me about any such thing?"

Jensen snorted. "He always said you were sneaky, even as a little girl. That you followed him around and tried to watch him. Of course, you know what he did with the jewels. You're bound to."

Her lip curled. "He lied. I did no such thing." Or rarely, like with the hollow tree. But there'd been times she'd sussed his secrets out just by the way he acted. Exactly the reason she'd found the money he'd stolen this summer. And returned to its owners. Most of it, anyhow.

She didn't see his fist coming at her stomach until it hit her. A blow that bent her over, gagging and coughing, the pain reaching the farthest nerve in her body. After a time, breathing hard, she stood erect again.

"Who told you about this so-called treasure, anyway?" She figured she knew. But to know for sure. In case...in case she survived.

At her question, he laughed. "Can you believe it? My boss. Dear old Eldon Masterson and Melvin Sr. cooked it up between them. Well, the Carvers first, the first time they came from back east. Yes. As long ago as that. Why else were they so persistent in trying to get the hotel? Certainly not to run the place.

"I learned about it after they convinced Eldon the story was true. He's going deaf, you see, and likes to bring me along to meetings with people like the Carvers. He doesn't want to miss what they say and trusts me to tell him what he misses." He let loose with another of those loud, scornful laughs. "Sometimes they do, sometimes they don't. It depends. He pats me on the back and says he needs me for protection and puts a little bonus in my paycheck. He doesn't do much active participation, you see. Personally, I find his squeamishness a bit hypocritical."

Bernie shook out his hand and stared down at it, almost as if it were disconnected from him. "He didn't like it when those two detectives were killed though. I lied and told him Melvin cut their throats, and he believed me." He tittered. "I do believe he got to worrying that he might be the next if he protested too much. And he was right to worry. He might still be next —after you. Or maybe after the sheriff's little brother."

Rio stared out over Jensen's shoulder. The horses were farther away now. For some reason, she found it funny that if Jensen didn't do something soon, he'd find himself afoot. Plodder, to her surprise, was almost out of sight, evidently determined to find his own way home after the rough handling, and the other animal showed signs of joining him.

A blow across her face rocked her head. Blinking, she stared hate at Bernard Jensen.

"Pay attention," he shouted at her. "Where is it? Where is the treasure?"

Her lips were bleeding, and she'd bitten her tongue. Her cheekbone felt as if it had shattered.

He gave her a minute to recover, smiling all the while. Then he said, "Well?"

Difficulty in forming words around her injuries slowed her reply. But she didn't falter. "You're a fool to believe another of Eino's lies. There is no treasure. Not now and never has been."

He slapped her again. "You're lying. Lying."

Rio sagged. Pain filled her head, and she seemed to be spinning. Spinning like a child's top. "Not lying," she said.

Jensen stared down at her. "It's almost a shame to kill you, actually. You do know you're the best cook in this entire county. Maybe the surrounding counties too." He shook his head. "Yes. A shame." And then he said. "But it's not going to stop me."

Rio's eyes were closing and from the whirl of vertigo all around her, she knew she was losing consciousness. Good, she thought. Good.

Far off, she thought she heard a dog. Not her little Boo, but a hound. Belle? Was it Belle?

But she could no longer stand, and as she slid, her back against the rock wall, onto her bottom, it appeared

Bernie Jensen heard the hound too. He'd turned to look behind him.

"Who is that?" He held his breath, then panted in quick little gasps. "Shit. My horse."

In a fit of new anger, his shoe cracked against her ribs. And then he was gone, running footsteps heading up the outcropping above her head, then the slide of loose stones tumbling around her.

———

THE MEN FOLLOWED THE HOUND, who followed Rio's scent. For a time, Belle led them along a well-trodden trail, where, as Benjie Akers assured the sheriff, they'd never have had a chance to find the girl if Belle hadn't been on the job.

"That hound of mine," he said with justifiable pride, "is the best in the territory."

But they hadn't actually found their objective yet.

Beckett wasn't inclined to argue, particularly when Belle, without a falter of indecision, broke off and headed into hills that grew steadily steeper, stonier, and the pathway narrower. For a while, there were signs of two horses. Confusing signs, with tracks coming and going, but it appeared Belle knew what she was doing and kept heading up. Right into Pyrite Canyon.

The men fell into a single file. Beckett behind Akers, with Jess Stoker and his two men after him. They didn't talk much until Akers called to his dog to rest her for a bit and give her water.

The men drank too, stomped their feet, and walked around to get the blood flowing.

Beckett checked the rifle in his saddle scabbard. All in order. Copying him, the others did the same.

"There's an old abandoned miner's cabin a couple miles up ahead," Jess said, and Benjie nodded.

"That'll be where they took her," he said and added grudgingly, "Good spot. I'da never thought to look there."

Beckett certainly wouldn't have known about an abandoned cabin without them. He was still a comparative stranger here. Thank the Lord for Belle.

The canyon narrowed. Timber was sparse along this stretch, the peculiar outburst of stones preventing room for tree roots to spread. The canyon wound around the outcroppings. Here and there, late afternoon sunlight glinted from the stones. Fool's gold, he realized. The reason for the canyon's name. He'd heard the first gold hunters in the area had been sadly disappointed after the first real assay, and most had turned their attention to the nearby timber.

Belle, who'd been lapping water from Akers's hat, suddenly looked up, her attention caught by movement ahead of them. She barked, much different than her trail song.

"What's that?" Akers said.

Beckett came to stand beside him, but not before he took his rifle from the scabbard. "Stay alert," he said. "We don't want any surprises."

Silence fell over the group of men as they waited, sharpened senses searching the top of the canyon walls and along the trail for an ambush. Someone muttered about having his throat cut, and Stokes shushed him.

Beckett sure as hell wished the man hadn't spoken. A vision of Rio as a victim rose before him, too difficult to push away until Akers said, "Look there. That's a horse got loose from somebody."

It was. A saddled horse, and as it ambled its way ever closer to them, he added, "Ain't that Pellow's old nag? It must be nigh on twenty-five years old. Surprised he'd still rent it out."

"Maybe somebody stole him." The man smothered a laugh. "Looks like the old feller wants to go home."

Jess Stokes had been keeping a close eye on the trail. "There's another. Anybody know if that horse belongs to Pellow too?"

"Think so," his man said. "I seen that bank feller riding it around a while back."

The information chilled Beckett, but confirmed his suspicions too. "Mount up," he said. His posse was becoming too genial for his liking. A woman kidnapped and two men dead was not an attraction to be taken lightly. They'd best be ready to defend themselves and Rio—if she was still alive.

His heart thumped, then went on, but felt out of rhythm.

They proceeded slowly. Within ten minutes, they met with the old horse, and a few minutes after that, with the second horse. There was blood on the old one's rump and down the left front leg. Not a lot. Not enough to drain a person. More like it had been wiped onto the hair. Beckett could only wonder who had been riding the horse.

"Tie them to that tree over there," he told one of the men. "We'll pick them up on the way back."

An elk almost ran into them as they rounded a twist in the trail. Horses and elk, a nice four-pointer, equally startled, it took a moment for Beckett to realize the tenor of Belle's baying had changed.

Benjie interpreted the change. "Means we're close. She smells what she's been sent to find." He started to say something else when a gunshot echoed off the canyon walls. He froze for a moment, said, "The hell," in a startled kind of voice and grabbed at his shoulder. Blood welled. Ignoring it, instead of going for shelter, he raced after his dog. "Belle. Belle. Out. Come."

Beckett couldn't see where the shots were coming from at first. Not until another shot raised dust from beside the dog. The gunman remained hidden, but the bullet had come within inches. She wasn't moving as fast, tired from her efforts of the day. Belle yelped and swerved. Benjie went on even as the next shot hit just in front of the dog, followed by another at him.

Beckett spotted the shooter now. A man lay at the top of an outcropping, the tallest point around. He had good cover, but even as Beckett watched, he raised up for another try at the dog—or possibly at Benjie.

Dismounting, Beckett raised his rifle and fired, sure his aim would be off. And it was. He missed and shot again. And missed again. But now the shooter's attention focused on him. The next bullet was meant for him. He ducked behind a boulder, finding it smaller than he liked as chunks of stone flew and drew blood from his ear.

Out in the open, Benjie reached his dog, swung from his horse, and picked her up. Beckett and Stokes, also with a carbine, kept up a covering fire as man and dog mounted again and raced back to shelter.

They were all breathing hard as Beckett reloaded.

He eyed Benjie. "That was a little foolhardy. How bad are you hurt?"

"I'll live." He petted his dog, hand trembling. "That sumbitch was gonna shoot Belle. Couldn't let him kill my dog."

"Now what?" Jess Stokes asked. "Whoever that is, he's got the high ground. And this is the only route through here. It'll take hours to go around and get behind him."

"Holy sh..." one of Stokes's men spoke up, sounding shocked. "Is that her? Is that Miss Salo?"

Five sets of eyes fixed on where the man, Beckett hadn't caught his name, pointed.

Twenty-Five

R io, barely able to move considering her aching ribs and the pounding in her head, didn't know what to do. The men—and she was sure Beckett was among them, although she couldn't tell at this distance, not with her swollen eyes—had no idea their bullets struck shards from the rocks rising above her. Or if they did, they were more intent on stopping Jensen before he got one of them. If so, she wished they'd improve their aim.

The sharp shards peppered her with what felt like needles. Blood seeped from the small wounds on her arms and hands as she tried to cover her head.

Why doesn't somebody shoot Bernie Jensen and end this? She wanted to scream at the men. On the other hand, she didn't want to remind Jensen that she was still below him, cowering as close as possible to the cliff-like side and its meager shelter.

A minute later, all the gunfire stopped. To Rio, with her eyes closed, the silence was every bit as ominous as the noise had been. Was everyone dead?

But no. At least Bernie wasn't. She could hear him rattling around above her and knocking little bits of debris to the ground. Metallic clicks indicated he was taking time out to reload his rifle while trying for better footing among the rocks. Or maybe just settling in. He was muttering to himself, rising once to an explosive curse. "Where's the rest of my ammunition? I packed some. Where is it?" There was a pause, then more muttering. "The horse. It's on the goddamned horse."

The horse, Rio remembered, that even now had passed beyond where her would-be rescuers hunkered down. They, too, judging from the ammunition already expended, were probably reloading.

She almost laughed. Would have if her ribs and stomach didn't hurt so much.

They were at a stalemate, with her cornered in between. And she was thirsty. So very thirsty.

The afternoon wore on. Only once did Jensen, who kept up a ceaseless tirade of invective railing against her, against Carver, against Beckett and the posse, and most of all, Eino Salo. After an interminable time, as Rio ran her dry tongue over split dry lips, something moved at the posse's stronghold.

Immediately, Jensen popped up like a prairie dog from its burrow and fired off two shots. Apparently hit, a man fell, then lay for a long moment before wriggling back under cover.

Not Beckett, Rio thought. The man's hat had come off, and he'd had hair almost as light as her own.

Time stood still. A deer wandered out to stand in the trail, right up until Belle, catching either its scent or seeing it, let out a long bellow. The deer ran, and as if he couldn't help himself, Jensen shot after it. Too slow, as it happened. The deer's white tail disappeared into a narrow crevice in the canyon walls.

The slant of sunlight leveled out as the afternoon waned. It must be hot, still, atop the outcropping, Rio thought. She was hot, unless a fever was taking hold. But no. Putting out her hand, she touched it to one of the stones. The stone had absorbed heat. It made her smile, thinking of Jensen up there, hot, thirsty, and afraid to move.

But he had shown himself to be a man who took chances. Breaking into her hotel during the night and killing two men with no one the wiser. A silent killer, in fact. One who used a knife. A knife he probably had with him right now. She shuddered. Rising up as much as her whirling head allowed, she began searching the ground around her for a weapon. A rock. A fist-sized rock she could wield with all her remaining strength. A rock with sharp, pointed appendages.

Once found, she gathered her choice in her lap and waited. Bernie Jensen—such a friendly sounding name for such a wicked man—would come for her soon. At first dark.

Beckett. If he cared for her at all, he needed to get here first.

———

"SAVE YOUR AMMUNITION, but be ready for a clear shot," Beckett told the men. He was sick of waiting. Sick with worry about Rio. He checked the rifle in his hand, also the revolver in his shoulder holster. "You fellas stay here. I'm moving in as close as I can get without him spotting me. But if you get a good shot, take it."

"I don't like it," Stokes said. "What'll we do if he shoots you?"

"I'd rather you think of what'll happen to Rio. She's first priority. Got that?"

Stokes flinched and nodded. "Blanche'll kill me if we don't get her back."

"In one piece," someone said, and there were nods of agreement.

From talking with folks, when Jensen's name came up those few times, Beckett had formed the impression that the banker's assistant probably wasn't an accomplished sniper. How many times had he missed hitting Belle? And even the graze Akers had suffered had been more luck than accurate aim. Fortunately, Jensen had completely missed Stokes's man who'd ventured out. Scared him plenty, though. Made him mad too, as he'd lost his hat.

Beckett didn't think they had time to delay any longer. The sun would be going down soon. Jensen, able to shimmy down from his viewpoint then, would try to get away in the dark. Chances were, he planned to kill Rio before he went.

And Beckett meant to stop him.

"Stokes, you're in charge while I'm gone." Face set, he stood, gazing out across the boulder-strewn stretch of trail between him and Jensen. Between him and Rio.

Jess Stokes stared at him. "There's a lot of ground open between here and there. Sure you don't want to wait for dark?"

"Dark is apt to be too late. He'll be on the move by then." Beckett studied the terrain a minute more. "The canyon walls are uneven along here. Even if you can't tell much from a distance, there are places to take cover. Remember the way the deer got away? We couldn't see where he went, but he found a way out somewhere."

Stokes gave a short nod.

Beckett found the first several steps the worst. They meant crossing an open area where he was fully exposed before he managed to slide into a crack between rocks. From there, progress became maybe ten feet at a stretch, taking time to figure out the best route. It seemed to take hours, though he knew it didn't. Finally, raising his head to see over the top of a rounded boulder, he caught a glint of the sun shining on metal. So Jensen hadn't managed to slip off anywhere. Not yet. Or not unless he'd left his rifle behind.

The angle, better from this new, closer location, provided him with a view of one of Rio's feet. A bare foot, and as he watched, she pulled it up out of sight. He sucked in air as if his lungs were starved. She was still alive.

Feeling renewed, he dove forward again, a little surprised when Jensen didn't shoot. Why? Did he want Beckett to come nearer? He hadn't had any luck killing anyone from a distance. Could be close up was his preferred method. The knife his preferred weapon.

So be it.

He still had fifty yards to go when he heard stones rattling down the side of the outcropping in a miniature landslide. The sound could only mean one thing. Jensen was making his move now. Only he wasn't trying to get away. Not on his own. It took only a moment for Beckett to realize his first thought had been right. Jensen intended to capture Rio again. Capture? Or kill?

She'd be either hostage or victim, a dare to him and the posse to stop him before he could slash her throat, just as he'd slashed Pope's and Heckert's.

He caught sight of the banker's assistant, only a dozen feet from the bottom of the outcropping. And his guess had been right. The angle he took proved Jensen was going for her.

Another slide of stone drew Beckett's attention. He saw Jensen miss his footing and hit the ground. He stumbled, caught himself, and came on, limping a little.

Did Rio see him? Would she be able to fight him off until Beckett could get to them?

He had to warn her. Beckett stood up, calling out. "Rio. To your left. He's coming."

Jensen must have lost track of him somewhere along the way, because he stopped a moment as if startled. But then he went on, limping but faster.

"Too late, Sheriff," he yelled. "You're too late. I've got her now." Laughing, he scrambled over a large boulder toward her like a scurrying badger.

And Rio stood up.

———

BECKETT CALLED SOMETHING. Rio wasn't sure what. She heard herself screaming, "Shoot him! Shoot him!"

Why didn't someone shoot him? Beckett was right there. Why didn't *he* shoot? Or those men with him. Benjie Akers, for one, known because she recognized his dog. Although, come to think of it, she hadn't seen if he even carried a gun. She couldn't tell who the others were, but it didn't matter. They had guns. Use them.

But then it was too late. A final three feet, and Jensen stood right in front of her, hidden behind the boulders that had given her shelter. His face was pocked with the same kind of marks Rio knew her arms and hands, and probably her shoulders bore. At least she'd kept her face covered. He hadn't. His was a bloody mask that made his scowl even more frightening.

She knew what he had in mind. Oh, yes, she did. And the rock in her hand that had seemed comforting earlier now seemed so inadequate she might as well drop it. But she didn't.

Small protection against the knife he pulled from a sheath on his belt. The knife, she figured, he'd already used to kill two men. They'd been sleeping, or at least unaware they should fear him. She knew better. And she'd fight to the end.

"You," Jensen said in a scathing tone. "This is all your fault. If you'd just told us where your brother hid the treasure, none of this would've happened."

She kept her eyes open and looked into his. "There is no treasure, buried or otherwise. There never has been."

"There is." It was a shout. He flicked his knife at her. "The Carvers. They knew. She told them so."

She? Rio had no idea who he might be talking about.

"She lied."

"Nooo." He howled the word, long and loud, and with that, leapt for her.

She'd known the drawn-out cry had been a forewarning. He slashed at her with the knife and without thinking, she struck at his moving hand with her stone. More by accident than aim, the stone connected.

He yelped. The knife dropped to the ground, but before she could follow up with another blow, he snatched it up.

"You'll pay for that." He glared at her, his teeth gritting behind open lips.

He looked like what a dog mad with hydrophobia must look. Fangs bared, frothing at the mouth with rage. Then he was on her. She twisted aside, smashing at him again and again with the stone, trying to hold him off with her bare hand, plunging her elbow to his midsection, striking her knee between his legs. Blood on her hand made the stone slippery.

Rio knew she was strong, but this time, not strong enough. The pain in her head, her ribs, her feet. The drug still slowed her reflexes.

"Beckett," she cried as Jensen raised his knife for the killing slash.

A killing slash that never happened.

As if by magic, Beckett—she knew it was Beckett even though her vision flickered in and out—scrambled around the boulder and grasped Jensen's arm before the knife descended.

The men grappled.

And Rio, to her everlasting embarrassment, fainted.

Twenty-Six

"**B**eckett!" Rio's terrified cry still echoed as Beckett caught Jensen's arm, wrenching the knife to the side. He was barely aware of her falling to the ground behind him.

"Not today," he breathed. "Not Rio."

"You then." Jensen faced him. He was a wiry man, stronger than he looked. And apparently without fear. He thrust Beckett's arm aside and came around with the knife again.

Somewhere, in his frantic dash to save Rio, Beckett had dropped his rifle when it grew too cumbersome to carry among the rocks. But he had his pistol, and dodging back from Jensen's wild swing of the knife, he drew the gun.

Jensen seemed not to see it. His maddened eyes were fixed on Beckett's face.

Seeing no choice, truthfully, Beckett didn't want one. The echo bounced off the canyon walls as he fired one bullet into the middle of Jensen's forehead.

With the knife still in his hand, Jensen's body dropped like a scarecrow released from its pole.

Moving slowly, Beckett holstered his gun and turned to where Rio lay, her eyes closed in her bruised and battered face. Kneeling, he checked for a pulse. Finding it, he swallowed hard and scooped her into his arms. Even in her faint, she moaned.

"You're all right, sweetheart," he murmured into her hair. "I've got you. You're safe." Raising his voice, he called out, "I got him, men. I'm stepping out. Don't shoot us."

Fifty yards or so down the trail, whoops and hollers celebrated their success, growing louder when they saw Rio in his arms. It faded when she remained unmoving.

"Is she alive?" Jess Stokes ran toward him.

At Beckett's nod, the noise rose again. He laid Rio under one of the few trees in the canyon, well away from where boulders at least partially hid the mess of Bernie Jensen's body.

Moments later, Rio awakened. She jerked, moaned at the movement, and opened one eye. The other, he saw, was swollen almost closed. Her cheekbone had a long gash, her lip was split and bloody. Her hand, from the rock she'd used to defend herself, bore deep cuts, and in his examination, he discovered her wrists were scraped and bore signs of being tied. Her feet, he discovered, looked like they'd been mauled by a bobcat. And cold.

"Anybody bring a blanket?" he demanded.

One of Jess's men had. They wrapped it around Rio, watching for her reaction. "Feels good," she whispered. Then, "Is he dead?"

"Yes." A chorus of voices answered her.

"Good," she said and closed the eye again.

Although Beckett would've preferred to stay close to Rio, duty drew him away. "One of you fellows ride back and bring up those horses. There's a body to take back to town."

At this, Rio stirred. "Two," she said.

"Two?"

"Two bodies. Melvin Carver is at a cabin a mile or so beyond where the canyon ends." Her voice was barely loud enough to hear.

"Carver? He's dead too?" Beckett stared down at her. "Why would Jensen kill him? Weren't they partners?"

"They were. But Bernie didn't kill him."

Beckett squatted back on his heels. "Then who did?"

"Me."

"You? How?"

At this, Rio's split lip quirked, starting another seep of blood. She didn't seem to feel it. "With a rusty ten-penny nail I found in the cabin."

The tale, Beckett decided later, made his own fight with Jensen sound pretty tame stuff.

Full dark had fallen before they started back to Painter's Bay with Rio and the bodies. Beckett, along with Benjie Akers, had gotten to the abandoned cabin with the old horse while there was still enough light to examine the cabin, the ropes, the gag, and most of all, Carver's body lying just where Rio had left it. The hole in the dead man's neck bore witness to her story of how he'd come to die.

Akers had told Belle, the dog having insisted on accompanying them, to stay outside. She stood in the doorway and growled as the two men viewed the carnage.

"That's some gal," Akers said, then quickly added, "I mean Miss Salo." He turned to his dog. "I don't mean you. But you're some gal too."

Beckett smothered his grin. Not that Akers was wrong. Both Rio and Belle were special.

It took both men to heave Carver's heavy body onto the horse and tie it on. Rigor mortis, in its beginning stage, had set in, which didn't help the process, and Akers didn't hesitate in letting Beckett know.

He muttered and complained and made a show of wiping his hands on his britches when they had Carver situated. "Made a deal to track the girl. Didn't expect to handle no dead men."

"Ever hear of civic duty, Akers?"

"No," Akers said. "What's that?"

"What you've just been party to. A successful search, which we owe to you and Belle."

His acknowledgment of the dog looked to please Akers's sense of worth. Important, Beckett figured, in case he had cause to call on the man and his dog another time.

They found the others ready to go when they got back. Someone who'd had the foresight to bring along a lantern lit the wick and held it up. "I'll lead. We can take turns with the lantern. Takes about three hours to town," he said to Beckett, who nodded. He hadn't been here long. All this was new territory to him.

Beckett and the posse rode into town around ten or ten thirty, having taken a longer route than going back to where they'd started from, but with a better road to follow. Rio, to Beckett's—and the other men's—great relief, had more or less recovered from her faint by this time. Though still lightheaded with a terrific chloroform-induced headache, she seemed to be regaining her strength as he held her in front of him in his saddle. It made for some discomfort to them both, but at least she wouldn't fall off.

Nobody talked much, and when they did, it was subdued. It had been a hard day.

But once, when his sorrel stumbled in the dark, Rio cried out. His arms had tightened around her.

He jerked away. "What?"

"My ribs." She took in short gasps of air. "Carver, he kicked me in the ribs a few times. I think they might be broken."

Bending around her, careful not to crowd, he muttered an imprecation. "I should've put a guard on you at the hotel in the first place. I thought they might make a try at you."

Rio made a funny sort of sound. "Not your fault. You can't be everywhere at once." She sounded just a little bitter. "Even Boo—" She stopped. "Boo. Is he all right? Why didn't he let me know? Did...did something happen to Boo? Carver told me he killed him."

Beckett knew there was no possible way she could miss the way he quit breathing just then. Or the way the muscles in his arms, passed around her to hold her and the reins, grew taut.

Slowly, voice shaking, she said, "Boo? Did they—Is he..." She didn't finish.

"They hurt him," he said. "As soon as folks at the hotel discovered you were missing and that your dog was hurt, Win came for me. We didn't know what else to do, so we sent for Dr. Clement. Doc fixed him up best he knew how. But as he made sure to tell us, he's a people doctor, not a veterinarian. And Boo had some of the same knock-out stuff they forced on you. God knows what it might do to a little fella like him. They most likely knocked him out first."

Her tears were already falling, warm drops on his hands.

"He was alive when we left. That's all I know." As assurance, it lacked something.

But there it stayed.

Only a few buildings were still lit as they entered town. On a weeknight in a town occupied by hard-working laborers, folks went to bed early and got up early. Beckett handed a five-dollar bill to Akers for his and his dog's service and disbanded the posse, asking Jess Stokes to stay with him. Their first stop was Mead-ows's undertaker's parlor, where light came from a ceiling fixture inside the porch. Bodies were delivered there for the embalming process. Meadows had an after-hours notification setup similar to the arrangement at the hotel.

Dismounting, and with Stokes holding the reins of the body-laden horses, Beckett pressed the button. Far off, a bell pealed. After a few minutes, Meadows, wearing a long robe over his nightclothes, cracked open the door. Seeing Beckett, he opened up and surveyed the group. His eyes lit at the sight of Rio sitting on Beck-ett's horse.

"By gum, Miss Salo. I'm glad to see you're alive," he said.

"I'm glad to be alive, Mr. Meadows," she replied.

"And these"—he gestured at the bodies draped over

311

the saddles—"are the ones who're guilty of this rash of killings?"

Beckett answered. "They are."

"I knew we done good, the doc and me, when we appointed you sheriff, Mr. Ferris."

With that, Mr. Meadows traipsed on out to the nearest horse and lifted the first dead man's head. The whites of his eyes shone in the dark as he gaped. "Bernie Jensen? Him?" Suddenly, he grinned. "Hah! What's Eldon Masterson gonna have to say about this?"

No one voiced an opinion, and he went on to the next horse and repeated the process. He peered closer. "This here is one of them out-of-town fellers, ain't it? Arrogant sons of..." He cast a guilty look at Rio and stopped what he'd intended to say. "Hang on a bit. I'll get a couple of stretchers, and we can take the bodies on down to the basement."

He retreated inside, muttering something about needing an elevator, seeing all the bodies he'd been tending to lately and how they were a heavy load for an old feller like himself to tote from here to there. When he got back with the stretchers, he'd donned his trousers.

Next stop was the doctor, where another of the nighttime lights kept visitors from tripping over any minor obstacles in their path. Clement called his wife, Molly, into service right away when he saw his patient.

Together, they checked Rio over while Beckett waited outside the room. When they let him back in, they identified a roster of injuries. Cuts, bruises, possible broken ribs, a black eye, and a deep gash on her cheekbone.

"But not much I can actually fix without bones to

set, bullets to probe, or wounded flesh to stitch." Dr. Clement patted her on the shoulder. "Best I can do is clean you up and offer some laudanum for the pain."

For a second, Rio seemed tempted, then shook her head. "I'd rather not," she said simply. "Tell me about Boo. Is he alive? Were you able to save him?"

At this, Dr. Clement twitched as if uncomfortable with the question. "Understand that dogs aren't my usual patient. I set his broken leg. That boy, Win, found some nice sticks to use as splints. He sanded them down smooth as a baby's bottom so they wouldn't scratch or pull hair. Last I saw, your dog was sleeping on a pillow, and the boy planned to stay beside him and keep him from moving around too much. Guess they're friends."

At last, Beckett had the pleasure—the relief—of seeing Rio's face light up.

Molly insisted, though no one actually tried to resist her, that they tuck Rio into bed in the hospital portion of the clinic. "We need to keep an eye on you," she insisted. "You've been pounded, knocked out, kicked, and drugged. You deserve some coddling. When did you last eat?"

Rio had to think. "Supper...last night. Was it last night?"

"It was."

Sure enough, hot—but not too hot, considering her sore tongue and split lip—sugared tea, soft toast, and a boiled egg were forthcoming. Minutes later, she fell asleep as Molly pulled a blanket over her.

Himself stumbling with weariness, Beckett had begun to regret running for sheriff. He'd as soon as not fallen onto the mattress beside Rio and slept there with her. But the night was not done yet.

His next stop was to return Pellow's horses to the livery and beg a boat for Jess Stokes to take across the bay. Jess's chore was to report to Win and the Golz family that Rio was safe and sound and tucked up in Dr. Clement's surgery.

Along with that, Jess had one more instruction: to make sure Harrison Fields remained until Beckett could get answers to some perplexing questions from him.They needed to put this treasure rumor to bed fast, before more people showed up wanting to dig holes on Rio's property. Stokes, possibly thinking of what Blanche would say, agreed.

Beckett watched as Stokes headed for the town docks. He shivered a little. Tilting his hat, he paused, thinking of how grateful he was that Rio wouldn't have to suffer the cold in that falling-down old cabin tonight. His breath condensed out in front of him as he set off on his final duty of the night. The destination caused him to check his pistol, only to find he'd forgotten to reload after the fight with Jensen. A situation soon remedied. Who knew what he might face when he got there.

Dr. Clement had told him where to find Eldon Masterson's home. A white picket fence surrounded the front of an imposing two-story house. Not a mansion compared to some he'd seen, but from what he could tell, probably the finest abode in Painter's Bay. A wrap-around porch accented the three sides of the house that he could see. Fancy woodwork painted a contrasting color accented gables and porch posts.

The building, dark and silent, gave him pause, but after a moment, Beckett dismounted and tied his sorrel to a wrought iron rail at the edge of the yard.

The gate creaked as Beckett lifted the latch and

made his way down a walkway formed of evenly set paving stones. At the front door, he banged a lion's head knocker several times. It was, after all, the middle of the night.

After a while, he banged the knocker again, following up by hammering a few times on the door with his fist. No bones about it, his anger had had many hours to grow strong. Right now, he didn't care a bit about disturbing the banker's sleep. Or his wife's, come to that.

They must've been heavy sleepers because as much as five minutes passed before the door inched open. A woman stood there.

Maid or lady of the house? Beckett found it hard to tell. He took a chance. "Mrs. Masterson?"

He guessed right. "Yes?" she said in a harsh voice. "Who are you? What do you want?"

Harsh, yes, but he sensed alarm too.

"I'm the sheriff. Sheriff Ferris. I need to speak with your husband."

She half-turned, her eyes shifting to where a staircase rose to the second floor. "He is asleep. Come back tomorrow." She started to close the door.

Easily remedied. Beckett stuck his foot in the opening and pushed the door wider. "Not tomorrow. Now." Ignoring her protest, he brushed past her into a vestibule. From there, he could see to the top of the stairs. Eldon Masterson stood there, clearly not asleep.

Caught, he didn't even bother to sound apologetic. "How dare you," he said. "Get out. I will speak to you tomorrow, if I must. And you may be sure this incident will ensure you never become sheriff of this county."

Behind him, Beckett caught sight of another man. A

corpulent man. He was sure of the man's identity. Melvin Carver Sr., waiting in the wings.

Beckett ignored everything the man had said. "Down here. Now. Call Carver down with you. The three of us need to have a conversation. I have news for each of you."

Masterson straightened. "Go to hell."

"That's not for you to judge. Mr. Masterson, I don't want to place you under arrest." Beckett tilted his head and spoke louder. "But I will if I have to. You too, Carver. I'm angry, and I'm tired right now. I don't want trouble. But we do need to discuss the recent deaths of several people, and we need to do it tonight."

The banker stiffened and turned to look at his houseguest, if that's what Carver was to him. Beckett's idea was that they were partners in crime. Something seemed to pass between them.

Still poised beside him, Mrs. Masterson gulped. "Dead men? What dead men?"

It was the first pertinent thing any of them had said.

"Did I say men?" He looked down at her and shook his head. "I said several people."

Oddly, it was Carver who took the first steps toward him. He echoed the woman's question. "What dead people?" His tone had turned apprehensive.

Beckett eyed him. "You may have heard Miss Salo was kidnapped last night?"

"Is she..." Mrs. Masterson faltered.

He didn't answer. Not outright. "We need to talk," he said, and it seemed Rio's name was the bait he'd needed.

It was as if the two men on the stairs were in competition to see who could descend the slowest.

Twenty-Seven

When Rio awakened, Beckett was sitting in an armchair the doctor had placed beside her bed. His dark eyes were closed, and he looked frazzled. He needed a shave too. Badly. Out of nowhere, it crossed her mind to think she was glad he did shave. She didn't care for beards or mustaches. Among other things, it always seemed they hid what a man was thinking.

Then the other reason she was glad struck her, and she knew she blushed. A beard or mustache would've made a barrier between her lips and his. That's if she ever got a chance to kiss him again.

She had killed a man. Killed him with a rusty nail and her bare hands. What would he think of her when he woke up and realized what she'd done? Would he be disgusted? And he didn't know about the other man she'd killed. No one knew except Quinn Callahan, and they'd made a pact never to mention where they'd buried him to anyone. To anyone, ever.

Her heart thumped uncomfortably just thinking of it.

What if Beckett never wanted anything to do with her again after all the trouble she had caused? All of it because of her half brother, Eino. From the look of things, she'd never be able to exclude him from affecting her life. Not as long as he lived, and maybe longer.

She sighed, then cried out as her lungs expanded and pulled at her abused ribs.

A light sleeper, Beckett shot up from the chair and leaned over her. "You're awake."

The pain from her ribs slowly ebbed. "I am. I think." Confused, she looked around. "Where am I? I want to go home."

Grunting, he sat back down. "I know, but Doc wanted to keep an eye on you. Make sure those ribs aren't causing trouble before he lets you go home."

She breathed in carefully and not too deeply, aware that not only her ribs, but her stomach hurt. She didn't even remember the kick to the stomach. "Depends on what he calls trouble. I can tell you they hurt." The hand cut by the rock had been cleaned and bandaged. Her cheekbone had one tidy stitch. Her lips had been coated with salve. Peeking under the blanket, she saw that she wore what was probably one of Molly's night-dresses since it was considerably larger than her own size. It revealed, she couldn't help noticing, more of her than she preferred. Funny how last night seemed a distant, unreliable memory. She didn't recall Molly stripping off her ruined nightdress, then dressing her in this one. And yet, Molly must have.

"What time is it?" she demanded. "Has Win let you know about Boo? Is he...is he..." She couldn't go on.

"No word yet." He stretched, tendons popping audibly, and scrubbed at his face. "I expect Win will stay with your pup, but Jess should be bringing one of the Golz ladies with some of your things soon. If the doc gives permission, we'll take you home then."

He eyed her as if sensing a certain wariness about her. "Do you want to talk about what happened?"

Did he mean killing Melvin Carver? Or about him having to shoot Bernie Jensen?

No. She wanted to forget. Rio couldn't meet his eyes. Looking down, she gave a quick sideways shake of her head. The time would come when she'd have to speak of killing Carver. She knew that. But not now. Not yet.

"All right," he said, his voice gentle. "When you're home and comfortable. Later. But we will have to talk about it."

"I know." And she did.

With that, Rio had to be content, her impatience growing as she waited. Time stretched, but at last the sound of voices outside the surgery announced the visitor she'd been waiting for.

It was Blanche, exactly as she had expected when Beckett told her Jess would be the boatman.

HARRISON FIELDS, sighing noisily, rested his arms on the table and glanced around at the others gathered in the dining room. He, more than anyone, looked to be dreading his part in this meeting.

Vesta White, her maid Bindle, and David Freeman had also drawn their chairs up to the table.

That left room for Rio, with Blanche helping her, to seat themselves. Jess Stokes was there to act as witness.

Not to be kept entirely out of the discussion, that left the hotel people, Turner, Marie, Eliza, and also Win, standing near the kitchen. Plenty close enough to listen and be party to the discussion if called upon. Or if not.

They all were waiting for Beckett who had spent most of the morning and the early part of the afternoon at the telegraph office in town. He'd only just arrived at the hotel and gone to stable his horse.

It was late afternoon. Rio had rested on her cot with Boo periodically wagging his tail and licking her unbandaged hand. He lay beside her, pointing his splinted leg as if it were a badge of honor.

Rio figured it was.

As for her, her aches and pains were not much diminished. She had no idea when she'd be well enough to get back to work, and she was sick of dealing with Vesta White, Bindle, and David Freeman. The sooner they all went back to wherever they'd come from, the better she'd like it.

Just as Harrison Fields heaved another of those loud, put-upon sighs, Beckett strode into the dining room. He carried a folder under his arm. Rio made a guess it contained the exchange of telegrams and notes regarding this situation.

Beckett's gaze sought hers. He flashed a wink and a quick smile as he hung his coat and hat on the rack just inside the door. That must mean he had answers as to why two men had been murdered, and why she nearly met the same fate.

Still, he kept his shoulder holster in place, reachable in case of necessity.

"Sorry to keep you waiting," he said, "but I presented this information to the commissioners and Judge Henry Button. They gave the okay to make a general announcement."

"Does this mean we can tell anybody we like?" Vesta asked. "For instance, my attorney, to see if I can sue?"

Beckett's mouth curled. "Who do you plan on suing? Far as anybody can tell, you don't even have a horse in this race. You're here on your own behalf on the off chance you could make money, whether by stealing an already stolen treasure, or by a bit of blackmail. That goes for anybody else who might be looking to go after Miss Salo and her place of business. In the judge's opinion, if anyone has grounds to sue, it's her."

Even Harrison Fields seemed disappointed. Hard to tell why. As for Vesta, Rio would've described her expression as furious, and maybe a bit apprehensive. Personally, she liked the idea of apprehensive.

Beckett noticed too. "Miss White? You're looking upset right now. Maybe you'd care to explain why."

Bindle shifted in her chair, as if she might like to jump up and take flight. David Freeman simply looked blank. Vesta shook her head. "None of your business."

"We'll see about that." Shrugging, Beckett opened his folder, took out a yellow telegraph flimsy, and read it before handing it to Fields.

Fields read it once, twice, looked up, and nodded before he spoke. "This is from my employer, New York State Senator Blackman. In it, Senator Blackman instructs me to cease my investigations immediately."

"What investigations?" It was Turner who asked from where he stood at the back of the room.

Fields glanced at Beckett before he answered. "Senator Blackman comes from an exceedingly wealthy family. In this telegram, he's given me leave to inform Miss Salo of certain aspects regarding her brother, but the rest of you"—his glance included Vesta and her party, plus the hotel employees—"need told only that any talk of stolen treasure is fiction. No treasure, which the senator is given to understand is supposed to consist of his family's collection of some rather valuable jewels, is missing. The family jewel collection is completely accounted for and secured in The National City Bank, where it serves as collateral for the Blackman businesses. Eino Salo most certainly did not steal the jewels and bury them somewhere on this property. The rumor is a complete fallacy."

Rio felt the most tremendous wave of relief—until she looked up and noticed Turner with his mouth open, as if to ask another question. She also saw Beckett shake his head once, twice. He wanted this meeting to close quickly. The way he shut Turner down indicated the fewer questions, the better. It was, perhaps, fortunate that Vesta wasn't paying attention to the hotel help just then. She was whispering to David Freeman and Bindle. Bindle shook her head as Rio watched, even as Freeman nodded.

But while maybe Turner couldn't ask questions, Rio didn't see that she needed to be so reticent and spoke up. "A fallacy, yes. But who started the rumor?"

Fields blinked. "I...uh...no one seems to know."

"Huh. Of course not." Her tone scathed.

Rio was pretty sure she knew. Someone who liked

to make himself seem more dangerous. Who liked to start rumors and collect blackmail to hush them up. Who didn't care whose reputation or livelihood he ruined. Who made jokes no one else considered funny.

In a word, Eino.

Fields had more to say. He went through the motions of clearing his throat, commanding everyone's attention again. "Senator Blackman apologizes for the trouble this has caused, although I daresay I personally don't see any reason he should. None of this is his fault. He shouldn't be forced to share this kind of personal information with you. But he has, which is extremely good of him. I expect all of this to be put to rest immediately. And forgotten. Are we agreed?"

He looked at Beckett for approval, and Beckett nodded.

Rio's temper flared, her injured ribs stabbing as she involuntarily took too deep a breath. "All this?" she said, aware of Beckett moving toward her, a worried look on his face. As if he'd like to warn her off asking questions just like he'd warned Turner. She blundered on.

"Two men were murdered in my hotel as they looked for this false trail of treasure. I, too, was almost murdered. Two other men are dead because of their own greed. All this? That's it? And I'm just to forget about it?"

She stood up. "Get out, all of you. Miss White, Mr. Freeman, Miss Bindle. You too, Mr. Fields." She named them off with fury in her voice. "I expect you all to vacate my hotel this very evening. There is a late train to Spokane leaving around midnight. I suggest you all be on it. And pay your damn bills before you leave." She had nothing to say to Beckett. Not at the moment.

Rio didn't wait to see her instructions followed. She went to her office-cum-bedroom and shut the door. If she had been able to stomp, she would have. Beckett followed until she heard Blanche stop him.

"Not now," she said. "I think she needs a good cry. In private."

Thank God for wise friends.

————

RIO HAD AN HOUR TO HERSELF. Yes, she cried, but only for a little while. It hurt her ribs too much to indulge in great sobs. She cooed over Boo and petted him until his eyes brightened, his tail wagged, and he seemed like his old self. She figured within a day or two he'd be dashing about on his three good legs, having learned to hold his splinted leg off the floor.

After the hour, Rio almost ignored the light tapping on her door. She'd have to face Beckett soon, she figured, no matter how angry and betrayed she felt. How he could simply say, in effect, get over it when she'd been snatched from her bed, beat up, almost raped, almost killed. *When she'd killed a man!* Who was this Senator Blackman to dictate how she should feel, anyway?

Abruptly, she stopped such thoughts and went to fling the door open. But it wasn't Beckett, it was Win who stood there. He flinched at the look on her poor, beaten face.

He should've seen it last night, she thought, when her left eye had been swollen shut. At least she could open the eye now. Partially, anyway.

"Yes?" she said coolly. Boo's greeting to him, three short barks, was a great deal warmer.

His feet shifted in a little dance. "I figured you'd want to know what Dr. Clement had to say about Boo. In case he didn't talk to you about it when you were there."

It was a poorly thought-out excuse, although in truth, the doctor had been quite reticent about discussing her dog, saying he didn't want to plague her with details. Evidently, he'd figured she'd had enough to bear.

So Win told her everything, including the fact he'd decided to become a veterinarian. "Beck says, yeah. Good idea." By the time he finished, he managed to work his brother into the conversation in such a way that Rio's anger had faded. But not entirely erased.

"So can he come in now? Please? He's feeling real bad about upsetting you." Win's eyes, almost as dark as his brother's, shone with sincerity.

She thought a moment. "Is Mr. Fields still here?"

Win nodded. "You want to see him too?" He seemed doubtful.

"Yes. Here in my office. Tell them to bring their own chairs."

He grinned. "Yes, ma'am."

Soon enough, the three were seated, perhaps a little too close for comfort around Rio's desk. She started.

"We've spoken before, Mr. Fields, of Mrs. Blackman, and of Miss Sally Blackman."

Fields blanched, then nodded, and Rio continued. "You spoke of watching my half brother dance with the Blackman ladies. You noticed, though didn't speak, of an attraction between first one, then the other, with

Eino. Or Evan, as I suppose you and the others know him."

Fields gaped at her. Of course. Just like the Carvers —and here her stomach clenched as she thought of Jr.— he had believed her an ignorant girl who had no idea of sophisticated gentility.

"When we spoke, I mentioned Eino's ability to dazzle a certain kind of woman. Right now, I'm not sure of which of the women was so bedazzled, but I suspect Mrs. Blackman. Am I correct?"

Fields didn't move a muscle. Rio shrugged. "I don't suppose it matters. Did they cook the scheme up between them? Or did she have the idea already in mind to steal her husband's heirlooms? I presume they are heirlooms. Those kinds of things usually are, I believe."

She fell silent and waited. Beckett's gaze flicked between Fields and her. He was smiling.

After a few moments, he turned to Fields. "You have to tell her."

Fields's face turned red as he clamped his lips. Until quite suddenly, he seemed to collapse. "Why not?" He shrugged. "I don't suppose you'll ever tell anyone. Who would believe you? Your word against a man like Senator Blackman?"

Beckett murmured, "You might be surprised."

It earned him a glare, but not from Rio.

"Mrs. Blackman was angry with her husband. She wanted to wear the ruby parure to the ball that evening, but the senator denied her. He made some excuse, but she kept at him and kept at him, until he finally had to confess that some of the jewels were paste. The rubies, for instance. The originals had been sold. And since a representative from Tiffany jewelers was to be at the ball, he didn't dare put the paste rubies on display. His reputation would be ruined if creditors learned of the deception."

Rio lifted a brow. Or tried, winced, and said, "And she told Eino."

"I'm afraid so. Between them, just to punish the senator, they concocted a scheme to put it about that all the Blackman jewels were paste. Unless, of course, Salo was paid to keep quiet. Serena...er, Mrs. Blackman, was to share. When Senator Blackman learned of the plot, he blamed everything on your brother."

"Half brother," Rio cut in.

Fields stared at her. "At any rate, in case Salo did as he threatened, in a moment of ill-advised panic, the senator reported the jewels stolen. By Evan Salo. Somehow"—and here he shrugged helplessly—"the story got added to. We don't know who started it. And it got around. Whispers about the Blackman treasure being buried here, at your brother's old home. And then, how you would know where. It helped the senator, actually, by taking the spotlight off him for the moment, by giving him a couple of choices on how to keep his creditors satisfied. He sent the Pinkerton agent here to provide an excuse for them suddenly reappearing at the proper time. And he sent me to keep watch over the whole affair."

And he added, in a perfunctory sort of way, "I'm sorry."

Rio was speechless. Beckett stood up, breathing hard. "I suggest you get the rumor turned around fast when you get back to your Senator Blackman. If ever another treasure hunter comes around here, he—or she —will hear the entire story. I'm sure it won't take long to spread."

"You can't," Fields said. "I told you. This is between us. Just us. The senator—"

"I can't think of a single reason Miss Salo should care about your Senator Blackman. If I was sheriff of his county, I'd arrest him." Beckett looked at Rio. "What do you want to do?"

Her mind whirled. She wanted this finished. She wanted to run her hotel, cook, and...and she wanted Beckett to love her. "Send out an officia announcement to all the newspapers that the treasure rumor was wrong. I'll only keep the secret as long as I'm never bothered again," she said.

Beckett nodded. "Now, get out. We're done." Not waiting, Beckett turned Fields to the door and pushed him out of the office. He glanced back at Rio. "I'll be back. We'll talk."

"Yes," she said.

RIO ABANDONED her office-bedroom in order to watch her erstwhile guests depart after each bill was paid. At that, it took two boats to get them all away. Turner took the oars to ship Vesta, Bindle, and all their luggage in one. Win rowed the boat with Freeman and Fields.

Rio didn't bother to wave, wish them Godspeed, or say, "Come again." She simply breathed as deeply as possible and retreated to the privacy of her room.

Beckett followed her in. Boo, on the bed, looked up.

Sinking onto her chair, Rio sighed. "What am I going to do? Do you think a newspaper announcement will keep treasure hunters away?"

He smiled ruefully. "There might always be a few around. But not like now. People will soon forget."

"This is Eino's way to get back at me, you know. I bet he started the whole buried treasure story just to plague me. That's probably why he showed up in the summer. Just to have cause to make people think he might've buried treasure here. Well, and to blackmail the senator, of course, who I'm sure paid him to let the treasure hunters and murderers come after me. That's just like him."

"I don't think he'll ever be back. I think he may be dead."

"Dead and having a last laugh." It came out bitter. She shook her head. "Oh Beckett, will I have to live the rest of my life with Eino and his many offenses hanging over me?"

Beckett took her hands in his, careful of the healing wounds. His dark, dark eyes held hers. "Whatever happens, I'll be with you, sweetheart. If you'll have me."

At first, she didn't understand. She stared at him, a one-eyed cockamamie look. "Have you?" Her voice shook.

He looked a little worried. "Yes. It'll mean Win too. I didn't think..." His voice failed.

And then it struck. "Beckett, are you asking me to marry you?"

He swallowed and nodded.

"Well, I'm saying yes," she cried, and tried to crawl onto his lap. It didn't work very well, and then the kiss

sort of went awry since, thoughtful fellow that Beckett
was, he tried to avoid the split side of her lip.

But they managed. They always would.

A Look At:

THE WOMAN WHO BUILT A BRIDGE: A WESTERN ADVENTURE ROMANCE

A 2019 Spur Award Winner

Shay Billings is pleasantly surprised when he finds a new bridge over the river, cutting miles off his trip into town. When he's ambushed and left for dead, the bridge builder—a mysterious young woman with extraordinary skills—jumps to his rescue.

January Schutt just wants to be left alone to hide her scars. Living like a hermit in a rundown barn, her life is turned upside down when she takes in the wounded Shay. And when she allies with him and a few ranchers to defend their homes against Marvin Hammel, a power-hungry tycoon intent on seizing their land and water, she finds herself in the midst of a battle over water rights. But has she chosen the right side?

Facing danger, newfound love, and difficult choices, January must discover her own strength and the true meaning of justice as she navigates the treacherous waters of loyalty and survival.

AVAILABLE NOW

About the Author

2019 Spur Award winner for *The Woman Who Built a Bridge* and 2020 Spur Award winner for *The Yeggman's Apprentice*, C.K. Crigger lives in Spokane Valley, Washington, where she crafts stories set in the Inland Northwest.

She is supervised by a feisty little dog with a Napoleon complex and ignored—except when he wants to lay on the keyboard—by a reclusive cat. Not satisfied to write only of the historical west, she also writes contemporary mysteries and dabbles in the speculative genre.

A member of Western Writers of America, she reviews books and writes occasional articles for *Roundup* magazine. *Buried Under Books* also features her book reviews.